"Why do you shiver so? Am I so very distasteful to you, Genevieve?"

She looked down, breathing deliberately, still infinitely aware of the strength and deftness of his hands, the heat of his body so very near hers. "Nothing could be further from the truth..." she began, then stopped for fear of what this statement might reveal. "My hands are simply tender and you startled me."

He frowned, looking down at the raw skin. "Forgive me, Genevieve. I will have more care."

Guilt assaulted her, but she made no effort to reassure him. For it was the tenderness of his touch that brought about her dilemma.

Even now as he stroked the cool cloth gently over her palm did she have to close her eyes to hide the thrill that coursed through her at the contrast between that cool cloth and the warmth of his own flesh...!

Dear Reader,

With the passing of the true millennium, Harlequin Historicals is putting on a fresh face! We hope you enjoyed our special inside front cover art from recent months. We plan to bring this wonderful "extra" to you every month! You may also have noticed our new branding—a maroon stripe that runs along the right side of the front cover. Hopefully, this will help you find our books more easily in the crowded marketplace. And thanks to those of you who participated in our reader survey. We truly appreciate the feedback you provided, which enables us to bring you more of the stories and authors that you like!

We have four terrific books for you this month. The talented Carolyn Davidson returns with a new Western, *Maggie's Beau,* a tender tale of love between experienced rancher Beau Jackson—whom you might recognize from *The Wedding Promise*—and the young woman he finds hiding in his barn. Catherine Archer brings us her third medieval SEASONS' BRIDES story, *Summer's Bride,* an engaging romance about two willful nobles who finally succumb to a love they've long denied.

The Sea Nymph by bestselling author Ruth Langan marks the second book in the SIRENS OF THE SEA series. Here, a proper English lady, who is secretly a privateer, falls in love with a highwayman—only to learn he is really an earl *and* the richest man in Cornwall! And don't miss *Bride on the Run,* an awesome new Western by Elizabeth Lane. True to the title, a woman fleeing from crooked lawmen becomes the mail-order bride of a sexy widower with two kids.

Enjoy! And come back again next month for four more choices of the best in historical romance.

Sincerely,

Tracy Farrell
Senior Editor

SUMMER'S BRIDE

CATHERINE ARCHER

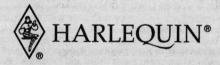

HARLEQUIN®

TORONTO • NEW YORK • LONDON
AMSTERDAM • PARIS • SYDNEY • HAMBURG
STOCKHOLM • ATHENS • TOKYO • MILAN • MADRID
PRAGUE • WARSAW • BUDAPEST • AUCKLAND

ISBN 0-373-29144-2

SUMMER'S BRIDE

Please address questions and book requests to:
Harlequin Reader Service
U.S.: 3010 Walden Ave., P.O. Box 1325, Buffalo, NY 14269
Canadian: P.O. Box 609, Fort Erie, Ont. L2A 5X3

This book is dedicated to God, with joy
and heartfelt gratitude for all things.

Chapter One

As his mount crested the last rise in the road, Marcel Ainsworth looked up. His gaze was unconsciously yearning as he watched the tip of the highest tower at Brackenmoore come into sight. Marcel viewed this first glimpse of home with both dread and longing.

Two years.

It seemed such a very long time to be away from home and his three brothers, yet he'd had no immediate plans to return. Or at least not until Benedict had sent for him. Though he did not know the reason for his eldest brother's summons, Marcel could not ignore it. Not from Benedict.

Leaving the family estate of Brackenmoore had not been easy. Yet when Marcel had done so, he'd felt there was nothing else he could do. What Genevieve had said to him that last day at Brackenmoore had forced him to act.

His chest ached even now at the thought of the longing and despair he had known. The temptation to act upon her words, to give in to the yearning he felt was far stronger than he could have imagined.

He could not give in to it. When he was but fifteen an incident had occurred that made him realize he could never succumb to the enticement Genevieve offered. It had been shortly after Benedict had dismissed Thomas, a young man who had worked as an assistant to Benedict's steward. Thomas had been Marcel's friend, but he had also been stealing from Benedict. When Marcel had gone to him and asked him why he would do such a thing, the older boy had looked at him with a contempt that rocked him. Thomas had told Marcel that he had done it in order to buy things for a particular young woman. He loved this damsel, would do anything to win her. And now, on learning of his dismissal, she had turned him away.

In spite of his own pain at the way his friend was treating him, Marcel had said that Thomas's love should have been enough, that he would now never know if she would have had him for himself alone. Bitterly Thomas had turned away, telling Marcel that he was in no position to make such a statement because he was an Ainsworth. As an Ainsworth Marcel would always get any woman he desired and he need do nothing of worth to achieve this, or anything else for that matter. Marcel had a name but would never know if *he* was wanted for himself alone. What Thomas said about women was true. Even at fifteen, Marcel noted they were more than eager for his attention, professed him to be witty and handsome when he felt awkward and shy.

Marcel had watched his friend go in silence, but the words had cut deep. They only reinforced what he had felt for most of his life, that he, Marcel, had accomplished nothing, earned nothing.

Benedict was the one who actually earned his position at Brackenmoore by selflessly caring for the lands and folk as their father had. Marcel would have been proud and fulfilled to serve that purpose, yet there could only be one heir.

He wished to hold such a position of responsibility. But he would gain it through his own efforts, not by marrying a woman who would have him for his name.

Surely Genevieve's feelings toward him had changed. Two years was more than sufficient time for her to see how unsuitable they were for each other, that her wish to be an Ainsworth was not reason enough for them to come together.

Marcel spurred his mount on. Early summer had urged the greenery along the roadside to shades so deep they near hurt the eyes and he could hear the call of crickets in the thick grass. Overhead in the clear blue sky the screech of a seagull reminded him of how, as a boy, he had wandered along the cliffs above the nearby sea and wondered what it would be like to fly.

Well, he had not learned to fly. But he had learned to sail and the sea had given him the freedom to go where and when he would. Still there was a place of longing inside him that had not been filled, a place where the images of a family, his own lands and contented folk dwelled. It was a place he had learned to ignore.

For the most part.

The dark and substantial shape of the castle ahead of him made him realize whence came a portion of that longing. Brackenmoore.

He knew the sense of love and comfort that pervaded the atmosphere inside, despite the stronghold's great presence of strength and power. Because of his choice for freedom he would never be a part of a family in that way again. There was ever a price to pay for the decisions one made in life. This was one he would accept no matter how difficult.

It had been his misfortune to find himself drawn to the wrong woman. But no more. Constantinople, Rome, Madrid—they were his loves and would remain so.

When he reached Brackenmoore, the guard at the castle gate hailed him. Marcel called out his own name with an unexpected feeling of reticence. It had been a very long time and he knew not how he would be accepted. He was humbled and gratified when the gate was immediately opened for his passage. Its opening was accompanied by shouts of welcome.

He shouted back a greeting, then quickly passed through and made his way to the stables. It was dark and Marcel had purposely timed his arrival for the hour of the evening meal, which meant there were few folk about the courtyard.

He told himself he wanted to see his family all together as he remembered them. His arriving when all would be gathered in the hall had nothing to do with wanting to avoid the possibility of coming upon Genevieve alone.

The wide, high-ceilinged hall was crowded as usual and no one seemed to pay him any heed as he made his way through the tables crowded with hungry castle folk. That might have been because he deliberately kept his face averted from anyone who glanced in his direction.

Marcel wanted to surprise his brothers. He continued on to the far end of the chamber, where the family table sat near the enormous cavern of the hearth.

As he drew closer he could not mistake his three brothers' dark heads. They were all there. The sudden wave of longing that swept through him at the mere sight of them made his chest tighten. He had known he missed them but had not realized how very much. Marcel had kept his mind and body busy in his quest to forget the compelling but unwanted infatuation he had felt for Genevieve.

Aboard the *Briarwind* it mattered not that he was the third brother of the powerful Baron of Brackenmoore. There he was captain, living by his own wits and talents.

But all the sense of accomplishment and satisfaction seemed as nothing, when his unknowingly questing gaze came to rest on a down-bent head. The breath seemed to rush from his lungs and his head felt light, even as an overwhelming heat filled his veins.

Genevieve.

God, but she was beautiful, even more beautiful than his fevered dreams had conjured. Her gold curls were covered by a cap of lush green velvet, the color of which made him think of soft moss and cool streams. Her dark lashes rested delicately against the curve of her high cheekbones, making him recall all the times he had looked down at her and discovered that she could not meet his gaze, that those creamy cheeks were flushed with—God help him—what he could only interpret as desire.

But that he had not realized until the last day. Before that time he had wondered, even secretly hoped that she might return his interest. Yet as soon as he'd realized she did, he'd known it could not be, especially as he knew the true reason behind it.

Genevieve was Benedict's ward, and heir to a great fortune. She possessed all that Marcel had secretly longed for as a boy when he began to realize the challenges and the rewards of Benedict's position as overlord. Not that he was in any way resentful toward his brother. Benedict had no more part in the placing of his birth than he. Marcel simply had not understood why he had been given a desire to see to his own lands and folk, yet not the right by birth.

Genevieve could bring Marcel all that he had ever desired, but he knew her genuine reason for wanting him. She desperately wished to be a true member of his family. She had admitted as much when she proposed marriage to his brother Tristan. That marriage had not taken place, as Tristan loved another, but Genevieve's desire had not changed.

His gaze focused on Genevieve once more. She was looking down at someone beside her, a gentle smile curving her pink lips. It was a raven-haired little girl.

As he watched, she said something to the child, and he noted the fact that it was his brother Tristan's child, Sabina. He was shocked and regretful to see that his niece had grown so very much in the two years he had been gone.

His attention went back to Genevieve at the moment she looked up. Her sea-green eyes narrowed as they swept over the crowded chamber and she brushed a stray curl from her creamy cheek. It was almost as if she were searching for something—someone.

As her gaze came to rest on himself, her eyes widened and her lovely mouth formed an O.

In that instant it was as if two years melted away. He felt the same overwhelming sense of longing and sorrow he had known the last time he had been with her. He had come upon her walking along the battlements, her fair brow marred by a frown of concentration, as she looked out across the snow-covered ground, which the army of her cousin, the dead Maxim Harcourt had only just vacated.

His heart pounded anew as he recalled the way she had looked up at him, her troubled frown turning to a smile. It was a smile of such soft and eager welcome that his heart had quickened. And the words she had uttered in that hopeful, breathless voice were burned into his mind for all time. "Maxim will no longer threaten Tristan and Lily, or anyone else here. He was an evil man, Marcel, and his death has also freed me from the fear that he will ever find a way to force me to return to Treanly. I shall be here with you all at Brackenmoore forever."

He had been surprised to find that she still feared that happening. She had been at Brackenmoore for years. But then she had gone on, making him look into those hypnotic green eyes. "There is something else you must know. I have released Tristan from his promise to marry me. It is Lily he loves. He only agreed to marry me because he thought her dead. He feels only as a brother to me as I feel as a sister to him.... You know that my engagement to Tristan was in aid of my finally and actually becoming an Ainsworth in truth." Her gaze darkened on his, displaying

a depth of emotion that rocked him. "That might still
be possible if..."

In that moment he knew Genevieve would take him
did he declare himself. Yet he could not do so, because she wanted him for the wrong reasons. The unmistakable signs of desire he saw in her eyes were
brought on by her admitted need to be an Ainsworth.

Marcel would be wanted for himself alone, not for
his family, however much he loved them.

The past faded away and he realized that, though
painful, his thoughts had taken no more than an instant. He also realized that after two years and so
many miles between himself and Genevieve, Marcel
could not deny that he still felt something for her. And
it was equally clear that though he had tried to convince himself otherwise, his feelings were far from
brotherly.

He felt a tightening not only in his chest, but in his
loins as he saw the way she flushed, the scarlet hue
trailing the elegant and well-remembered column of
her throat. It then swept down over the full curves of
her breasts above the tight bodice of her green velvet
gown. Feeling the tug in his body, Marcel knew he
was on dangerous ground. He forced his gaze away
and when he glanced back, she was looking down at
her hands.

Try though she might, Genevieve could not still the
sudden erratic beating of her heart.

It was he—Marcel.

And looking far more masculine and confident than
she had remembered. She had not known what it was
that caused her to look up only a moment ago, yet she

had felt something, a sense that all was as it should be—but not.

And there he was, with his dark hair grown slightly longer, his blue eyes, which seemed so familiar but also older, more cynical. Those eyes, which she had thought of so very oft in these two long years, had offered comfort and compassion. She nearly cringed now as his blue eyes raked her with a remote and unreadable expression.

There was another difference in him, something so subtle that it could not be measured in the length of his hair, nor the bronze cast of his skin, nor the slightly rolling gait he had adopted. It was a difference undeniably deeper and could more likely be ascertained in the way he held his head and shoulders.

She felt that somehow Marcel had come to a bigger place within himself. It was as if this castle, these lands, would never be vast enough to hold him again.

This understanding was at once frightening and fascinating, for it seemed as if he was the Marcel she had known, yet not that Marcel. He had become somehow mysterious and new and completely unpredictable.

Dear heaven, she did not know what to do with her hands, with her completely scattered emotions. Genevieve risked another quick glance at him and saw that he was once more moving toward them, his expression self-confident, his strides assured.

He no longer looked her way and gave no sign that he had been moved by the sight of her.

And why should he? she asked herself. Why would a man such as Marcel Ainsworth show even the least interest in her?

Simple country maid that she was, in spite of her great fortune.

An overwhelming and at the same time shocking despair swept over her. As if from a very long distance she heard Benedict say, ''Good God above, look who has arrived days before we expected him.'' Peripherally she was aware of her guardian standing and holding out his arms in welcome.

It was clear that he had realized his brother's arrival with joy, but Genevieve could not share in his pleasure. She sat in dejected silence as the next few moments passed in a clatter of introductions and cries of welcome.

No one seemed to note that Genevieve failed to join in the chaos, for there was much to occupy them. Not only had Benedict married and had a child, an auburn-haired daughter named Edlynne, there was an announcement to make of his wife Raine's new pregnancy. Marcel had also acquired another brother in that marriage. Benedict proudly introduced Raine's brother, the now thirteen-year-old William.

Then it was Lily and Tristan's turn to display their second child—a tiny boy named Aidan. Marcel hugged them all, including his youngest brother Kendran, who was near grown to be a man. He ruffled Aidan's dark curls and kissed him on the forehead. Marcel then lifted an excitedly dancing Sabina up into his arms to place a resounding kiss upon her soft cheek before setting her back down, while congratulating Raine and Benedict on their upcoming birth.

By the time anyone got around to looking at Genevieve she had nearly managed to master her emotions. She smiled, albeit stiffly, and moved forward as Benedict turned to her.

Not sure what she would do, Genevieve extended her hand. "Marcel. It is so good to see you home at last." She was quite proud of the fact that her voice remained even despite her inner turmoil.

He took her numb hand in one large warm one for such a brief moment that their flesh barely touched. "It is good to see you, as well, Genevieve."

But though that touch had been brief, it left a tingling of awareness along the length of her fingers and she felt her face heat. She found herself glad that Marcel immediately turned back to Benedict, his voice deep with concern as he said, "I came as soon as your letter arrived."

Benedict replied quickly, "There was no cause for alarm. I had simply decided that it was time you came home."

Marcel appeared both relieved and rueful at this admission. "Well, I am home and gladly so, though you might have told me in your letter."

Had it been so very simple to have him back at Brackenmoore? Genevieve wondered silently. If only she had known, she would have come up with some pretext to have him sent for long before now.

Immediately she told herself her thoughts were sheer madness considering his obvious disregard for her. All the secret dreams she had held close to her heart in these two interminable years had been for naught. There was nothing for them. He was a stranger, a stranger with a life that had nothing to do with her.

Benedict waved toward his own place at the table.

"Sit. I am sure you have hunger after your journey. You have arrived just in time."

Genevieve said hurriedly, "I will see that another plate and cup are brought. I will fetch some of the wine that Maeve has set aside for special occasions, as well."

Benedict halted her. "Nay, sit, Genevieve. I will send one of the servants."

Genevieve was quite aware that the servants would come at Benedict's call, but she would have been grateful for any excuse to be away. Any excuse to keep from having to sit at the table with Marcel. Yet that was exactly what she must do, for she could think of no way to avoid it. Quickly she took her place beside Sabina, fussing over the child's meal though there was no need to do so.

She could do no more than listen distantly as the others continued to converse while they took their places with Marcel, now in the position of honor—directly across from her.

Only briefly could she glance in Marcel's direction for fear of his seeing the yearning she knew was in her own eyes. Yet even in a glance she saw that his shoulders filled the same space Benedict's had. Encased in the black velvet of his houppeland, his shoulders looked so broad and powerful. She had not recalled them being so very wide.

Benedict spoke, his query drawing her undivided attention. "May I ask how long we shall have the pleasure of your company, my brother?"

She looked to Marcel, who was watching Benedict now so she was free to let her gaze focus hungrily on the blue of those heavily lashed eyes. He shrugged.

"I fear not long." Was she wrong or did his gaze flick briefly to her? Or was it the pain that sliced her at hearing his words that made her wish he had some care for leaving her? She forced herself to pay heed as he went on. "My crew is unloading cargo, but I must arrange for another."

Benedict threw up his hands. "Can that not wait for some time? You have made a fortune for both of us."

Marcel shook his head, his gaze earnest on Benedict's now. "My concern is not for myself. I must also think about the livelihood of my men. As Baron of Brackenmoore you understand that."

Benedict subsided. "I do. And your conscientiousness does you credit though I cannot be glad for it. At any rate you must promise to return ere two years have passed in future."

Again Genevieve felt as if his gaze flicked toward her as he replied, "Aye. That promise I will make and keep." There was no doubting the sincerity of his tone as he went on. "I have missed you…all, and Brackenmoore."

In spite of the strange catch in his voice, the words sent a spiral of warmth through Genevieve, even though she told herself they were not meant for her.

Tristan looked up from the other side of the table, with a frown. "Look you, Benedict, is that man not wearing a plaid?"

Genevieve followed the direction of his gaze and saw that there was, indeed, a man garbed in a plaid making his way through the tables. He also wore a white shirt and a pair of sturdy leather shoes.

Benedict stood as the dark-haired young man

reached his side. "I am Lord of Brackenmoore. What business have you here?"

The man faced him with a respectful nod. "The guard at the gate bid me enter this hall when I told him whence I came."

Benedict shrugged. "Speak freely then. From whence have you come?"

The man nodded his dark head respectfully. "I am come from Scotland, my lord. I have a message from the Lady Finella."

"Aunt Finella," Kendran said. "We have not seen her in years. Not since before Mother and Father went to Scotland and were lost at sea."

Even after all these years, Genevieve could see the pain that came to the four brothers' faces at the mention of their parents' deaths. Though she had mourned the loss of her own mother and father, the deep sorrow had passed long ago.

Benedict took a deep breath and held out his hand for the message. "I thank you, sir, and hope you will take your rest here with us."

The young fellow smiled wearily, running dusty hands over his shirtfront. "I will, my lord, but I must take your answer back to the lady with all haste, as she has bid me."

Marcel saw the lines of fatigue about his eyes and mouth. "Certainly, but as Benedict suggested, you must rest before we ask you anything more. You are exhausted," Marcel said.

Benedict nodded in agreement, and Genevieve found herself moved by Marcel's thoughtfulness toward the messenger. "I will first read and discuss the letter with my brothers before questioning you."

"My thanks, m'lord. 'Tis true. I am that tired."

Benedict raised his hand to the head woman, who stood overseeing all from beside the huge hearth, a wide smile upon her well-known countenance. "Maeve."

She came forward quickly. "Aye, my lord."

"Please see that this young man gets a hot meal and some rest in a quiet place."

Maeve nodded. "I will that, my lord." She turned her assessing but kind gaze upon the Scotsman. "Come with me, my man. I'll see you fed and put to bed as if you were a swaddling lad." With that she led him away.

Marcel addressed Benedict. "What has Aunt Finella to say?"

Benedict broke the seal on the roll of parchment, scanning quickly. "Good God."

Kendran said, "What is it, Benedict?"

Benedict turned to them, his expression grave. "Aunt Finella's grandson is being held against his will."

Tristan rose to stand beside him, his own eyes scanning the page quickly. "What?" He, too, grew grim faced.

Genevieve watched as a clearly worried Benedict raked a hand through his thick hair, his gaze going to Raine and away. "She requests our aid."

Raine replied evenly, "Then certainly we must give it, my love."

Marcel spoke up. "Someone will have need to go to Scotland."

Genevieve felt a sinking sensation in the pit of her stomach. And though she knew she had no right, nor reason, to make such a request of heaven, she prayed. *Please God, not Marcel. Not now.* In spite of the fact that he clearly was not interested in her, she was greatly reluctant for him to go.

Raine looked at her husband with resolve. "You must do what you must, Benedict."

He cast her a loving and grateful glance.

Lily spoke up, as well. "And so must you, Tristan. She is your aunt, our family."

Kendran cried, "I will go."

Benedict squared his shoulders. "Methinks we had best take this discussion to the library."

But Genevieve knew as she looked at Marcel, saw the resolution on his handsomely chiseled face, exactly how the discussion would end. He confirmed her suspicion by saying, "You know I am the man to go, Benedict."

An unexpected ache blocked her throat. She reached out to take up her cup, her hand made uncharacteristically clumsy by her agitation. Instead of grasping the cup firmly by the stem as she intended, she barely got hold of the bowl of the cup. She watched with horror as it tipped and the wine flowed across the table, directly into Marcel's lap.

Marcel gasped as the cool wine met his lap.

Genevieve cried out, as well, jumping to her feet. Without thinking, she raced around the table, her eyes widening with horror when she saw the spreading stain on his dark green hose. She reached a helpless hand toward him, and Marcel sucked in his sharp breath. "Nay."

She paused in midmotion, her eyes meeting the blue ones so close to her own. As when she had first seen him in the hall, there was no reading his expression, which was as mysterious and unfamiliar as the sea he had made his home.

She felt as awkward and inexperienced as a baby calf in the face of his coolness, his utter foreignness. His fascinating maleness.

No longer did Genevieve care what the others thought. She could not remain here in the hall with his unreadable and oh so tormenting eyes upon her. After turning on her heel, she exited the hall, not caring in the least what they might make of her flight.

Marcel sat in the library at Brackenmoore with Benedict, Tristan and Kendran. Looking across the table at his brothers, each in turn, he gave an unvoiced sigh. He knew he was the one who must go to Scotland. He also knew that there would be resistance to the idea, because he had only just returned home.

Yet his attention was not fully on that, nor on Benedict, who sat rereading the letter on the other side of the table, which was littered with books and parchments. As it had always been. The book-strewn chamber was, like the rest of Brackenmoore, exactly as he recalled it.

Except for one thing—Genevieve. She seemed somehow more vulnerable and uncertain than she had even through the painful time when Tristan was rediscovering his love for Lily. Marcel had been so angry with Tristan then. It had taken Marcel some time to realize that love knows its own rules and Tristan was driven by the force of his love for Lily. Genevieve had understood that the familial relationship she had with Tristan was no match for such love. She had shown a strength and maturity that had drawn Marcel to her like the tide to the shore.

Today she was a very different woman from the one in his memory. She seemed far more uncertain. Marcel had seen deep vulnerability in her eyes just before she ran from the hall.

In some part of himself he had wanted to get up, go after her and tell her he was fine, that a little spilled wine would not hurt him. And in another part of himself he had known that he could not go after her, that his intense reaction to the mere thought of her touching him had been far too disturbing.

Marcel had convinced himself that his coming back here would not cause difficulty, especially after so much time had elapsed. But the heat that had rushed through him at the moment of seeing her and then again, even more powerfully, as he barely touched her soft, cool fingers, told him otherwise.

His gaze went to Benedict, whose blue eyes, which were so like his own, seemed to weigh him too carefully. Perhaps this letter from Aunt Finella had arrived just in time.

With that in mind, Marcel said, "I take it you wish to debate the matter of my going to Scotland." He had known there would be a discussion when Benedict had said they must come to the library. During his life here at Brackenmoore, all meetings of any significance had been held in the library.

Benedict nodded. "Yes. First let me say that I appreciate your offering to go to Aunt Finella. But you must see that I cannot accept your offer. You have only just arrived home this very day."

Marcel gave an offhanded grin. "How could I not

go, Benedict? You and Tristan both have families. Kendran—'' he looked at his youngest brother with an apologetic shrug ''—is still a boy.''

Kendran groaned in frustration. ''I am no boy.''

Benedict grimaced, but spoke diplomatically. ''Nay, not a boy. Yet not old enough, nor experienced enough, to carry the authority the situation is sure to demand.''

Kendran folded his arms over a chest that was broadening with each passing year. ''You were looking after Brackenmoore at my age.''

Marcel spoke for his eldest brother. ''That is true, but 'twas only because he had no choice. Be grateful that you have the freedom to experience your youth.''

Kendran glared at him. ''Someday I shall show you all that I am capable of more than you can imagine.''

Tristan arched raven brows. ''You would be surprised at how much we can imagine.''

Benedict shook his head, though there was no mistaking the smile in his eyes as he listened to his brothers' exchange. He then sobered quickly. ''Enough. We must discuss this, and there is no time to squander on prideful debate. Aunt Finella's letter is quite clear in her concern over young Cameron.''

Marcel watched as Tristan and Kendran nodded, each of them having read the missive when they first arrived in the library. ''I am the logical choice.''

Benedict frowned. ''I wanted you to know my Raine, our Edlynne, and Raine's brother. Spend time with them.'' The pride and love in his voice could not be mistaken and Marcel realized that there was indeed a change in his brother. He seemed less tense, more content, as if the responsibilities of his position did not rest quite so heavily on his wide shoulders as they had in the past.

Could the love of his wife have affected him so very greatly? Marcel could be nothing but glad for him, even though he felt an unwanted stab of envy—knew an unwanted vision of Genevieve, her green eyes alight.

Benedict said, "Things have not been quite the same since you left."

Marcel forced himself to concentrate on the gratitude he felt at being so greatly missed. "I am not offering to go lightly, my brother. It was indeed time that I become acquainted with your Raine, not to mention the other additions to the family. When next I come home, which I vow here and now will be soon, I will outstay my welcome." He laughed deliberately in spite of his sadness over leaving them.

Benedict leaned back in the chair, assessing him closely. "You are determined."

"I am." Marcel did not meet his questing eyes. "I have no ties to bind me to one place as you have. It would be utter selfishness on my part to do aught but accept this responsibility. My home is on the sea now and she will not lie wakeful, awaiting my return as your families would." Not caring for the slight wistfulness in his tone, he quickly added, "I have done well there, made a good life for myself."

Gravely Tristan said, "Is there nothing here to bring you back home permanently then?"

Marcel did not look at him, for he feared that Tristan would somehow see that the words gave him an instantaneous image of Genevieve. It was not a subject he was willing to discuss. He knew that Benedict had

had suspicions about what was happening between them before he left, but he had not interfered, a fact for which he had been grateful.

Marcel did not want any interference now, from any of his brothers, no matter how much he loved them. He knew that his decision to put aside his feelings for Genevieve was the right one. For both of them.

He spoke hurriedly to forestall any more talk. "In view of the situation I believe I must leave as soon as possible. I will go by sea and take that exhausted Scotsman back with me."

Kendran stood. "Surely not ere morning."

"Nay," Marcel shook his head. "I would not leave before then." He pointed at the one small window. "'Tis soon that full dark will be upon us."

Tristan motioned toward the door. "We'd best get back to the others. They will not want us keeping you to ourselves."

He nodded and told himself that he was doing the right thing.

Yet as he followed Kendran and Tristan to the door, Benedict halted him. "Marcel."

He paused and swung around to see the expression of deliberate resolve on his brother's face. He asked, "What is it, Benedict?"

Benedict frowned, took a deep breath and said, "Roderick Beecham has made Genevieve an offer of marriage."

The words hit Marcel with the power of a gale-force wind. He could not hide his shock. "But how? When?"

Benedict spoke softly. "A few weeks gone. They

met at a tourney last year. Obviously he was quite taken with her.''

Marcel turned his back and forced himself to reply with deliberate calm. ''Beecham is a good man, honorable and strong. There are none better. And there is no doubt that he is her equal in status and property, as he will become a baron on his father's death.''

Benedict replied, ''Aye, he is a very good man. Thus I…Marcel, you cannot play the role of merchant captain forever. You are a nobleman and in that guise would be of great use to us here at Brackenmoore. With my own and Raine's brother's, not to mention Genevieve's lands to administer—''

''Nay, Benedict, I am not needed here.'' He swung around. ''But I am needed aboard the *Briarwind*. There I am a simple sea captain, but I am respected for my own efforts, my own wits, not my name. And you will soon be rid of the responsibilities of Genevieve's lands.''

Benedict frowned. ''I did not—''

Marcel forestalled him with a raised hand, unable to hear another word with the knowledge of Genevieve's marriage to another man making his heart beat so painfully in his chest. ''Your pardon, Benedict, but I will thank you to say no more on this.''

Without another word, Marcel left the room. He needed some time to get hold of himself, to think on what was really disturbing him. To accept that Genevieve would be with another man.

Yet as he strode down the hall, he brought himself up short. Of course she would marry. Had he thought she would spend the rest of her life alone simply because he had gone away? She was a beautiful woman, one who deserved to be loved. He could never wish aught but the best for her.

He had a sudden and unwanted vision of the uncertainty in her eyes as she had looked at him before running from the hall. As always her distress moved him. He did not want her to think that they could not be friends. Perhaps it would be of benefit to both of them if he were to speak to her before he left Brackenmoore, make his position clear. He did not allow himself to think, for even a moment, that he simply wanted to see her once more before he went.

Chapter Two

Genevieve sat in her chamber staring out the high arched window. It was a very warm night, and the breeze that passed though the open window did little to cool her heated cheeks.

She cast a listless glance about the large stone chamber. It slid over the new moss-green samite bed hangings and draperies, the massive dark furnishings, the chests that contained her many garments, shoes and fine jewels. There was gold in the velvet purse she kept in her jewel chest. Though Benedict oversaw her inheritance, she had complete and unfettered access to all.

These signs of wealth offered little comfort this night. All she could think on was the fact that Marcel was home, that he seemed to have made no more than casual note of her existence. While she was as—

She started as a knock sounded upon the door. She called out, "Who is there?"

She recognized Lily's voice as the other woman spoke. "It is me, Lily."

Genevieve answered the door, her wary eyes meeting Lily's gray ones. She said hesitantly, "Enter, Lily. You know there is no need for you to knock." Though she had come to love the gentle black-haired woman in the past two years, she was not anxious to discuss what had occurred in the hall, which was exactly what she feared the other's presence foretold.

Genevieve attempted to hide her agitation as Lily came in and stood quietly, her hands folded before her. Her demeanor only further convinced her that the other woman had something difficult she wished to say. At long last she asked, "Are you well, Genevieve? In the hall you seemed…"

Realizing that she simply could not speak of her confused feelings about Marcel, Genevieve quickly forestalled her. "Please, Lily, you came to Brackenmoore with your own secrets. I respected that. I ask that you respect my need to keep some things to myself, as well."

The other woman bowed her elegant dark head, her gray eyes soft. "As you wish. Should you ever wish to talk I will listen."

Genevieve nodded, her gaze grateful but resolute. "There is naught to tell. I am well and will be so."

Lily met her gaze once more. "You are loved by all of us, Genevieve, will always be the sister of our hearts."

With that Lily left the room.

Genevieve was glad, for she would not wish Lily to see her sadness. How easily those last words had fallen from her lips. How Genevieve wished that she was indeed a sister to this family.

She had first visited Brackenmoore with her parents when they stopped here on a journey north from their own holdings. Benedict's family had been friend to hers. That brief stay had been one of the happiest times of her life. She did not well recall Marcel's parents. Her memories were of the boys and the joy and freedom she had known with them, wandering the forest, wading in the sea, exploring the cliffs. She had never forgotten those experiences though she had been no more than seven.

At that time, she had not taken any particular note of Marcel. He had been one of the four magical and carefree creatures who had played with her and shown her their world for two whole days. Two days in which she had not heard her mother cry even once.

It had not been until just over two years ago, long after Benedict had taken her in and made her his ward that she had begun to see Marcel as anything but one of the Ainsworth brothers. He had been kind to her, shown concern for her when others were lost in their own troubles. And her feelings for him had changed. She had found herself looking at him in a new way, feeling a strange stirring when he was near.

She had never felt anything like that toward Tristan, no matter how certain she had been that their marrying was a good idea. To be an Ainsworth was all she had really wished for in her life. Until she had come to care for Marcel.

Though Genevieve knew the Ainsworths loved her, none of them could ever understand how it felt to be on the outside, to want above all else to truly be one of them.

But she was not.

Before she had run away to Brackenmoore, her life had been very different from what it was now. And more unhappy than she had ever admitted to anyone. Somewhere in her mind was the belief that if she could only become an Ainsworth, she would be able to finally and completely erase the years before she had come to live here.

It had been for this reason that she had felt distress at learning Tristan was still in love with Lily, whom he had believed dead. Genevieve had never begrudged them their happiness, not for one moment, only mourned the death of her own dream.

Yet when she had realized her feelings for Marcel, her hope to be an Ainsworth in truth had once more come to life. Not that this was the reason for her feelings for him. That she knew. It had simply meant that her hope was reborn.

Now Marcel had returned, a Marcel she no longer felt she knew. Yet he was so very handsome and even more compelling than before. She had made a complete fool of herself by spilling wine all over his lap. Her cheeks burned at the very thought.

Hearing the door open again, Genevieve did not turn from the window. "I am fine, Lily. As I told you, you need have no concern for me."

A deep voice replied, "It is not Lily."

Swinging around with a gasp, Genevieve saw none other than Marcel standing just inside the doorway. "What are you doing here?" Her eager gaze ran over him, so tall, so strange and familiar at the same time, so very handsome with his black hair, the color of which seemed to intensify the blue of his eyes.

He took a deep breath, closing the door behind him before he said, "Genevieve…" He took a step toward her then stopped. "I had to come to see you."

She caught her own breath, the sound of her name on his lips making her realize anew just how much she had missed him, the sound of his voice, his gentle strength. She tried to answer evenly, but her own hopes, her irrepressible reactions to him brought a huskiness to her voice. "Why, Marcel?"

Marcel came toward her. "There are things I wish to say to you. Things that, I believe, must be said."

What was he talking about? Could it be what she most desired in the secret recesses of her heart? Did he feel what she did?

As he began to speak, she understood that all these thoughts had simply been wishful thinking on her part. "Firstly, let me say that I want you to know that my presence here at Brackenmoore need not make you uncomfortable. There is no need to avoid me or to be nervous of my presence."

She drew herself up, her heart thumping as she blushed. "What makes you think I am nervous of your presence?"

He shrugged. "Your spilling the wine." Inwardly she cringed. As he continued, she felt torn between pleasure and embarrassment. "In all the time I have known you, you have never been aught but graceful in your every movement. Even when you first visited Brackenmoore at seven."

Genevieve settled on incredulity. She was not usually awkward, but she had to have been so at times as a normal seven-year-old. She took his statement as an overzealous effort to put her at ease with her clumsiness in the hall.

Yet as Marcel went on, she forgot all but the utter embarrassment caused by what he was saying. "I know that before I left we had a particular...that we had certain feelings for one another. I realized soon after my departure from Brackenmoore that we had simply been drawn together through your troubles over your engagement to Tristan. I want you to know that all is forgotten. I do not harbor any feelings that would make our having a friendship difficult and my hope is that you feel the same. Any fear that you might have about my having feelings for you that are more than brotherly may be laid to rest.''

Genevieve could say nothing as his meaning found purchase in her mind, feeling as though a dagger had been stuck into her heart. He was letting her know in clear terms that he had no romantic feelings for her and that she should not harbor any such feelings.

How could he talk to her this way? Did Marcel think to put her in her place, to make certain that she did not pursue him and cause him embarrassment?

Well, he need not worry there. She had no intention of pressing herself upon him.

It was, in fact, the last thing she would do.

She drew herself up to her full height, which unfortunately was not great. "Have no worry on that score, Marcel. I thought no such thing. I was simply embarrassed at having ruined your homecoming and I felt I might cry. Yow know that I have never cared to display my emotions before others.''

He frowned, and she wondered at his expression before he said, "I should have realized. Benedict has told me of your coming marriage to Roderick Beecham.'' He smiled stiffly, even as she felt a ripple of shock run though her at his words. She was hard-pressed to concentrate as he said, "You have my congratulations. He is a fine man."

Genevieve simply stood there, staring at him. It was true that Roderick Beecham had sent an offer of marriage. And that Benedict has said he would make a very fine husband. It was also true that she had, although flattered and moved by the proposal of such a gentle and handsome man, declined. He had written back and indicated that he would still be willing should she change her mind.

She did want a husband, children.

Yet in her heart Genevieve had known that she would never change her mind. She could think of no one save the very man who now stood before her and told her that he had no such feelings for her.

Genevieve offered what she hoped was a bright smile. "Thank you so very much for your kind wishes."

She saw a strange and unfathomable expression pass over his handsome features as he said, "I am sorry that I will not be in attendance and you must be assured that I will be thinking of you on my journey to Scotland and after—"

She spoke too quickly, her shock evident. "You are the one who is leaving for Scotland then."

He nodded. "Aye."

She felt a jolt of renewed sadness, in spite of her resentment about his attitude. Genevieve asked, "When?"

He grimaced. "Immediately. A rival clan has kidnapped Aunt Finella's grandson. They refuse to negotiate with her and she has turned to us, as we are her only family. We cannot ignore such a request."

Genevieve looked at her hands as the seriousness of the summons sank home. "I see. Then surely you must go even though it will mean that you must be away from your family again so soon." Her gaze met his. "It is very good of you to do this."

Marcel shrugged, as if uncomfortable with her praise. And as in the hall, she could not help noting how wide his shoulders seemed to have grown.

"You have never met Aunt Finella, have you?" he asked.

She shook her head, distantly thinking that this was just one more thing that set her apart from being a true Ainsworth. Genevieve had never had an aunt of any kind. Knowing he was expecting a reply, she said, "Nay. I have not met her."

He nodded speaking casually, "I recall her being quite the eccentric though it has been many years since I have seen her. Since before Mother and Father died. It will be good to see her again after all this time, but the fact that her grandson has been kidnapped will not make for a happy reunion."

Genevieve murmured, "I will pray that he is returned to her well." In spite of his declaration that he did not wish her to harbor any feelings of attachment to him, she could not deny the mad thrumming of her pulse as she looked into those dark blue eyes.

Obviously completely unaware of this, he continued. "I have never met my cousin. When Aunt Finella was last here it was with her husband, who was also Cameron. He was a great bear of a man with a craggy red beard and hearty laugh. Some time before our parents died, actually. It was as they were returning from a visit to her that their ship floundered and they were lost.'' She heard the regret that entered his voice as he spoke of his parents, though the accident had occurred so many years ago. She knew that Marcel had been young when they died, as she had been when her own parents passed just before she was fourteen. They had been killed in an accident that would not have occurred had her mother not been having one of her ''spells'' and gone bathing in the lake on a dark, stormy night. Her father had gone in after her and both of them had drowned.

Her parents' deaths had resulted in her being sent to her cousin Maxim Harcourt. That despicable knave had attempted to force himself upon her. Genevieve had escaped him and his keep with one thought in her mind, that of getting to Brackenmoore.

Looking at Marcel, feeling her stomach tug at the sheer masculinity of him, seeing the lean line of his jaw, which seemed to beckon her lips even now, Genevieve knew that she must take hold of her feelings for him. She was not willing to jeopardize her place in this family because of an unrequited infatuation.

Surely that was what she would be doing by holding on to any romantic notions about this man after he had made his feelings clear. If Marcel wished to put what they had once felt aside, she would do so as well. After all, she reminded herself, he was leaving again. The tightness that came to her chest made her wonder if she was as indifferent to him as she told herself she was.

Deliberately she smiled at him, aiming to be as bright in her manner as possible. ''I do appreciate your coming here to see if all was well with me, Marcel, especially as you are leaving so soon and your time at Brackenmoore has become doubly precious...to us all. I am most well and contented as things are between us. Your presence here in the future will cause me no unrest.'' It was suddenly very important that he believe this, that he did not again stay away for two long years.

Marcel viewed that smile, heard the cool civility in Genevieve's voice and felt a completely unexpected twinge of irritation. He was glad that she accepted what must be, was very glad indeed to hear that she was not harboring any untoward notions about the two of them.

She seemed, in fact, to be happy about the offer of marriage from Roderick Beecham. It was a fact that made Marcel less pleased than it should have.

If only they could go back to the way they had been before their being thrown together had changed the way they... He sighed.

His gaze ran over her as she looked down at her clasped hands. He took in the sweet arch of her cheek, the dark fringe of her lashes, the lovely curve of her mouth, the slender length of her neck and the delicate golden curls that escaped her head covering at her nape. The idea of twining his fingers in those curls was somehow more intimate than he would ever have imagined. His gaze dipped lower to where her breasts pressed above the square neckline of her gown.

Genevieve made him think of a warm fire on a frosty evening, of candlelight and downy pillows and soft white sheets, of...

The sound of his own muted groan startled him and Marcel drew himself up, feeling a strangling tightness in his chest. He wanted the sea, the roll and pitch of his ship, the sounds and smells of exotic ports.

Perhaps, it was best that he was leaving immediately, given his own unexplainable reactions to the woman before him. He spoke far more gruffly than he had intended. "Well, this will be good-bye then."

The shock on her face could not be mistaken, for she blanched and swayed. "Now?"

He was not happy with the way his voice softened in reaction to her shock. "Nay, not this very eve but on the morrow. Far before you rise."

He looked away from her, his stomach tightening at the sadness in her gaze.

"I am sorry for being so foolish." She turned her back to him. "You have no idea how I...we have missed you."

Though he could not see her face, Marcel was aware of the catch in her voice, the pain. Before he knew what he was going to do, he had moved to put a hand on her slight shoulder.

The moment he touched her, he felt a piercing heat enter his body and, as she swung around to face him, he saw that she too had felt it. Her green eyes were wide with shock, and another emotion that he could not fail to recognize. It was the same emotion that had sent him from the keep two years ago.

As if through a dream he saw her reach toward him, felt the light pressure of her slender fingers on his chest. His body tightened and all he knew, could think of, was Genevieve and his own undeniably powerful reaction to her.

It had been too long. There had been too many nights when he had lain awake thinking of her, wondering what would have happened that last day at Brackenmoore if he had just turned to her, just...

His arms closed about Genevieve's pliant form. His lips found hers as her sweet womanly shape seemed to mold itself to his.

Genevieve felt as if she had waited for this moment her whole life. No matter what she had tried to tell herself over the past two years, she had never, for one moment, stopped wanting this man. Marcel—his mouth was firm and hot on hers, the taste of him so heady, and more wonderful than she had even dreamed. His hands on her back were strong and sure, molding her to him, and she wanted to cry out with joy that he was finally touching her, kissing her as she had longed for him to.

She gave a husky gasp and whispered, ''Marcel.''

When his tongue flicked over her lips, she opened to him, welcomed him into her, felt a spark of something hot and fluid move in her lower belly. This was Marcel, the man she had longed for with each aching part of her as she lay in her lonely bed. She raised her hands to hold the back of his head, threading her eager fingers through his thick black hair. She strained into him, increasing the pressure of their kisses with a growing urgency, knowing a sense of pleasure as his hips pressed in to her.

Marcel drew her closer to the length of his ardent and increasingly eager body, running his tongue over hers, reveling in her responses to him. Never, even in his most heated dreams, had Genevieve been this pliant, this responsive, this enticing.

He was infinitely aware of his own readiness, the aching need of him. As his manhood pulsed against

her belly, she gasped, wriggling closer to him. Awed
and humbled and undeniably aroused by her response,
Marcel felt an indefinable something expanding inside
him. It radiated out through his body, rippling in wave
upon wave of not only pleasure but also a tenderness
so overwhelming that he was dizzied and shaken by
it.

When her hands clasped his hips, Marcel closed his
eyes on the resulting flash of heat that throbbed in his
belly. He reached up to slide his hand between their
bodies, closing around the firm weight of her breast,
hearing her cry of yearning and reveling in it.

Genevieve was on fire, her blood turned to a molten
river of desire—a desire for something she could not
name. But as her breast seemed to swell beneath his
questing hand, she realized that her body knew what
she wanted, knew and was more than prepared to seek
the answer to this indescribably delicious longing—
this all-encompassing need.

Marcel was at first only distantly aware of a stran-
gled gasp that came from neither himself nor the
woman in his arms. Breathing heavily, he pushed back
and looked in the direction of the sound.

Lily stood in the entrance to the chamber, her fingers covering her mouth in obvious surprise, but he
could see no hint of condemnation in those gray eyes.

As her gaze met his, she spoke hastily. "I…forgive
me."

Marcel felt Genevieve start and he reacted instinc-
tively, pressing her face protectively against his chest
as Lily went on, her expression seeming to display
approval. "I did not know that you were…I thought

Genevieve was alone. I will speak with her on the morrow.''

With that, Lily was gone.

That approval made Marcel realize just how wrong he was in what he was doing. He had no right to hold this woman, kiss her, and lead others to believe that he had feelings for her. Not only did his life at sea lie as a barrier between them but there was also her future marriage to Beecham to consider. He took a deep breath, concentrating on easing the erratic beating of his blood, calming the fierce need in his belly.

Finally Marcel let his arms fall away from Genevieve's and stepped back. Dear God, what had he done?

He could not meet the probing weight of her gaze, as he spoke. "Forgive me, Genevieve. I..." There was nothing he could say that would not make things worse. His assurances that he felt nothing for her that was not brotherly seemed very foolish now.

He squared his shoulders and went to the door. He paused only briefly when he heard her plaintive cry of "Marcel!"

"There is nothing to say, Genevieve. I am very sorry."

He was more sorry than he could ever say. Sorry that no matter what his resolutions now and the last time he had been with Genevieve, he still had no power to resist his attraction to her.

It was best that he was leaving in the morning. Not only for himself, but for both of them.

He could only pray that time and her marriage would eradicate the wildly confused feelings that existed between them, for he had no wish to hurt her.

The sorrow in her voice as she had spoken his name could not be missed.

Though he felt a tug to return to her, he would not allow himself to do that. He would go back to the sea, to the life he had made for himself, where he was sure of what he wanted and why.

Genevieve could only stand there staring at the closed door in stunned silence, her heart beating so fiercely and painfully that it felt as if it might surely break through the wall of her chest.

Why had Lily come?

The thought was immediately followed by a horrified thanks to God she had done so, for if she had not... Genevieve was afraid to even contemplate what might have occurred. She had been past reason and sanity, aware of nothing save the way it felt to be kissed and held in Marcel's strong arms—save her own desire for him.

Surely he felt something, too.

Yet his distress at Lily's having seen them together was more than evident.

Genevieve put her hands to her head, her headdress falling unheeded to the floor as she ran her fingers through her too heavy hair. She gained no relief from her anguish, only a horrifying certainty that her feelings for Marcel were stronger than they had ever been.

Stronger, the word was such an understatement. Heaven help her, she loved him. All these long months when she had tried to convince herself she did not care for him in that way had been nothing more than a lie. A lie to hide the truth of her own feelings from herself, for surely she had loved him all along.

Marcel's reaction to her told her that he was not immune to her, no matter how he might wish otherwise. Even she, as innocent as she was of such matters, knew that his kisses had been far from indifferent or even brotherly.

Why should this displease him so? Whatever could make him wish to deny the depth of passion and sense of deep connection that had overtaken them?

They were surely the same unknown reasons that had made him leave Brackenmoore two long years ago.

If he would only talk with her she was sure his reservations could be overcome. Surely her love for him would be enough to turn his passion to true caring. The problem lay in the fact that he would have to be convinced to tell her what was troubling him, why he was holding back from her. His departure in the morning would severely limit any opportunities for them to speak.

Who knew how long Marcel would remain gone this time?

If they were apart, she could have no opportunity to overcome his unexplained reticence, make him see that with her love as a basis their feelings could grow. There was no conceivable way for a man to kiss a woman the way he had Genevieve lest he have some feeling for her.

Suddenly Genevieve knew what she had to do. She could not allow Marcel to walk out of her life again.

She would simply have to go to West Port, board the *Briarwind* and go to Scotland with him. Then she would have an opportunity to convince him that they belonged together. How she would manage this feat would take some contemplation, but Genevieve was not afraid of either planning or executing the deed.

She had escaped from the unwanted advances of her cousin Maxim Harcourt by running from Treanly in the dead of night, when she was barely more than a child. She would find a way to get to West Port and board that ship.

Her love for him would be her guide.

A few hours later, Genevieve wrapped her hair tightly in a wide strip of fine cloth and tucked it into a floppy velvet cap of William's. As she stepped into the other garments she had taken from William's chamber, Genevieve knew a moment of regret. She did not care for the idea that she had taken his clothing without permission, but she dared not bring him into her confidence. She was very sure that he would only tell his sister Raine, and Raine would certainly stop her.

It seemed like a sign of some sort that neither William nor Kendran had been in their rooms. Maeve had informed her that both of them were in the hall with the others, visiting with Marcel.

Maeve's expression had plainly shown her surprise that Genevieve was not there with them. It was to her credit that the head woman had held her tongue concerning the subject. A most unusual restraint.

Surely these occurrences were a portent of the fact that she was doing the right thing. All would be absolved when she and Marcel returned together.

Her feelings for Marcel were the only thing that mattered. The members of this family knew well that in the name of love one must ofttimes overcome difficulty and sometimes even behave in ways that one never would in other circumstances.

Of all those involved, she was most concerned about the reaction of Marcel himself. She was well aware that he would be angry when he saw her. Of that she had no doubt, but she meant to hide her presence until they were well at sea and hopefully give them an opportunity to talk before he could return her home. Surely he would forgive her once he had seen the truth, that they must be together. He would realize that the two of them must be together, marry and have children, who would grow to adulthood in this wonderful loving family.

Her heart swelled at the very thought. Anything, any hardship she had to face was worth her eventual union with Marcel. For she could not doubt that it would come.

It was this thought that bolstered her courage as she wrote a note and left it with one of the serving boys. She had addressed it to Benedict saying very little more than that she had gone after Marcel. More than that she did not disclose, though she suspected that Benedict knew far more of her feelings for Marcel than he had ever said. She could only pray that the boy would do as she had instructed and show it to no one until it was too late to stop her.

Her courage stayed with her as she went to the stable and took one of the horses. The one she took was Kendran's horse, which she had apologized for in her letter. She hoped that in the dark and in her boy's garb, she would be mistaken for Kendran. All knew that he had an occasional nocturnal tryst and he was far less likely to be challenged at the gate than she was.

Yet she could not deny a lagging of her determination as she rode out from the castle gate, having gotten no more than a wave from the guard. It was very dark outside the castle walls, the moon being only a curved sliver in the early summer sky. The horse knew where the trail lay this close to the castle, but Genevieve was suddenly less certain about farther out from there. Though she had been to West Port on more than one occasion, it was not by any means a common destination.

The night she had escaped from Treanly it had been in absolute desperation, feeling that nothing could be worse than remaining in the clutches of her predatory cousin, Maxim. Her memories of being at Brackenmoore had burned like a beacon in her mind, lighting her way during the night.

Now the heavy darkness and the looming shapes of the trees as she moved farther away from the protective mass of the castle were somewhat disturbing. Only the belief that she and Marcel would soon be together kept her going.

Marcel stayed in the hall as late as he could, smiling, talking and drinking. He told stories of his adventures at sea to the wide-eyed amazement of Raine's brother, William, and Sabina, not to mention the genuine interest of the others.

He could not miss the fact that Genevieve stayed away. Nor could he help seeing the way Lily watched him, her gray eyes assessing.

While one part of him was glad of Genevieve's absence and that he need make no pretence at treating her with polite civility, he felt sick, with himself and the Fates. He should not have touched Genevieve, should never have kissed her. He had simply not been able to stop himself.

Why could he not get over whatever mad attraction he had for her? Perhaps it was just being back at Brackenmoore, where the memories of his youthful infatuation with her lingered. Perhaps he was simply lonely from being so long from home.

He was not in love with Genevieve. Genevieve, who was to wed another man. No one had mentioned the forthcoming marriage again and for that he was grateful, for he was not sure how well he could hide his unwanted discontent over this from his brothers.

His stomach tightened each time he thought of her with Beecham—his hands touching her…he groaned. The sooner he got back to the *Briarwind,* the better.

Feeling a gentle touch on his shoulder, Marcel looked down. Sabina stood watching him with steady regard in her gray eyes, which were so like her mother's. "You are sad, Uncle."

He hugged her quickly. "I am not sad, dear heart. I am happy, happy to be here with you all."

She smiled up at him. "I have missed you, Uncle."

Feeling a lump rise in his throat, he ruffled her soft dark hair. "I am so glad that you remember me, sweeting."

She grinned, her small face lighting up. "Mother and Father and the uncles, they speak of you always."

Marcel felt a wave of love sweep over him. He might be gone from here, but he was not forgotten. He held out his arms. "Are you too big a girl to sit upon my lap?'' She came into his arms without hesitation.

Glancing up to see the affection in his family's eyes as they viewed this, Marcel again felt an overwhelming sense of love for them. His sadness at saying good-bye to them only made controlling his emotions all the more difficult. He did regret leaving them again, in spite of his certainty that he was only doing what was right—in returning to his life aboard the *Briarwind*.

His choice had been made two years ago. The sea had been good to him, taught him things about himself that he had not known. The responsibilities of command rested well upon his shoulders. Marcel had found the place where he alone was in control of the decisions that were made, and accountable for them.

The men who sailed beneath him treated him with a respect born not of his name but his abilities. They did not know he was an Ainsworth.

He'd resisted the urge to take a woman who wanted him for that name alone, and gained all through his own efforts. He would not now regret his decision. No matter how alone it made him feel.

Chapter Three

The arrival of the first creeping light of dawn just happened to coincide with her entering the town of West Port, and Genevieve did so with her head down. She knew that her horse would mark her a young nobleman, but she did not wish to press fortune by hoping that her face would not give her away.

The narrow streets were not busy at this early hour of the morning, but she knew they presently would be. This was a fishing, shipping port. Men who worked the sea did not linger long abed.

After stabling Kendran's stallion at a reputable hostelry she made her way to the docks. The heels of William's oversized boots clumped noisily upon the wooden walk, and she tried to go more quietly while keeping in mind her need for haste. She had no trouble locating the *Briarwind*. It was a large three-masted merchant ship with a wide belly that she had seen on more than one occasion since coming to live at Brackenmoore. Along with the usual clutter of sailing paraphernalia, the deck bore a large structure at one end and what she knew was the captain's cabin at the other. Genevieve was sure that once she got on board she could find a place to hide.

The sounds of male voices told her that at least a portion of the crew was up and about. A stack of barrels and wooden crates rested along the dock near the stern of the ship. She ducked in amongst them.

As she looked up over the side of the ship, she began to grow more nervous and uncertain, for there were more people up and about than she had at first thought. Several men were milling about the deck, exchanging jests and conversation as they worked, braiding ropes and stitching sails.

There was no way she could simply step across the gangway without notice. What would she say if someone attempted to stop her from going aboard?

As the question ran through her mind, a man came toward the gangway. With a silent groan of frustration she ducked behind a barrel.

She had delayed too long in making sure Kendran's horse was taken care of. Now what was she to do?

Marcel left Brackenmoore with a heavy heart. He rose long before dawn, saying good-bye only to his brothers, who were clearly saddened by his leaving. Marcel could not help seeing the way Tristan watched him the whole while that he was making ready to go. He was fairly certain that after they had sought their beds only short hours ago, Lily had revealed what she had seen in Genevieve's chamber.

Thankfully, Marcel was spared from having to explain what had happened between him and Genevieve. Tristan, in spite of his steady regard, kept his opinion of the matter to himself.

As he left the keep alone, the Scot having refused to return by sea, Marcel told himself he was glad that he had not seen Genevieve. Another meeting would serve neither of them, for he had nothing to say that could possibly improve the situation.

He had gone a short way down the road when he found himself pausing to look back at the castle in the distance. He could not deny his sadness—not entirely due to his leaving his family.

That kiss. His body burned at the memory of it. It had been more powerful, more shattering than anything his wayward imagination had been able to conjure in his waking hours or in his restless dreams.

Squaring his shoulders, he went on, determined this time to leave his feelings for Genevieve behind for good. She would be much better off with Lord Roderick Beecham. A more honorable and suitable man could not be found.

Unfortunately, this thought did not bring the peace he sought. He felt only an aching emptiness.

With a growl of frustration, Marcel prodded his mount to a gallop. All he needed was an invigorating ride to clear his mind.

Marcel was still riding at a gallop when he entered West Port some hours later, having made the journey in far less time than he'd expected. He moved through the port without paying much attention to the bustling activity around him. He had to see to the outfitting of his ship, and in short order.

He was not sorry for the pressing haste of his mission. He only hoped it would help keep his mind from thoughts of Genevieve and the way she had felt in his arms as the hard ride from Brackenmoore had not.

Resolutely he went about the business of ordering supplies. Although the journey to Scotland was not a long one, he never set out without enough rations to see them through untoward circumstances. It cost him extra to have his goods delivered with such speed, but he was assured that all would arrive at the *Briarwind* within the hour.

Leaving the horse at the establishment where he had hired it, Marcel then made his way to his ship. As he approached, he experienced the same rush of pride that he felt each time he saw her.

She was a fine vessel, which his father had purchased from a Venetian shipbuilder. In her he'd sailed throughout Europe and the Holy Land. They'd carried English wool and Arabian spices, and Chinese silks in the hold. The captain's cabin was visible from where he stood and forward of that on the starboard side was the galley, and the pen for the livestock that provided fresh meat for the crew. In the forepeak was a small chamber for the bow watch. In between was an ordered jumble of spare sailing parts, benches, spars, casks, chests and so on.

He was not at all surprised to see the amazement on the face of his first mate, Harlan, as he stepped up onto the gangplank. Harlan dropped the rope he was repairing and came toward him, that tall, deceptively slender frame seeming poised for action as always. He spoke with no small measure of surprise. "Captain, why are you returned so soon?"

Marcel shrugged, explaining the situation hastily. When he was finished, Harlan asked, "So we will set sail immediately?"

"As soon as the supplies I ordered arrive."

The first mate frowned. "Some of the men are not aboard. They have gone into town as you said they could."

Marcel rubbed his forehead. "See that they are found and told to come back now."

Harlan nodded his sun-streaked blond head. "Very well. Jack and Harry are aboard and none too worse for wear. I'll send them out to look for the others."

Marcel nodded with approval. He knew the men would not be pleased, many of them very likely nursing sore heads this day. It could not be helped. He would make an effort to see they were compensated next time they put into port.

Without wasting another minute, he turned and addressed all within earshot. "We leave as soon as the ship is seaworthy. I'll be in my cabin mapping our course."

Genevieve watched Marcel arrive, approaching the ship with a confident stride, and felt the uncontrollable pounding of her heart. After he was aboard ship, she heard the deep and achingly familiar timbre of his voice as he spoke to another man.

It felt so good just to be near him. She told herself that she was glad she had come, even if she had spent the past hours huddled behind a barrel. The fact that she still had no idea about how to proceed did not completely quell her anticipation at being with Marcel soon.

She was weak limbed at the possibility that he might soon hold her—kiss her again.

Abruptly she tore her mind from that distracting and all too stirring prospect. There was much that must fall into order before such an event could ever take place.

Her desperate gaze scanned the dock for some answer to her difficulty, and she saw a man approaching, pulling a cart laden with crates much like the ones that were piled near her. He stopped and ran an assessing eye over the *Briarwind*. He lifted his cap, scratching his head as his gaze then went to the heavily loaded cart.

Before he had moved from this position an even larger cart loaded with barrels moved up behind him. The driver bellowed, "Delivery for the *Briarwind*. Move out of my way."

The first man spun around scowling. "And what do you think I'd be doing here?"

The second man frowned in return and said, "Get yourself unloaded and out of my way then. I've other work this afternoon."

The first man looked back toward the ship. "I'd be happy to, if someone would only come to help me."

Genevieve watched a tall and undeniably handsome blond man come to the side of the *Briarwind* and look out at them, and an idea came into her mind. The blond man left the ship and, along with the carters, began to discuss the unloading of the goods. When he turned and called out, "Come, the wagons must be unloaded," two other men left the ship and moved toward the carts.

Hastily, before she could lose her courage, Genevieve slipped out into the open, moving quickly to take one of the crates from the cart. It was so heavy that she gasped in surprise. Yet she forced herself to hold it, breathing carefully.

She had to appear to be a laborer. Hopefully, the carters would think her part of the ship's crew. The crew would imagine her to have come with one of the carts. Thus would she get onto the *Briarwind*. After that, it would simply be a matter of finding a hiding place.

The two roughly dressed sailors went to the first cart and took a crate each. Genevieve fell in line behind them. To her utter amazement neither the carters nor the blond seaman paid her any attention at all. She was able to follow the seamen, right to a hatch in the middle of the deck.

Genevieve knew that she would not be able to carry the heavy crate down the ladder that rose up from inside, though the men seemed to have no trouble as they went down ahead of her. Holding her breath with terror, she dropped the crate on the deck and ducked behind the mast, her heart pounding like a drum in her chest.

One of the men came up, saw the crate and scowled, looking about as if perplexed. Then with a shrug, he shouldered it and disappeared down the ladder once more.

Soon both of the sailors emerged from the hole and went back across the deck. When they reached the gangway, Genevieve cast a careful look about. The carters and the other man were still talking, but they were turned the other way, obviously discussing the goods that had been brought.

It was now or never. Taking a deep breath, Genevieve raced toward the hatch. Holding that breath and knowing she dared not pause to look behind her, she took a tight hold of the sides of the ladder and scrambled down it.

Spinning around, Genevieve could see that she was in the hold. The inside walls of the ship were lined with all manner of goods that would be needed to make long voyages—extra ropes, canvas, even extra lanterns hung from the posts. There were also all sizes of containers besides the three wooden crates that had been brought from the carts.

Hearing the sound of voices approaching above, Genevieve raced down the center aisle and lodged herself behind a pile of goods at the front of the ship. This was accomplished none too quickly for the men brought more supplies down into the hold.

Several others had now joined the two, who had begun the unloading. They formed a sort of line as they transferred the cargo into the hold.

The next hours passed in an agony of frustration and anxiety. Her frustration stemmed from being inactive for so very long, and anxiety from her fear that one of the sailors would come too close and discover her hiding place. In spite of her agitation, she was somewhat awed at their efficiency as they packed the space so tightly there was no more than a narrow walkway down the center when they were through.

When finally they had finished and closed the hatch above her, Genevieve heaved a great sigh of relief. Yet when the boat began to move some time later, she knew a renewed sense of trepidation as well as relief, her stomach clenching at the realization that she had succeeded.

She was aboard the *Briarwind,* and it was moving.

Just what might happen now she was afraid to even contemplate.

Genevieve grew cold as the day wore on. It was very damp down in the hold. She was afraid, though, to leave her hiding place for fear of being discovered should someone open the hatch unexpectedly. She did not believe they had gone far enough to make Marcel believe that he must go on to Scotland rather than take her home.

Surely all they needed were a few days together to work out whatever was making him hold back. Surely when he learned that she loved him…

The pure happiness she felt at the possibility of his returning her affection in even a small measure, at the notion of his letting go his reservations and completing the lovemaking they had begun at Brackenmoore was incentive enough to stay where she was. She could not reveal herself yet.

But after another interminable stretch of time, the cramping in her legs and lower back grew unbearable. She bit her lip with indecision. The hold was empty of all save her. Surely it would hurt nothing to walk about a bit.

Slowly, listening for any sound from above, Genevieve stood. The tingling in her lower limbs told her just how badly she had needed to move. Gingerly she exercised each muscle until the sensations eased.

Cautiously she stumbled about in the darkness until she found a lantern, and the implements to light it, hanging at the bottom of the stair. With a sigh of relief, she looked about. As she had seen earlier, a narrow pathway ran down the center to the stair, which led to the upper deck.

Genevieve began to pace this trail. Then as time passed and her body felt more itself, she began to be aware of another form of discomfort. That of hunger.

It had been many hours since she had thought of eating anything. Her stomach growled, as if now demanding its due. Putting a hand over her belly, Genevieve looked about the hold.

She knew that many of these containers would hold food. Why should she go hungry when surrounded by such plenty?

Sometime later, she leaned back against where she had sat down to eat and sighed. She had pried open a barrel with a bar she found hanging nearby. It had offered only salted fish, but her hunger had improved the taste.

Though she had no idea how much time had passed since she had come aboard the *Briarwind,* Genevieve was fairly certain that it must be well into the night. The tiredness she felt told her that she had been down there for many hours.

Again she sighed. What a day it had been, and after no sleep the previous night. Surely there would be no harm in closing her eyes for just a few moments. If none of the crew had come down to the hold in the evening hours, it was quite unlikely that they would do so at night.

She extinguished the light. Then using her arm to cushion her head, Genevieve lay down at the far end of the path…

The next thing she knew she was looking up at a heavily lined masculine face that contained a bulbous nose and a pair of watery gray eyes. He spoke roughly as he scratched his wiry gray head. "Now, what have we here?"

With a gasp of shock, Genevieve sat straight up, her own voice husky with sleep and horror as she cried, "Who are you?"

The man laughed gruffly. "It's me who'll be asking the questions, lad. What are you doing here?"

"I…" She hesitated, realizing that she was still wearing her masculine garments and this fellow thought her a boy. For reasons she could not name, she did not disabuse him of his mistaken notion.

"Well?" he prodded.

Now that she was found out, Genevieve could only think of getting to Marcel. "Take me to your captain."

The man took her by the arm and hauled her roughly to her feet. "That I will, young man, but I'm not thinking he'll be glad to see a stowaway. Especially one who refuses to answer the questions put to him."

Genevieve did not care for this mauling in the least but decided to let it pass, for the man did not know who she was. When he nudged her ahead of him up the stairs, she pushed his hand away and went up with her head held high.

It was not yet full light on deck and a dark bank of cloud on the distant horizon seemed to make the light even dimmer. As she peered about she did not see any other signs of movement on deck. Her captor jerked his head toward the cabin at the stern of the boat and said, "Go on, no dawdling. You wanted to see the captain. Get to it then."

Genevieve did not acknowledge him but moved in

the direction he had indicated. As soon as she had spoken with Marcel, this lout would mind his manners.

When the sailor pounded loudly upon the closed door, Genevieve felt a momentary anxiety. There was no question in her mind that Marcel would be surprised to see her. The possibility of his being angry was very great, as well.

Hopefully he would not remain so for long.

The heavy oak door opened abruptly. Her heart turned over with a sudden and unexpectedly deep yearning as her gaze came to rest on the man she had come so far to be with. Marcel's midnight-dark hair was tousled from sleep and the long white shirt, which was all he wore, lay open to expose his muscular bronze chest. Her heart thumped and her fingers itched to touch the smooth flesh.

Having never seen so much of him before, it was a moment before Genevieve was able to raise her gaze to his shocked and disbelieving blue eyes.

Before he could say a word, the sailor spoke. "Sorry for disturbin' you, Captain, but I found this lad stowed away in the hold when I went down to get some supplies for breakfast."

For a long moment Marcel did nothing, then without warning, he grabbed her arm and jerked her inside the cabin, telling the other man, "I will see to this, Charley. Go on and get the meal ready for the crew."

Although she had not expected his reaction to be welcoming, Genevieve did not care for this manhandling, especially as she had taken far too much of the same from the sailor. As Marcel slammed the door, Genevieve said, "Although I understand your surprise, please refrain from grabbing me that way, Marcel. And you will have to tell that man he must mind his manners in the future. He was somewhat rough with me, though I must allow him some measure of leeway as he does not know who I—''

Marcel interrupted as he swung around to face her, putting his hand on his lean hips. ''What are you doing here?'' His shirt parted even further, exposing the smooth bronze flesh of his chest.

She could not deny that it was very difficult to phrase a reply when her eyes seemed to be riveted to that golden flesh. With a great force of will she raised her gaze to his angry one. ''I...I can explain. But give me a moment.'' She found she had great need to collect herself. She had not expected him to be quite so enraged. After the kisses they had shared, she had thought... He seemed a stranger again.

His voice was raised to an angry pitch. ''I am waiting!''

Marcel had never spoken to her in such a tone and her surprise began to give way to irritation. She frowned. ''I will thank you to have a civil tongue in your head, my lord.''

Marcel moved toward her, his brow creasing in a fierce scowl. ''A civil tongue in *my* head? You are not in the position of giving orders here, Genevieve. You will answer me now. Why are you aboard this ship?''

Genevieve stared up at him, knowing that though Marcel was certainly overreacting, he had some justification for wanting to know what she was about. Deliberately she took a deep breath. ''Please, let us calm ourselves. You have every reason to expect a reply. Only let me think of how best to explain.''

She was glad when he seemed to ease back somewhat, though the determination was not gone from his countenance. She took another breath, for it was not easy to speak of what had passed between them, especially in the face of his anger. "I...after the way you ki—"

A feminine voice interrupted her from the fore end of the cabin. "I think it best if I do not overhear this conversation, Marcel."

Genevieve swung around to see a dark-haired woman peeking out from the edge of a wide folding screen. The bed, which lay directly behind her, was not completely hidden.

Spinning about again, Genevieve faced Marcel with what she knew were shocked and disillusioned eyes. In spite of her wish that he would not know how very hurt she was over finding him with another woman, she could make no effort to hide it.

His brow creased as his gaze met hers and he reached toward her. "Genevieve, I..."

She forestalled him with a raised hand. "Nay, do not touch me." Hastily she turned to the other woman. "Please, come out. I am very sorry for disturbing you. I did not know you were here."

The other woman moved cautiously out from behind the screen, and Genevieve could not be blind to the fact that she was exotically beautiful. And that she was dressed in no more than a white nightgown, which though admittedly not revealing, was nonetheless a nightgown. Her long dark hair fell in a tangled mass to her hips and her liquid dark brown eyes were filled with unhappiness, her gaze going from Genevieve to Marcel and back again.

Genevieve was unable to meet the other's eyes. The white nightrail did not completely disguise the pleasing shape beneath it.

A piercingly painful emotion made her chest tighten and she could not look at Marcel. Had she actually convinced herself that she loved him? Obviously that was nothing more than an excuse to come here, an excuse to ease the ache of longing he had awakened in her body. For even now, knowing that she was disgusted by him, she could not help realizing that he was so very tall, so very undeniably and compellingly masculine. The cabin seemed far too small to contain his powerful presence as he stood with his shoulders back, his feet planted wide to accommodate the rolling of the ship. She was also aware of her body's reaction to his all too fascinating masculinity.

And she hated herself for it. All this time she had waited for him—longed for him.

He had found another. Even when he had kissed her, this woman was here waiting for him. Genevieve felt a wave of sympathy for the other woman. It was not her fault Marcel was a blackguard of the worst order, for she was most likely completely unaware of his perfidy.

Marcel could not quite believe his eyes. Genevieve. It only made matters worse that, for a brief moment, as his gaze had first alighted on her that his heart had raced with joy. Immediately it was replaced by irritation.

He forced himself to concentrate on the fact that she had, as yet, not explained what in the world she was doing here aboard the *Briarwind.*

He was just getting ready to reiterate this fact when there came another pounding at the door. With a grunt of irritation, Marcel strode across the chamber and jerked the door open a crack. "Yes."

Harlan stood in the opening, his hazel eyes filled with apprehension. "A storm is brewing, Marcel. It's coming up behind us quickly. You can see it on the horizon."

Vexation and concern filled him. The summer storms along the coast could be horrendous and were not to be underestimated. Now that he paid attention, Marcel was aware of the rising sound of the wind.

This was the last thing he needed now. He closed his eyes and took a deep breath. "I trust preparations are under way."

"Aye."

Regretfully Marcel changed the subject abruptly. "I am in the midst of a little problem. I will attend you shortly."

Harlan's gaze searched the chamber behind him, though Marcel knew he would see little through the narrow opening. The first mate said, "Charley said there was a stowaway."

There was, indeed.

Marcel answered as evenly as he could. "Aye, a lad. I have decided to make him my cabin boy. Now as I said, make the ship secure."

If the man who had become his friend in the past two years thought there were anything unusual in Marcel's tone or actions he gave no indication of it as he nodded, then turned and made his way across the deck.

Grateful for this small favor from the heavens, Marcel closed the door firmly. He did not wish to try to explain anything in detail at the moment. The first mate was far too perceptive and Marcel first had to think of precisely what he was going to say.

This whole nightmare would be far clearer when he knew the reasoning behind Genevieve's mad act. One thing was unfortunately and undeniably obvious. With a storm rising, there was no way they could turn around and take Genevieve back to Brackenmoore at the moment.

It was ever in his mind that his parents had died in such a storm. Angry as he was with Genevieve he would not risk her safety.

Marcel looked at Constanza where she stood. Her brown eyes fixed rigidly on Genevieve's back, and he saw the unhappiness in her brown eyes, her unmistakable pallor. It was obvious that Genevieve believed they were lovers. Marcel knew how embarrassing this must be for Constanza, who was a still-grieving widow.

He was ashamed to admit that he had, until the moment she stepped from behind the screen, completely forgotten her presence in his shock at seeing Genevieve. The lovely and infuriating Genevieve, who had occupied his every waking thought since seeing her again at Brackenmoore.

He knew a great sense of sympathy for Constanza at having been placed in this position. Yet he suddenly realized that he could possibly use Genevieve's misinterpretation of their being here together to his advantage. Her mistaken belief that he and Constanza were lovers had clearly angered her. This brought him a sudden revelation as to what Genevieve was doing here. What woman would not be angry at finding a man with another woman when he had kissed her, touched her the way he had at Brackenmoore?

For that must be why she was here. He would be daft to pretend that their embraces had been anything but compelling. But it was obvious to him that even a physical reaction such as they had shared could not be acted upon. Their lives had gone in opposing directions.

Did Genevieve understand this?

Clearly she did not, but she could not jeopardize her coming marriage for such madness. Nor he his peace of mind.

Aye, he would use her anger to protect her. It created a boundary between them he would not easily cross. And her coming marriage would act as a deterrent to him, for he had a distinct feeling that he would have need of one. But how his gaze lingered on the slender line of her back, her hips, and he recalled how good it had felt to run his hands over them...to have her...

Roughly he pulled his thoughts back to the present. He must get hold of himself.

Marcel regretted that Constanza would be involved in his deceit. He determined to explain all of this to her when they had a moment alone. Though who knew when that moment would come as he would need to keep Genevieve close by, for fear of her giving away her disguise. He genuinely did not wish the men to know he had *two* women aboard.

Though the crew were a good enough lot, it was highly unlikely that the roughest of them would think it fair for him to have two of what they had none of. Especially when he had abruptly cut short what they had believed would be several days of shore leave.

He spoke with resignation. "Unfortunately, the storm has postponed our discussion. But make no mistake, we will continue, however unpleasant it may prove."

Genevieve looked at him with chagrin. "I can tell you in this moment that I am sorry I have come here and I wish to go home."

He shook his head. "It is impossible. You heard what Harlan said. A storm is coming. We will have to go on. You, Genevieve, will stay in this cabin with Constanza until I have time to sort this out."

She sputtered, "But—"

He cut her off with a motion of his hand. "Nay, I will not discuss it now. You have gotten yourself into this. You will not even consider doing aught but obey me. You will continue to wear your disguise, for I will not explain my having two women to my men. They do get lonely aboard ship."

He saw color stain her cheeks as she realized just what he was saying. "They would not dare."

"No," he informed her immediately. "They would not dare. But I prefer not to be forced to confront the matter. I have enough to occupy my mind."

He was moved by the relief she tried to hide. He was aware of the fact that Maxim Harcourt had tried to force himself upon her when she was in his care, though she had refused to reveal any details of that ordeal. He had no wish for her to fear being in such a position again and was, in fact, sickened by the very idea that she would feel such anxiety.

But he did not wish her to know the degree of his reaction. Quickly he turned to Constanza. "Genevieve will stay with you in the cabin this day and share the bed with you each night. I cannot have her sleeping out on deck."

Genevieve spoke up hurriedly. "I could not—"

His brows arched. "You certainly could and you will. It was your decision to come aboard, Genevieve. You will simply have to accept the consequences of that." He looked at her for a long moment and saw the displeasure on her face. "Unless, of course, you do prefer to sleep on deck."

She scowled at him fiercely. "Nay, how could I possibly prefer that? But—"

"Then it is done." He moved to the table where he had been going over his charts when Charley first pounded on the door—before his life had exploded in chaos with the arrival of the very woman he so desperately wished to put from his mind.

He could feel the seething anger of Genevieve at this very moment, but he did not acknowledge it. He must show an appearance of indifference no matter how difficult it might be. She must return home and marry Roderick Beecham, leaving him to the life he had worked so hard to make his own.

He was glad that he had already folded his own blanket and tucked it in the chest beneath his padded bench. There was no sign that he had not spent the night in the bed with Constanza.

His regretful gaze went to Constanza's unhappy

face. Again he resolved to explain his reasons for putting her in such an awkward position as soon as possible.

Now he had to go out and secure his ship against the storm that had begun to rage as loudly as the one in his heart.

Chapter Four

As she watched the other woman disappear behind the screen, Genevieve felt her stomach churn with rage toward Marcel. What madness had ever possessed her to believe he wanted her, that he was anything other than a black-hearted knave?

She recalled her first sight of him in the great hall at Brackenmoore the previous day—thinking that he had changed. He had indeed changed, and more than she had imagined. The Marcel she had known would never kiss her as he had when he was in love with another woman. For surely he was in love with Constanza.

He had her near him. Poor Constanza, Genevieve could not even look at her as she came from behind the screen, now garbed in a heavy velvet gown. Marcel had betrayed her as surely as he had betrayed Genevieve.

For was that not what he had done by kissing her, touching her the way he had? And she, fool that she was, had cared for nothing but the feelings that were racing through her own body. She had been able to think of nothing beyond the mad thought that her physical reactions meant she was in love with him.

Her miserable gaze flicked back to Constanza. She had not known that he was bound to another.

The other woman was watching her closely and Genevieve could not hold that gaze, for fear of the woman's reading all that had passed between her and Marcel. She suspected that Constanza knew more of the truth of the situation than she had been told.

Loving Marcel as she must, Constanza would surely feel that something was wrong between Marcel and Genevieve. Loving him as she did, and feeling that he loved her in return.

Genevieve's heart twisted in her chest at the thought of their feelings for each other. Again she told herself that she was a fool, a poor mad fool. It did her no good to pine for a man who loved another, who had not had the decency to make his position clear before kissing her.

Hopelessly she moved to stare out the portal.

The other woman's gentle voice interrupted her tortured thoughts. "You must be tired and hungry. Sit and I will get us some food, *por favor.*"

Genevieve spun around to look at her, knowing that her surprise must be obvious. "You are concerned for my comfort?"

The other woman's brown eyes measured her with a surprising depth of kindness. "Of course. You have been through much."

Genevieve looked away. She did not know what to say, could not even understand her own tumultuous emotions. She went to the long bench beside the table and sat down, drawing her knees up to hold them tightly against her.

Misery gripped her, making her throat tight and her chest ache. She was determined not to cry. Not in front of Marcel's woman.

Marcel's woman. The thought only increased her pain.

Until just short minutes ago she would have given anything to be Marcel's woman. Now there was nothing she wanted so much as to get away from here, to never set eyes upon him again.

But that was impossible. When night fell she would be sleeping in this chamber with both Marcel and Constanza. She was, in fact, to sleep in the bed they had shared.

'Twas an unbearable thought.

Worse yet, Marcel had demanded an explanation as to why she had come here. Genevieve could not tell him of her mad delusions of being in love with him. The fact that she had come to her senses did not lessen her shame.

Unfortunately, it was through no one's fault but her own.

Again Constanza's soft voice interrupted her. "I will get the food now. As the storm worsens it will become impossible."

Genevieve looked at her then. She seemed quite knowledgeable about what would occur during the storm and not in the least concerned. How long had she been on the *Briarwind?* Genevieve could not bring herself to ask, but she could not completely restrain her curiosity about Marcel's mistress as she again took in her exotic beauty. "Your English is very good, yet it seems as if you are not English."

The woman nodded, her gaze disconcertingly assessing. "*Sí.* I am originally from Spain."

Genevieve could not stop herself from going on, though the subject was not an easy one to bring up. "Is that where you met Marcel? Where you and he…"

"No." She gave Genevieve a last indecipherable look and left the cabin.

Marcel looked up from tying off a rope to see Constanza standing behind him waiting for his attention. The winds whipped at her long dark hair, and her brown eyes were no less stormy than the sky above them.

He was not surprised.

He had fully expected that she would require an explanation for his allowing Genevieve to believe they were lovers. He had not thought she would demand one now with the storm beginning to rage around them.

The moment his gaze met hers, she said, "What are you about, Marcel? Just now Genevieve was asking me questions about us and I did not know what you would have me say. Why did you allow her to believe we are together, that we are…?"

He was acutely away of the other hands working nearby as they secured the ship. He did not wish them to overhear.

His gaze came back to Constanza's face. How could he even begin to explain this to her? He spoke hesitantly. "As for what you should tell her, I would not ask you to lie, yet…"

She shook her head. "I cannot do so."

He frowned. "You do not understand how things are between myself and Genevieve, for it is more complicated than any words I have to offer. Can you not accept that I know it is for the best to allow her to believe this? I do not wish her to imagine that there is any chance for the two of us."

Her full lips set stubbornly as she held her wind-tossed hair away from her face. "I owe you much, my friend, more than I could ever repay, but I do not believe I can do this. Her eyes, they look at me with such…"

Marcel grimaced, drawing her aside. Luckily the crew, even those closest to them, seemed to have no care for their conversation. He could speak freely. "She imagines that there is something between her and me."

She shrugged with obvious irony, saying, "And with good reason, for even I can see as much."

He felt his lips thin as he shook his head. "You do not understand. Genevieve is not for me. We are of different worlds. I am captain of this ship. She is a wealthy heiress, a noblewoman. I cannot allow her to act on a physical attraction that could well destroy her life."

Constanza's mouth rounded. "Oh, I see."

Marcel knew momentary guilt as he realized what she would be thinking, which would be that, when he referred to their being of different worlds, he meant their social status. Constanza, like the others on board the *Briarwind,* knew nothing of his own noble heritage.

He pushed his guilt aside. Constanza's cooperation

in this matter was necessary. What he said of his own and Genevieve's lives being too different was no less true simply because it was based on his own personal need to have his own life. A life that he had made by his own hard work.

Without meeting her gaze, he said, "Now you understand."

She nodded, though with obvious reluctance.

Relieved at her acquiescence, however grudging, he looked about them, waving a hand toward the rising sea. "I will talk with you on this again, if you wish, but now I must see to the *Briarwind*."

Again she nodded. But she did not go before adding, "I do not know how you know this young noblewoman, but I now see why you do not sleep at night, why you do not look to the woman who would welcome you. Yet she has left all she knew to come to you. Surely it means that she loves you very much. Perhaps love is all you require to see your differences through?"

His lips tightened, not bothering to tell her that the attraction he and Genevieve shared had nothing to do with love. He knew the physical reactions that had flared up between them had been fueled by Genevieve's deep-seated desire to become an Ainsworth. As far as his own desire was concerned, well, she was a very beautiful woman.

He cast these thoughts aside and replied, "'Tis unthinkable. I will thank you to refrain from mentioning this again. I have long since made my decision on this matter. Genevieve and I are not for each other and, as soon as my duty in Scotland is done, I will be taking her home where she belongs."

Constanza made no comment on this statement, only nodding her head sharply in reaction to his curtness and moving away. Telling himself he was glad to have this interview ended, he went back to his duties.

Genevieve did not see Marcel again that day. The storm rose to a fever pitch outside and the seas became so wild that she could see nothing beside a gray blur beyond the portal.

She was glad that she had forced herself to consume a small portion of the bread and meat Constanza had brought on a tray. Not much time passed before the sea became so rough that the ship began to toss wildly beneath them.

Though the pitching caused her stomach to roll, it also made conversation difficult. A trace of seasickness seemed a small price to pay if she could avoid speaking with Marcel's woman.

Not long after the full force of the gale hit them, the cabin door opened and the man Marcel had addressed as Harlan entered. His gaze skimmed over Genevieve where she sat with her knees pulled up to her chin on the bench and passed on to Constanza.

He spoke with obvious concern. "You are well?"

She nodded, her gaze skipping to Genevieve. "We are both well."

He looked again at Genevieve, still showing little interest, then back to the other woman. "That is fine then. I...we just wanted to make certain." The tall, slim man raked a rough hand through his sun-streaked blond hair.

Genevieve was aware of his lack of interest in herself, for why would he greatly concern himself with a young stowaway? She noted the tension between him and Constanza, but she realized that they must be anxious about the storm. Perhaps Genevieve herself would be more apprehensive if she were not so preoccupied with her own distress at discovering Marcel loved another.

Costanza looked down at her hands as she said, "That was most kind of you. You must thank Marcel for sending you and go now tend your own duties. Do not concern yourself further. We are safe here."

He frowned and nodded jerkily, then swung around and left them.

Constanza stood there for a moment, watching the closed door before turning to Genevieve. "It was very good of Marcel to send him, was it not?"

Genevieve swallowed hard before answering. "Aye, it was. He is a considerate man." Even she could hear the strain in her voice, for she was very sure that Marcel had not been concerned for *her* safety when he sent his man. This further proof of his care for his mistress only made her throat tighten.

She felt nothing but relief when Constanza nodded politely and went to tend some purpose of her own behind the screen.

The hours of silence gave Genevieve a great deal of time to think on exactly what she would say by way of explaining her presence aboard the *Briarwind*. But she came no closer to coming up with a reasonable justification.

She told herself it was because she remained too disturbed by the fact that she must share this small space with Marcel's woman.

As the evening wore on, Constanza came out from

behind the screen and again tried to engage her in
conversation despite the noise of the wind and crash-
ing waves. Genevieve could not bring herself to chat
politely. Her heart felt like a heavy weight in her chest
and every breath of the air in the cabin Marcel shared
with the lovely Spaniard seemed to sear her lungs.

With a long, considering look that ended in a helpless shrug, Constanza went to bed.

When Genevieve did grow tired she did not join the
other woman where she lay in the bed. Instead, she
stretched out upon the long bench beside the table,
covering herself with her cloak.

She only realized that she had finally fallen asleep
by the fact that she opened her eyes to see Marcel's
face leaning over her. That he was not pleased was
more than apparent in his blue Ainsworth eyes.

He waved an impatient hand, the other riding a lean
hip. She could not help noting that he was quite distracting in his snug-fitting black trousers and hose. "I
thought I had made it clear that you were to sleep
with Constanza."

She reared up, pushing backward immediately when
the motion brought her too close to the bare wall of
his chest. Though she had avoided actually contacting
that smooth golden expanse, her eyes fixed upon it.
Genevieve's blood seemed to thicken and heat in her
veins.

Yanking her gaze away with an act of will, she saw
that a white shirt such as he customarily wore lay in
a wet heap on the plank floor. Her gaze skittered back
to that bare chest and away. Deliberately she swallowed as her eyes met his. She was careful to keep
her voice even in spite of her agitation as she an-

swered, "Pray accept that I will not sleep with your..." Genevieve paused, unable to speak deprecatingly of the other woman despite her anger and disappointment over everything that had happened.

He scowled blackly at the unfinished sentence but made no remark on it. "Would you prefer *me* to sleep with her in yon bed?"

She could not prevent a horrified gasp. "Nay, I—"

He nodded knowingly. "Just as I thought. You must realize that even I require sleep."

She stood, moving away from him as she tilted her nose high. "Of course." She waved toward the now vacated bench. "Please, be my guest."

"Oh, no," he reminded her coolly. "It is you who will remember that you are *my* guest."

Marcel turned his back on her and reached down to pull the top up on the bench, which she now realized doubled as a storage chest. He took out a dry shirt and pulled it over his head, bringing some relief to her wayward thoughts. He then withdrew a thick blanket and slammed the lid back down.

She watched as he lay down upon the bench and spread the covering over himself.

He was oblivious to Genevieve. He simply pillowed his head on his arm and closed his eyes without saying another word to her.

Aghast that he would dismiss her so easily, she moved to stand beside him. As if sensing her there, he opened his lids and looked up at her, his expression reluctantly resigned. "Pray, what is it now, Genevieve?"

As he spoke, she was aware of the exhaustion in his face. In spite of her anger, she felt a stab of sympathy. He had battled the storm for many hours, though from the quiet that had fallen it seemed to have abated. Her anger deflated, she shook her head. "Go to sleep."

In spite of his exhaustion, it was some time before Marcel did finally fall asleep. He could not stop thinking about the way she had looked at him, how her eyes had darkened to the color of rich moss as they slid over his chest, seeming to leave a trail of heat in their wake.

God help him, Marcel had not been able to prevent his own reactions, the tightening in his belly, the quickening in his loins. For in spite of everything, she was not indifferent to him and he seemed to have no ability to quell his responses to her desire.

Though that was precisely what he must learn to do. Until such time arrived, he was determined to keep her from seeing that he wanted her still.

No matter that it continued to prove as difficult as it had during their confrontation this morn.

When at last he did sleep it was only fitfully. An indeterminate time later he opened his eyes and saw that it was not daylight. His gaze immediately came to rest upon Genevieve. She was seated on the floor atop her cloak, her resentful gaze trained upon himself.

The moment she realized he was awake she leaped to her feet. Her concern as she looked down at her hands was more than apparent.

Carefully hiding his agitation at her obvious uneasiness, he sat up and rubbed the grit from his eyes with a thumb and forefinger. Absently he glanced around the cabin for Constanza.

Interpreting his action correctly, Genevieve said stiffly, "She has gone out on deck. She did not wish to wake you."

Her tone told him that she considered such thoughtfulness overdone. Perhaps he had been wrong this morning and simply confused with exhaustion when he'd thought she looked at him with desire. It did appear that all she felt toward him was animosity.

Perhaps it was his own desire for her that had made him think...aye, mayhap it had been. He barely felt the answering jab of disappointment this time and assured himself that he was coming along well.

Yet he had no more wish to be ruled by her anger than her passion. As his gaze traced her stiff form, he told himself he would not be ruled by her clearly disapproving opinion of him.

His wary eyes swept her again. Gratefully he took in the fact that she was still wearing the boy's cap and garb. As he did so an unpleasant suspicion swept through him and he found himself asking without thinking, "You did not cut your hair?"

She shrugged, frowning at his sudden change of topic. "Nay, I did not think of it. 'Twould have made keeping it in this hat easier. Though it has proved roomy enough, it is hot." She scratched at her nape as she spoke.

What was he to do with her? he asked himself even as relief washed through him. It would simply be a shame to ruin what was an undeniably lovely feature.

He stood and rubbed the back of his neck. What

little sleep he just had had left him stiff and he could feel her watching him, assessing him.

Taking a deep breath, he brought his hands down to his sides and faced her squarely, not wanting to show any hint of uncertainty. "Genevieve, we must talk."

She drew herself up to her full height, which still meant that her head did not reach past his shoulder. But there was cool steel in her green eyes as she said, "Aye."

He could not deny a sense of admiration at her directness, but he did not wish for her to know that.

Turning her back to him, she added. "Oh yes, we must. I wish to tell you why I came aboard the *Briarwind.* It is because I..."

The long silence that followed this statement prompted him to say. "Because you..."

She swung around to face him. "Because I too long for adventure. I wish to see some of the world and since you were going to Scotland and I had never met your Aunt Finella, I thought that would be a fine place to begin."

This was far from anything Marcel might have expected her to impart. It was certainly quite different from what he had assumed. For a long moment he could summon no reply as he stared down at her.

When an annoyed expression clouded her lovely face, he realized that he was staring and spoke more forthrightly than he had intended. "You did not come here so that you and I could..."

She gasped with unflattering horror. "I should say not. I thought that we had discussed all that back at Brackenmoore."

"But that was before I kissed you."

She blinked as if stunned by his remark, then looked him straight in the eyes. "It is you who must answer to that if it plagues you, Marcel, not I. I have forgotten it. And I would think—" she cast a quick glance toward the bed "—you would have good reason to be sorry for that kiss."

He could hardly believe what was happening. The unpredictable damsel had turned the tables upon him. He sputtered, "What of your marriage?"

She looked away, shrugging casually. "I will see to that when I am ready."

He watched her for a long moment, wondering if her coming after him might have something to do with her willingness to abandon poor Roderick on the chance that the Ainsworth name could still be hers. He said so. "Did you imagine that I might be willing to make your desire to have the Ainsworth name a reality because I had kissed you?"

Her head jerked up, her eyes flashing daggers. "You assume too much."

Though he searched her face carefully, he could find no hint of prevarication. He saw nothing but a possible heightening of color along her cheekbones. That could be brought on by the very fact of speaking of such discomfitting subjects as his having kissed her.

He was, in fact, not unperturbed at the conversation himself. Nor was he, if he were completely honest with himself, unmoved at her easy dismissal of the passionate embrace they had shared.

He didn't imagine himself in love with her, no never that. But he was well aware that their kisses had moved him more than any other in his life.

Her gaze found his again and she spoke with cool rebuke. "You must certainly cease worrying about what I am about, my lord. I would think that you would not find the hardihood to concern yourself with my life, as you surely have all you can manage in concentrating on your own relationship with Constanza."

He nearly winced at the words, unnerved and angered by her utter willingness to allow him to take all the responsibility for what had happened between them. He also balked at her obviously damning assessment of his behavior toward Constanza.

Well, her condemnation would have been deserved if he was involved with the Spanish woman, but he was not. Yet under no circumstances was he willing to admit that now. He would look like a fool.

He would carry on with the charade until he returned Genevieve safe to Brackenmoore. That could only be done after things had been resolved in Scotland.

Be that as it may, Marcel had suffered enough reproach from the woman before him for one day. He spoke more sharply than he had meant to. "You say that Scotland seems a good place to begin your life of adventure?"

She flinched at his tone, but answered haughtily enough. "Aye."

He shook his head. "'Twill be the beginning and end of any adventure that I have a part in. Know you this, my fine adventuress, I will not be taking you on with me once I have done what I can for Aunt Finella. I shall take you back to Brackenmoore forthwith."

She cast a disdainful glance around the cabin before

meeting his gaze. "That will suit me full well, my lord. I find this particular adventure has less appeal than expected."

Marcel realized he was scowling again, that he had scowled more since finding Genevieve aboard his ship than he ever had in his life. What a fickle, unpredictable, self-indulgent creature she was.

For a long moment he could not reply. All these years he had known this woman—or at least thought he had.

Now he found that she was someone completely different from all he had thought of her. The Genevieve he had known had been a being apart from others—gentle, beautiful, and so delicate that she must be protected from unpleasantness or hurt of any kind.

Somehow in the years he had been gone, she had become a willful woman, a creature unknown to him. And regretful though he might be to admit it, she seemed for a moment far more mysterious and intriguing than ever with her eyes flashing headstrong defiance and undeniable arrogance. This knowledge was far more disturbing than he cared to admit even to himself.

Deliberately Marcel gave himself an imaginary shake. He had managed to go quietly mad over the course of the last hours. He could not be more attracted to Genevieve on learning that she was obstinate and willful.

The light of morning did seem to paint a lovely gilded sheen over her face and neck as it slanted through the portal. It also glowed upon her lashes and brows, her lips...

Suddenly realizing just what he was thinking, Marcel closed his eyes on the sight of Genevieve, on his own reactions to her.

Good God, what was wrong with him? He must wrest control of these feelings—and without delay.

He swung away. "Unless you have something more of import to say I have work that needs doing. There will be much to set to rights after the storm. There has been some serious damage to one of the masts and I must determine whether or not the repairs can be made aboard ship."

Her tone was clearly startled. "I...nay. I have nothing more to say."

He moved toward the door without looking her way. Her voice stopped him as he reached for the latch. "Marcel, I...is there not something I can do? I am going mad with naught but my own thoughts to occupy me." The frustration and regret in her tone told him just how difficult this admission was to make.

Although her situation was completely her own doing, he felt a stab of sympathy. He turned and nodded, noting that her gaze did not meet his as he said, "I will see if I can find something for you to do, though 'twill likely not be anything you are accustomed to doing as we must keep up the pretense that you are a lad. Aside from that, there is no stitchery to be had aboard the *Briarwind*."

She drew herself up, her lips thinning as she said, "I understand that, Marcel. I am not a simpleton, whatever you might think."

Marcel felt a momentary regret that he had offended her with his last words. He had never doubted her intellect, had, in fact, always had a great respect for her mind. He said, "I did not mean to imply such a thing. I regret that you would think thusly."

Her gaze met his and, for a moment, he thought he saw a hint of vulnerability before it was quickly masked by a cool courtesy. "Pardon me for taking offense. Considering the circumstances, I suppose we must make some attempt to get along in the next while. We have known each other for so long."

To his utter self-disgust Marcel was more offended by this show of politeness than he would have been by anger. Her offer of civility was painful.

He could not help thinking of the way it had been before he left Brackenmoore, of the talks they had had about all manner of subjects, the walks they had taken, sometimes falling into silence but never into indifference. He went on softly. "There is no need for you to work, or take care of anyone in order to prove that you have worth, Genevieve. That has never been questioned in my mind, nor in the minds of anyone at Brackenmoore."

As he said the words, he knew how true they were. All her care of those who loved her was appreciated, not expected. She was loved for her own self, could she but see it. Yet she could not, for if she could she would never have felt she must become an Ainsworth in order to make herself whole.

Clearly oblivious to his thoughts, she replied with a stubbornly raised chin, "I am to act the part of cabin boy. No cabin boy would be allowed to lounge about. I have made my choice in coming here. I will accept the consequences of that choice."

Her tone was cool and displayed no hint of the

friendship they had once shared, in spite of her previous words.

Feeling unexplainably bereft, he could not find it in him to answer her but with a sharp nod. "Very well then, but please remain here in the cabin until I can arrange something."

She answered with an equally sharp nod.

Abruptly he swung about and left her, his heart heavy and tight in his breast.

Chapter Five

Genevieve had never been so miserable. This was doubly difficult to accept with aplomb as she had hoped for something so very different from the situation she found herself in. When she had taken her future into her own hands and stowed away aboard the *Briarwind,* she had thought...well, that no longer mattered.

She had spent the day plaiting rope. A proper task for a cabin boy no doubt, but not so very easy for a noblewoman with soft hands. Those hands were hurting so badly now that she did not know what to do with them. No matter how hard she applied herself to taking her mind from the throbbing ache of them, it did no good.

Genevieve knew she could have simply left the task undone. Marcel would not have berated her. Yet she had not been able to bring herself to set the work aside.

Genevieve had been the one to ask Marcel to give her something to do. She would carry on.

Besides, the task of plaiting the rope had kept her mind from her own unhappy thoughts. Somewhat.

It gave her something to think on other than the cold expression in Marcel's eyes as he had told her to remain in the cabin until he found something to occupy her. His curtness told her very clearly that he did not wish to be bothered with her.

His manner left Genevieve feeling very grateful that she managed to conceal her agitation as she told him that incredibly ridiculous lie about coming aboard the *Briarwind* in search of adventure. She could only be glad that Marcel so deeply disliked the notion of her wanting him that he would believe such a transparent falsehood.

Luckily Constanza had appeared a short time after he had left, giving Genevieve something else to occupy her. She had been the one to show Genevieve where she was to work—just outside the door of Marcel's cabin. Two crates had been arranged close together, obviously one was to act as a seat and the other one, which was topped by the materials she would require, was to act as a table. Constanza had also shown her how to plait the rope before going off on some business of her own.

Not long after Genevieve had begun, Marcel and his first mate had gone into the cabin. They had been too deep in their conversation about navigating through small islands and shoals to pay her any heed. With the constant rush of the sea sounding in her ears, she was unable to make out the specifics of their conversation once they were inside, though she was able to recognize the deep timbre of Marcel's voice each time he spoke. This did little to aid her in her desire to put him and all things concerning him from her thoughts.

The other hands seemed to pay her no more than cursory attention as they went about their work. Though she could not see that there was anything particularly amiss, it seemed that there was still much to do after the storm. At least it appeared so from the level of activity on deck.

They scrubbed the deck and unwound rolled-up sails in order to allow them to dry in the sun. They coiled and uncoiled the ropes, and a myriad other tasks with an efficiency that was somewhat awing.

When they stopped working to answer a call to eat, she remained where she was. Genevieve did not believe that Marcel would wish her to go with them to the wooden structure at the opposite side of the ship.

Just moments after the last of them had disappeared inside, the cook, who had first discovered her presence down in the hold, came out with a laden tray. He brought it to the captain's cabin and, as he thumped upon the door, she felt his deeply scowling gaze upon her.

Genevieve kept her own head down as he entered then came back out again, but she was aware of his close regard. She clearly recalled Marcel's admonition to keep her true sex secret.

A few moments later a rough cough brought her gaze up in surprise. Once again, it was the cook. Silently his craggy brows pulled together in what she could only begin to think of as a permanent glower, and he held out a heavy wooden bowl.

As she smelled the surprisingly delicious aroma rising from that bowl, her stomach growled loudly. Genevieve reached out to take it as the old curmudgeon grimaced crookedly, his brows not parting as he said, ''I thought as you'd be hungry.''

She answered, ''Thank you,'' careful to keep her voice low, and he hobbled away with that uneven gait of his.

For some reason the utterly unexpected kindness from the dour cook made her eyes sting for a moment. Quickly she took a deep, calming breath.

Genevieve did not cry.

With a determined sniff, she began to eat the savory fish soup with the heavy wooden spoon that rested inside the bowl. It tasted far better than she would have expected, or mayhap she was very hungry. Or mayhap it was the cook's compassion that made it so.

That surprising event had occurred quite some time ago. During the ensuing hours, Genevieve had found her fingers working ever more slowly as the skin became more and more abraded, the pain from those abrasions harder and harder to ignore.

When the door of the cabin finally opened and Marcel and Harlan came out, Genevieve glanced up then bent to her work once more. Only as Marcel's shadow fell across her did she look up into his blue eyes.

For a moment they simply stared at each other.

At last he said, ''You must be tired. Surely you must feel that you have more than proved your willingness to work and can rest now.''

She gave a quick nod. She then waited until he had turned away to go about his own business before setting aside the rope she'd held in such a way that it effectively hid how damaged her hands were. She did not wish Marcel to see how shaky and sore they were, having no desire to give any hint of weakness.

When she stood, it was not without ginger care. Her back and legs were somewhat stiff from sitting on the wooden crate. With a sigh of relief she went into the cabin, holding her raw hands together carefully. Sighing again, she collapsed onto the bench beside the table.

Marcel entered the cabin and carried the tray to the table where he and Harlan had spent hours going over the charts earlier in the day. The trip to Scotland was not a long one, and would only take a matter of days with good wind. Even with the storm, they had not been much delayed. But it was a somewhat difficult journey as there were many small islands and shoals that must be avoided along the way.

Constanza had opted for eating with the crew, and Harlan had assured Marcel that he would see to her. Marcel knew that it was not easy for the Spanish widow to be in the same room with Genevieve, given what Genevieve believed of her, for there was no more virtuous woman than Constanza. Harlan, who was the only member of the crew to know of Constanza and Marcel's true relationship, would see that the men treated her with respect.

Marcel's gaze searched the cabin for Genevieve. At first he did not see her, then something, an inner awareness directed his gaze to the narrow shelf that ran along the front of the cabin beneath the portal. She was seated there, her back to him as she gazed out the portal, which would offer little in the way of interest as night had fallen over the sea.

He set the tray upon the wide oak table and said, "Come, I have brought food."

She turned to him then and Marcel realized that he could read nothing of her expression in the pressing shadows inside the cabin. Quickly he moved to light more candles, telling himself that it was only prudent to have some idea of what the damsel was thinking at all times.

When he finished, the room was brighter, shadows hovering only in the more remote corners. Moving back to the table, he saw that Genevieve was now standing looking at the bowls of soup, bread, sliced meat and cheese.

Yet she made no move to eat.

He went toward her, wondering at this sign that she might be angry with him. He frowned. She should not be angry with him. He could think of not one thing that he might have done this day. Was it not she who had made the pronouncement that they must be civil to each other?

The thought of how coolly she had treated him while making this pronouncement still prickled. Yet he was determined to set aside his own irritation in the hope of making a peace.

Resolutely he ignored her confounding behavior. He motioned toward the bench beside the table. "Sit, eat. You must be hungry."

She looked up at him and away, conspicuously keeping her hands behind her back as she shook her head. "No thank you, I do not wish for any just now."

Against his will, Marcel felt his ire rise. "Come now, you are the one who said we must not be at odds. Are you too stubborn then to break bread with me,

Genevieve? We have been near to being brother and sister for years.'' He was not at all pleased with the way his conscience rebelled at this statement.

She did not know that the suggestion of their being akin to brother and sister could not be further from the truth in his mind. He had no intention of telling her.

She stared up at him in obvious distress. ''I am not refusing to break bread with you, Marcel. I...'' She stopped, biting her lip as if distressed and still making no move to join him.

Because of her obvious agitation, he took a deep breath for patience. ''Pray then what are you doing?''

She looked down at the floor again. ''I simply have no hunger, thank you.''

She continued to stand there with her hands behind her. In spite of her boyish garb he could not help seeing how the heavy blue wool stretched tight over the fullness of her bosom in this stance, nor did the soft fabric of her trousers completely disguise the gentle roundness of her hips and bottom. His body tightened, and he forced his tortured gaze back to her pale but lovely face, which was framed by the floppy velvet cap. Her lips and nose were pink from the fresh sea air. It was completely beyond him how anyone had been fooled as to her true sex. He could only be grateful for the men's blindness.

Those green eyes with their heavy fringe of lashes were near mesmerizing, in spite of the fact that she was staring at him as if she wished to be anywhere but here. This did not soothe his agitation as she repeated, ''I am really not in the least bit hungry.''

He stood with an impatient sigh, coming around the

table toward her. "That cannot be. Charley told me you have eaten nothing since very early in the day. I should have seen to the matter long since."

She shook her head. "You need have no worry for my comfort. I am quite well."

It was true that Marcel had been concerned when he spoke with the cook. He had been beset by guilt that Charley and not himself had been the one to concern himself with her well-being. Marcel had been far too occupied in concentrating on not thinking of her when he had so much work to do. This had proved disturbingly difficult with her sitting just outside the cabin.

Though he was a sour-looking fellow, Charley was ever one to feed stray cats on the docks when they tied up. It did not surprise Marcel that he would have a care for a lad who seemed too shy to eat with the crew. He could feel his own gaze softening as he looked down at her, for of a certainty there was something of the lost kitten in those green eyes at the moment.

Genevieve bit her lower lip as she stared up at Marcel. She could think of nothing to say to this, could think of little save the warmth that seemed to emanate from his powerful body even though he had not touched her. She looked down, feeling the weight of blue eyes on the top of her head.

She did not wish Marcel to know how she reacted to his nearness. Nor did she wish him to see how sore her hands were.

She had washed them in the basin near the bed and knew the abrasions were not so very terrible. But the wounds, however shallow, were painful and had made her fingers so stiff that she did not believe she could eat without revealing the pain.

Marcel spoke again and, in spite of the gentleness in his gaze only a moment ago, this time it was with obviously leashed impatience. "Pray discontinue this exercise in avoidance and tell me what is amiss and without further delay."

His tone sent a wave of irritation through her, drawing the strength of defiance from the depths of her sadness and pain. Her narrowed gaze met his. "How dare you speak to me thusly, Marcel? You have no right." She was so angry that she started to bring her hands out from behind her back to shake one in his face, then recalling her injuries, quickly tucked them back behind her again.

But not quickly enough, for he said, "What are you hiding behind your back?"

Before she could even move to prevent him, he had reached out and pulled her hands from behind her. His gaze widened as he saw her abraded hands.

After a long moment, he looked into her face. "Why would you hide such a thing?"

Her answer did not come easily as her jaw was so tightly clenched. "I did not wish for you to see."

"Why?"

She shrugged. "I do not require your pity, my lord. Nor anyone's. I am quite capable of taking care of my own hurts."

There was another long silence, but Genevieve did not look at Marcel even though it stretched until she thought she might scream. Finally he spoke, his voice so soft she could barely hear it. "Pity is something I will not give you, Genevieve."

His tone seemed strange, almost tender, and she felt an unexpected and unwanted tingle of awareness. Unable to stop herself, she looked into his eyes, seeing that he had turned so his face was now cloaked in shadow.

His tone was rife with disapproval in spite of the softness as he said, "I did tell you that you need not work at all."

She scowled. "And I told you that a cabin boy must not remain idle for the whole of the day, not if you wished to avoid comment. And it was you who told me that you wanted me to continue to play the part I had adopted."

He then asked, with obviously forced reason, "Why did you continue when your hands became sore?"

She shrugged again. "I chose to. I am not so helpless, Marcel, nor thoughtless that I do not know a cabin boy must pull his weight. It would be a strange thing, indeed, if he began a task and quit it only moments later."

She halted abruptly, feeling a strange thrill go through her as his gentle fingers traced the ill-used skin on her palms. She took a quick, shallow breath, her gaze fixing on the top of his down-bent dark head.

He seemed to be unaware of her attention as he cradled her sore hands in his, but his tone was matter-of-fact when he ordered, "Sit down. I will see to them."

She stiffened. "I have done so. I will be fine."

He made a noise, which she could only interpret as exasperation and, swinging around, led her toward the section of the cabin where the bed lay. Genevieve had no choice but to follow as he held securely to her wrist.

Yet he did not hold her tongue and she sputtered, "Marcel."

If he heard her he gave no indication of it, but continued forward with purpose. When they reached the bed, he pushed her down upon the coverlet and turned to pour fresh water into a basin on a shelf beside the bed. He then took a clean cloth from a small chest on the floor next to the bed and wetted it before turning back to her.

Genevieve curled her hands close to her stomach. "I tell you I do not need..."

Again he ignored her, taking hold of one hand and drawing it toward him as he sat down next to her on the edge of the bed.

She tried one more time. "Marcel, I do not want..." But the warmth of his long fingers closing around hers made a shudder pass through her that even he must have felt.

Horrified, she looked into his eyes as he turned to her. But his words made her realize that he had completely misread her reaction. "Why do you shiver so? Am I so very distasteful to you, Genevieve?"

She looked down, breathing deliberately, still infinitely aware of the strength and deftness of his hands, the heat of his body so very near hers. "Nothing could be further from the truth..." she began, then stopped for fear of what this statement might reveal. "My hands are simply tender and you startled me," she prevaricated.

He frowned, looking down at the raw skin. "For-

give me, Genevieve. I did not mean to cause you hurt.
I will have more care.''

Guilt assaulted her, but she made no effort to reassure him. For it was the very sweetness of his actions, the tenderness of his touch that brought about
her dilemma.

Even now as he stroked the cool cloth gently over
her palm did she have to close her eyes to hide the
thrill that coursed through her at the contrast between
that cool cloth and the warmth of his own flesh.

When he finished washing the first hand and
reached for the other, Genevieve was forced to lean
close to the solid wall of his shoulder. For a moment
she remained stiff and tried her best to keep her body
as rigid as possible where it touched his. The gentleness of his touch and the obvious concentration in his
face as he looked down at what he was doing lulled
her.

She was being foolish to hold herself so stiffly.
Marcel was paying no attention to her beyond caring
for the wounds. Slowly she allowed herself to lean
against him, taking a comfort from the solid strength
of him that she had not expected.

As she did so she told herself that she should not
be surprised by her reaction. This was Marcel. She
had lived in the same keep with him, had taken meals,
celebrated joyous as well as sad occasions, shared
laughter.

More than anything she realized that she regretted
the loss of these things. Surely it would have been
wonderful to find that he cared for her, that she could
be a real part of his life and his family's, to become,
in truth, an Ainsworth. What she had not considered

was that her desires might lead to a ruin of the friendship they had known.

It had been difficult being here with him and remaining aloof, behaving as if he were a stranger, and worse, almost as if they were enemies.

No physical attraction was worth losing him and the relationship they had shared. She must, and would, put her willful passions behind her, especially after assuring him they did not exist.

Clearly it was what Marcel wanted, as well.

If she did, for a time, continue to react to his touch in a way that neither of them wanted, she would keep those feelings to herself. She had no choice if she hoped to salvage something that meant so very much to her.

Yet as he continued to minister to her hands, she became aware of a growing tightness in her chest, a warmth in her belly that she did not wish to acknowledge. She ground her teeth together tightly, telling herself that this was Marcel—her friend.

This self-resolve did not make her feelings dissipate and Genevieve looked to Marcel, relieved at seeing how preoccupied he was with what he was doing. Again she allowed herself to relax against him.

His dark hair was thick and silky looking where it brushed the vulnerability of his nape, making her heart ache with longing at the intimacy of this moment. Genevieve closed her eyes, breathing deeply and deliberately but knowing her actions would not make the sweet yearning in her breast disappear. She was not sure that she wished it to. During the two long years he had been gone from her, she had yearned so very intensely for even one hour in his presence, to see his smile, hear the rich deep sound of his voice. And now here he was in the flesh, even more heady and intoxicating to her senses than she had imagined.

So precious were these moments here at his side, his gentle hands tending to her hurts. Perhaps, she told herself, there was naught amiss with what she felt as long as she kept it close to her. Surely, if her attraction did not leave her own mind, there was nothing to feel guilty about, nothing to castigate herself for.

Marcel was, after all, a very handsome man. She allowed her gaze to pass over his face, taking in the clearly defined Ainsworth features, which were evident in his high cheekbones and strong jaw. Her gaze lingered on the deep black fringe of his lashes, the raven hair that seemed to absorb the light of the candles.

Her gaze slid over his wide shoulders, which were encased in heavy burgundy velvet. It traveled down to his wrists, seeing the bones that were sturdy and strong but not thick. Those wrists led to fine strong hands with wide capable palms and long, supple fingers.

How good those hands had felt on her back when he held her close to him as he kissed her that night at Brackenmoore, how knowing. The warmth in her belly increased and she shifted slightly.

He looked over at her. "Have I hurt you again?"

Genevieve saw that his blue eyes seemed darker than before, but she was too consumed by her own responses to him to wonder why. She lowered her gaze, shaking her head quickly. "Nay, you did not." She was not blind to the breathless quality of her own voice.

She could feel him watching her for another long moment, and her gratitude was great when he finally turned away. But his doing so did not ease the growing ache inside her, nor slow the increasing tempo of her heart, nor deepen the quick shallowness of her breathing.

She was grateful, but also bereft when Marcel rose abruptly and took several strips of fine white cloth from the same chest. When he came back, he seemed to sit a bit further from her.

Genevieve frowned at her own disappointment, sharply telling herself that she was crazed.

As he began to wrap one of the cloths around her left hand, she saw that his hands now did not seem as steady as they had before. From somewhere inside her came the unexpected yet shockingly powerful thought that he was not as indifferent to her as she had imagined.

If her heart had been beating quickly before it now began to feel as though it were a drum pounding in her breast. That quivering of his hands was such a small sign, dared she even heed such a sign, believe it could mean that he was as moved by their nearness as she?

Again she was assaulted by the memory of the one embrace they had shared, the sheer passion of it. Did he never touch her again she would take those feelings, those memories, to her grave.

Looking at him closely, afraid to give credence to what her instincts were telling her, she saw a flush of color had risen along the golden skin of his throat. Before she even knew that she was about to do such a thing, she heard her own voice whisper, "Marcel?"

Slowly he turned to her, and finally she saw her answer, there in the deep indigo darkness of his eyes. His desire.

Her stomach tightened and her lips parted.

Marcel's gaze fell to her mouth, saw the parting of those perfect pink lips. He swallowed to dampen his own suddenly dry mouth.

"Genevieve."

Was that his voice whispering her name? The sheer wanting in that one word made him shudder.

Catching her breath, she leaned toward him. Without knowing that he was going to do so, Marcel closed the space between them with his own lips.

Genevieve was drowning, her mind reeling as his lips, so oft thought of, so vividly recalled, came into contact with hers. So sweet, so stimulating was the contact that a piercing shaft of heat raced through her though their bodies touched at no other point.

When his arms came around her and pulled her close to his hard warmth, she thought she might surely expire from the sheer and unadulterated thrill of it. She was shaken by the wonder of being in his arms once more when she had never thought that such a thing could happen again.

She was completely lost in the pleasure of this embrace. His lips slanted across hers and, when his tongue begged entrance, she gave it. Willingly, joyfully, her own inexperienced tongue twined with his in a dance that she learned to follow quickly. Her breasts seemed to swell and become more sensitive against the hardness of his chest as his hands slid confidently down the length of her back to settle on her hips. She squirmed restlessly, pressing herself closer and closer as an ache that was impossible to ignore began to grow in her lower belly.

There seemed no relief for her discomfort. His kisses and the able pressure of his hands only seemed to increase it.

Marcel felt as if his head was swimming, his pulse racing like a raging river in his veins. It was as if every part of him were alive to the taste and feel and warm, soft scent of the woman in his arms.

Gently he lay her back upon the bed, never breaking the contact of their mouths. So readily did she react to that gentle pressure that it was as if her own body was joined to his by some invisible link that connected their two separate selves and made them one. One in need and pleasure.

With her soft form resting beneath him, he brought up one hand and closed it around the swell of her breast. She gasped against his lips, her back arching as her nipple hardened beneath his palm.

Driven by his own pulsing reaction to her response, Marcel slid his other hand up beneath the wool houppeland and soft linen shirt she wore. He connected with the softness of her belly, spreading his fingers over that velvet flesh with wonder.

The fluttering of her belly as he touched her made him press his hips more closely to hers. She reacted in kind and he took a sharp breath as his manhood reared in response.

Genevieve felt as if she could not breathe, could not think of anything save the steadily rising passion inside her. Her every nerve called out with longing and anticipation as that gentle hand on her belly slowly slipped up along her ribs, then closed around her naked breast. She cried out then, arching her back as her thighs clenched around the sweet ache at their joining.

"Marcel, Marcel," she cried out his name as his mouth left hers to leave a hot trail of longing across her neck. When he dipped his head to the collar of her houppelande she reveled in the thrill that made the hairs stand up along her nape.

He pulled the cloth down and nuzzled the top of her breast, which he continued to hold in his large warm hand. She whimpered, her breath coming in shallow gasps and it seemed as if her body begged him to nuzzle lower, to do something to...

Heaven help her, she did not know exactly what he would do, only that she wanted his mouth on her breasts.

The words he whispered against her ear made her shudder with desire. "I want to see you."

"Yes," she gasped. "Oh yes."

When Marcel reached down and grasped the hem of her garment she did not demure, but raised her hands over her head. The houppeland was removed in an instant and she kept her arms high as he now reached to take off the linen shirt she wore beneath it.

It was as he leaned to kiss her before removing it that her hands came into contact with a very similar fabric, clenching around it convulsively. At first her passion-befuddled mind did not grasp what her fingers were curling around.

His kiss was so distracting, making her heart hammer in her breast.

But then as Marcel leaned away, for how could she be holding her shirt in her fingers when he was about to take it from her, to dispense with the barrier between her flesh and his lips...

And then, in a vivid flash of recall it came to her, where she had seen such a fabric before. Constanza. It was her nightrail. The one she had worn the first time Genevieve had seen her.

Dear heaven, Constanza.

With a horrified groan, Genevieve folded her hands across her chest just as the unsuspecting Marcel made to raise her shirt. Her action successfully blocked him and he looked up into her eyes, his own dark with passion and confusion.

Before he could speak, she said the one word that must bring him to his senses. "Constanza."

He started away from her as if struck, rising to stand with his back to her where she lay upon the bed. Seeing this, and the way he raked a shaking hand through his hair, made Genevieve's heart ache. That he was sickened by what they had just done was obvious. Although it hurt her to see how upset he was, Genevieve told herself that she must be grateful that they had come to their senses before things had gone any further.

Before...God help them, someone had come in and discovered them....

Quickly she sat up on the bed and searched for her houppeland, which she found lying on the floor beside the bed. She slipped it over her head, aware that Marcel was moving away from her to gaze out the portal.

With awkward fingers she tucked her hair into the velvet cap, just as the door behind her opened.

Genevieve did not want to look around, did not

want to see who it was. But as the silence lengthened, she realized that she must.

Constanza stood in the doorway, her eyes flicking back and forth between them. That she was aware of the tension in the air was obvious in her dark brown eyes.

The Spanish woman said hesitantly, ''Perhaps I should go?''

Marcel swung around with what Genevieve could see was forced calm. ''Nay, there is no need. There is nothing you need be absent for.'' He motioned toward Genevieve. ''Genevieve's hands were not up to the task of plaiting ropes.''

Genevieve looked down at her hands with a guilty start. She had completely forgotten her injury. The bandage Marcel had begun to put on had long since fallen away.

Constanza came toward Genevieve with an expression of concern. ''May I do something to help?''

Quickly Genevieve grabbed one from the bed and began to apply it to her own injury. ''There is no cause for concern. I am near finished and it is not so bad as that. Marcel has already done too much.''

At his muffled grunt, she glanced at him and saw how he had taken her statement. She closed her lips on any explanation, though she felt that what had happened was certainly more her own fault than his. He had simply reacted to her own desires. For she was in no doubt of the fact that she had wanted what had occurred, wanted it desperately no matter how she had tried to convince herself otherwise in the past days.

She flicked another glance toward Constanza and saw the sympathy in her brown eyes. Quickly she looked away, feeling her face heat even more than it had been. Guilt rose up in her like an inky stain. She had no right to kiss Marcel, to touch him. He belonged to this gentle woman.

Genevieve could not help considering how hurt she would be if he was hers and betrayed her. Heaven, how hurt she felt even now, and he did not. How greedy and possessive she felt of his hands, his mouth, all of him.

She spoke through tight lips, unable to look at either of them. "I am very tired now."

Constanza said, "You must go to sleep then." She moved to the bed and pulled back the cover.

Looking at the bed, the last thing Genevieve wanted to do was get into it. How could she sleep in the bed where Marcel and Constanza had…?

Where she and Marcel had just…?

But how could she refuse? And where was she to lay her head if she did?

With an abrupt nod, Genevieve moved to the bed and lay down fully clothed. She did not care what the other two made of her silent refusal to disrobe. Her ability to behave as if nothing was wrong had been completely submerged in her confusion and hurt.

When the other woman pulled the quilt up close over her shoulder, Genevieve felt the sting of tears behind her lids, the kindness nearly being her undoing. She refused to shed those unwanted tears.

As when she was a child and all seemed to be in chaos around her, Genevieve told herself that she must go inside herself. Only there could she find a place where none of it could touch her, where she need rely on no one but herself.

Yet even as she went over this familiar pattern of thought she realized that her heart still ached, that Marcel still belonged to another.

Marcel felt Constanza's gaze upon his back, but he refused to look at her. With deliberate casualness he went to the table and poured himself a glass of wine from the pitcher on the tray.

He immediately realized that it might not have been wise to bring attention to the tray of food, for it was obvious that none of it had been touched. He knew Constanza would not miss this detail. Glancing at her from the corner of his eye as he raised his cup to his lips, he saw that she was indeed eyeing the still laden tray.

Again he felt her gaze upon him, but he did not want to talk. The passionate embrace he had just shared with Genevieve was still too vivid in his mind, too powerful, too moving to set aside.

He did not know why Genevieve affected him this way, only that she did and that he must wrest control of his reactions to her if either of them was to know any peace. For he was not blind to the fact that the same desires drove her. Clearly he had been right that in spite of her coming marriage, there was still some part of her that wished to be an Ainsworth, however unconscious that desire might be.

"Marcel?"

He looked up to see that Constanza had come close, her eyes searching his, clearly troubled. He shook his head.

With too much care he placed the cup back on the

table. He spoke with equal care. "There are some
things I must see to on deck."

With that he turned and left the cabin, closing the
door quietly behind him. Closing the door on the eyes
of his friend whose gaze told him far too clearly that
all was not well with him, in spite of his every wish
to the contrary.

Chapter Six

After that night Genevieve did her utmost to avoid Marcel. But it was not plausible to think that she could do so with complete success aboard the ship. He was simply there, in the cabin going over his charts, on the deck checking the direction of the wind, or giving instruction to the crew in a tone that was both civil and commanding.

No matter where she turned, there he was. His constant presence meant that she was unable to even hope for any relief from her tormented thoughts and emotions. She had told him that she did not want him and yet she had… What must he think of her?

Meals in the captain's cabin were a lesson in silence and discomfort. For two nights Constanza was the only one to even attempt to make conversation and when she finally questioned Marcel on his obvious preoccupation, he scowled at her and said that he was simply concerned about navigating the coastline.

That had seemed to mollify her in no way for her darkly assessing gaze had fallen upon Genevieve. Genevieve had nothing to say on the matter.

She knew that it was his guilt and regret over what they had nearly done that caused his preoccupation. The degree of regret he displayed convinced Genevieve all the more that his love for Constanza was strong.

The next eve, Constanza did not come to the cabin for the meal. Genevieve assumed she had chosen to sup with the men. The painful experience of sitting alone with the taciturn Marcel, who left without saying a word after taking only a few bites, made Genevieve think quite seriously of joining them.

But Marcel's warning about the men could not be forgotten. The events of her past would not allow her to do so. She knew how men could be, smiling on the surface and seemingly civil, while underneath their hearts burned with secret malignancy.

The last night she had spent at Treanly with her cousin Maxim was fixed in her mind for all time to come. Even though he had not succeeded in his attempt to rape her, he had come far too close for her to ever put herself in a position of possible danger again.

Yet her efforts to avoid Marcel, while never being alone with a member of the crew, brought her into constant contact with Constanza. The Spanish woman spent most of her hours in the cabin, either sewing, reading or keeping the chamber tidy.

Although Genevieve did not wish to be with the other woman, considering her own guilt over her actions with Marcel, she had really no choice. The fact that her hands were not completely healed did not help. She had no wish to sit on deck attracting the attention of the other crewmen with her idleness.

By the fourth day of the journey, the cabin seemed far too small, the air far too close. As Genevieve paced the confined space she found herself growing more and more restless, her guilty gaze fixing upon the partially concealed bed too often.

Genevieve was infinitely aware of Constanza, who sat close to the portal, sewing the seam of a garment that could only belong to Marcel. Her gaze raked that easily recognized houppeland of brown velvet, and a sense of possessiveness jabbed at her. Though she could not quite restrain these feelings, she knew she had no right to them.

Marcel was Constanza's lover, not hers.

That was just fine with Genevieve. The way he continued to treat her made her more certain by the hour that she was much better off without him.

Perhaps, she told herself, she would even reconsider Roderick's offer of marriage when she returned to Brackenmoore. She was beginning to realize more and more clearly that she wanted a marriage, a family and life of her own.

She wanted to be held and caressed.

Yet as these thoughts passed through her mind, Genevieve knew she would not do this. Roderick deserved better than she would be capable of giving him.

A husband deserved more than her confused feelings for Marcel would allow her to give. She would only marry when that changed. Change it would, if she had any say in her future. Hanging on to these unwanted feelings for Marcel would gain her nothing but heartache.

She was brought from her reverie by the sound of

the other woman's voice. "I am going out for a walk on deck. Is there anything that I might get for you?"

Genevieve shook her head sharply. "Nay, I am fine."

She could feel Constanza's gaze, so dark and thoughtful upon her. The Spaniard had a way of looking at her that made her feel as if all her secrets were revealed.

Firmly she told herself that this was not possible. Constanza might, indeed likely did, suspect that there was something between Marcel and Genevieve, but she could not know it.

Hurriedly she reminded herself that there was no longer anything for her to know. There would be no more contact between them.

The regret she felt at knowing she would never be held in Marcel's arms again must be forgotten. She heard the sound of a heavy sigh and realized it had come from herself.

"Genevieve?"

She looked at Constanza, wondering if that sigh had brought the other's attention to her again. She acknowledged that it had when Constanza asked, "Are you sure you are well? You seem…" She shrugged those white shoulders, which were revealed by her low-cut gown of scarlet velvet.

Ruefully Genevieve raised her bandaged hands. "I fear I grow mad from having naught to occupy me."

Constanza gave a sympathetic smile. "They are healing more quickly than I expected but unfortunately are not equal to more than the lightest of activities. I am not surprised you grow restless at the restriction."

Genevieve watched the other woman as she spoke, saw her genuine sympathy. She was not able to deny that Constanza was both beautiful and sweet of nature. 'Twas no wonder Marcel cared for her. As her gaze ran over the exotically lovely face, she found herself asking. "How is it that you came to know Marcel?"

The Spanish woman looked up with an astonished expression at this abrupt change of topic. Yet she spoke with resignation. "'Tis not an easy tale to tell, Genevieve, but one which I agree you must hear." Her dark eyes became distant. "I met Marcel shortly after my husband died nearly a year ago."

Genevieve exclaimed, "Your husband?"

Constanza flushed slightly at her shock. "Does it surprise you so very much that I would have been married?"

Genevieve looked down, contrite. "Forgive me. I did not mean—"

Constanza interrupted, "Of course you did not. It is I who should ask for forgiveness. It is just that my circumstances here aboard the *Briarwind* have made me...protective of my..."

This time it was Genevieve who interrupted. "Let us not talk of that, but of your husband and your meeting Marcel." She meant this most wholeheartedly. She did not wish to even think of the difficulties, nor the benefits, of Constanza's position as Marcel's mistress.

Constanza seemed happy to comply with her request. "My George, he was English, a successful merchant. I met him when he first came to visit my father on business in San Sebastian. I was seventeen then, and my George, forty." Genevieve was not blind to the true affection in her tone as she said, "He was older, *sí*, but a very kind and gentle man. Also very handsome. I fell in love with him in an instant. When he asked my father for my hand I begged him to agree. My father was sorry to see me depart from our home but wanted me to be happy."

Her tone was even more wistful as she went on. "It all happened so quickly there was little time to speak of anything save our love. It was not until we came to England that I learned that my George had a child from his first marriage, a son, named Burford. From my first meeting with him I knew that Burford did not approve of our marriage. But he was near a grown man then at nineteen, and soon made his own home with his wife, whom he wed not long after my arrival in England. George and I were so happy for eleven years. There were no children, but I continued to hope. That is until my George became ill. Only then did I realize that our days together were numbered, our hopes for a child together, our future, gone. For the doctors gave little hope, saying that it was his lungs." She raised damp eyes to look at Genevieve. "Burford and his wife moved back into our home to be with his father, though his dislike of me was still in evidence. George died only weeks later." She paused for a long moment, wiping at the tear that trailed down her cheek with the back of her hand. "Burford waited no more days before casting me out with only the clothes upon my back."

"Dear heaven," Genevieve exclaimed. "Was there nothing you could do? No one who could help you?"

"No. I had left my father, who was my only living family when I wed George. He was, by this time, long dead. My husband and I had lived a quiet life together and I had no one whom I would presume to ask for such a favor. I had no monies of my own and no claim to my husband's fortune. Yet I found myself wandering the city aimlessly as I tried to conceive of a way to support myself.''

Genevieve knew that Constanza's son by marriage could do as he liked as far as she was concerned, but that did not ease her outrage at the unknown Burford. That he could treat his father's beloved wife so badly was inexcusable.

She was distracted from these thoughts as Constanza said, ''It was on the second day of my wandering the city, wondering where I was to find food and shelter that I met Marcel. I actually fainted dead away on the street in front of him. When I awoke he was bending over me.'' She looked at Genevieve with obvious chagrin at the memory, before going on with great respect. ''Marcel insisted on knowing my situation. When I told him, he bought me a meal and offered me a place here aboard the *Briarwind*. What else was I to do? I had nowhere else to go and he is a kind man, like my George.''

Genevieve was not able to hold her gaze as she asked, ''You mean he offered outright for you to…?''

Constanza gave a soft chuckle. ''Oh nay, not that, not Marcel. He offered only a place to lay my head.

''He said that he had need of a woman servant to clean and look after his things, though I soon learned that it was simple human kindness that had prompted him.''

Genevieve did not know why learning this relieved her. For in spite of finding that Marcel had not been knave enough to enlist the helpless woman as his mistress in the beginning, their relationship had clearly grown into that. Forcing herself to face the other woman again, she spoke with compassion in spite of the agitation she felt at this realization. "You could do nothing but what you did in accepting Marcel's offer. It is no wonder that you came to care for him. He is a good man."

Constanza faced her, her eyes regretful. She said, "Genevieve, I...I need expl—"

Wondering at the strange expression on the other woman's face as she halted, biting her full lower lip, Genevieve could not help feeling as if she had been about to impart something of grave import. Genevieve prodded, "Aye. Is there something else you wish to say?"

Constanza shook her head. "Nothing, there is nothing." She swung around and left the cabin with a pensive Genevieve staring after her.

Marcel looked up from the helm of the ship to see Constanza standing at the top of the ladder that led from the deck. The expression on her face was far from peaceful and he was not surprised when she said, "I must speak with you."

He could feel the surprising weight of Harlan's gaze as he nodded jerkily. Marcel turned to the first mate and instructed, "Take the helm." He did not stop to consider the reason for his mate's intensity as he followed after her. He was more concerned with what Constanza had to say, for he was certain it would concern Genevieve, a fact that made him feel very reluctant to have the discussion.

He certainly did not wish to speak in front of Harlan. Though he genuinely liked and respected his first mate, he preferred to keep the private side of his life completely separate from his role as captain of the *Briarwind*.

Constanza led the way down the ladder, her movements near as agile as his after the months she had spent aboard ship. At the bottom she turned to him. "I will not spend your time with niceties, *mi amigo*. I have come to say that you must tell Genevieve the truth."

After a quick glance about them, he took her arm and led her to a more secluded section of the deck. He wasted no more time in getting to the point than she had. "I cannot do that. I will not."

She put her hands on her hips, her eyes narrowing. "You can and you must. I will not play the villainess in this. She is in love with you."

He took an involuntary step backward as the words hit him like blows. "Did she tell you this?"

Constanza frowned. "Nay, she did not. But 'tis true."

He took a deep breath and let it out slowly before answering. "She is not in love with me. You do not understand any of it."

She shook her head. "*Sí*, I do not understand and know so very little of you even after the many months I have been with you. Yet from soon after my coming aboard your ship I have known that there was something wrong, an emptiness inside you. I had thought that you might have been hurt by someone you loved. I believed that you might eventually come to confide your hurts to me as I have mine to you." She looked up at him with genuine concern in her deep brown eyes. "I know you are a good man, Marcel, that you took me in and cared for me when I had nowhere to go and no one to help me. I thank you for that and I owe you much."

He stopped her with a raised hand. "I did not ask you to keep silent on our true relationship because I felt you were indebted to me. You are not. Anything I have done for you was willingly and painlessly given. It is easier to give when one has much." He halted himself. Even Constanza knew nothing of his status as the son of a noble house. He wished to keep things as they were. Once Genevieve had been returned to Brackenmoore, his life must go on as before. He wanted to be respected for his own deeds here. Not because he was the third son of the house of Ainsworth.

She was shaking her head. "I believe you, *mi amigo,* and would have refused your request if I thought you did so. But you must understand that this deception is very difficult to continue, especially as I do not know the reason you keep the truth from Genevieve." She scowled at him. "You have too many secrets. I do not know why you wish for this young woman to believe the worst of us when you obviously have feelings for her."

His lips thinned, for he did not know a way to deny this that would not sound like too eager a protest. Yet he tried. "I do not have feelings for her."

She smiled knowingly, shaking her dark head. "You cannot convince me of that no matter how hard you try."

He replied stiffly, "Again I tell you I cannot explain."

"Is it because you believe this life too difficult for her?"

Marcel's lips thinned. He had no wish to discuss this or even think on it for that matter.

Constanza went on, "Anyone who had a care to truly look at Genevieve could see she is not used to hardship—her speech, her carriage, those poor hands. They are not accustomed to doing even the simplest of menial tasks."

Experiencing an unexpected sense of affront on Genevieve's part at her assessment, he said too hastily, "She is actually quite accustomed to keeping busy, and has spent most of her life running a large house…"

He stopped himself as he saw her eager interest, then abruptly and deliberately changed the subject. "Your pardon. There is no need to defend her to you."

Constanza was not willing to let it go at that. "So you have known the lady for a long while."

He did not reply, simply looked at her.

"How do you know her, Marcel? What was your life before you became captain of the *Briarwind?* I have asked Harlan and even he, your friend, knows nothing of you before he signed aboard as your first mate two years ago."

Still he made no move to answer. He was ever conscious of the fact that he did not want anyone here to know of his past, did not wish to become an Ainsworth in their eyes, and thus separate from them.

With a sigh of impatience, Constanza said, "I begin

to see, in spite of your continued silence. You have fallen in love with a lady who is above your station and she, returning your feelings, has run after you.''

He said, ''I mean to return her to her home as soon as my tasks in Scotland are completed.'' He told himself not to feel guilty about allowing Constanza to believe falsely. He was not willing to compromise the life he had made for himself by telling her the truth.

He went on with careful reason. ''You need not keep up the pretense that we are lovers indefinitely. We will arrive in Scotland within the next few days and I will take Genevieve with me whilst I see to my business.''

She nodded. ''Very well, then, I will not tell her, though it becomes more difficult by the day.''

He forced himself to attend her as she went on. ''She seems a fine young woman, your Genevieve, and is kind to me in spite of what she believes of the two of us. It is unfortunate indeed that the two of you come from different worlds. When she is gone, though, we must speak, there are...'' She took a deep breath. '''Twill wait.''

Marcel could only be grateful for her cooperation, his mind too full of his own disquiet and confusion about his feelings for Genevieve to long ponder her capitulation. He looked out over the vast expanse of the sea, not experiencing the familiar rush of belonging that he had known in days past. He felt for the first time since becoming captain of this ship that he did not completely belong.

Yet he did not completely belong to his former world, either. He could not live the way he had with no responsibilities to test his mettle and show him his true nature. Which was exactly what this life at sea had done. He had found the core of strength within himself.

Constanza had said that was it unfortunate that he and Genevieve came from different worlds.

Yet there was no other way.

Genevieve could not stop thinking about the story Constanza had told her, about how the other woman had no one but Marcel. Marcel, whom Genevieve wanted. For want Marcel she did, with every fiber of her being, no matter how she attempted to prevent it. Just the sound of his voice was enough to set her heart to pounding. Knowing that he was sleeping there only a few feet away from her, hearing the softness of his breathing in the darkness as she imagined the rise and fall of his smooth golden chest near drove her mad.

She knew what she felt was wrong. The Spanish woman had no one and depended completely on the charity of the man who loved her.

Genevieve, who had so much in the way of material wealth, felt she had nothing as long as she was bound by this hopeless longing for a man who did not want her.

Genevieve sighed. She had spent most of the morning pacing the cabin, wandering about listlessly. Then with a groan of utter frustration she tore the bandages from her hands and went to the door.

She could bear no more of her own company, even if it meant facing Marcel in the light of day. Her abrasions were healed well enough to do something—anything.

Out on deck, Genevieve saw that the sun was fairly

high in the cloudless blue of the sky. Many of the crew were working with darkly tanned bare chests. She was aware of a few casual glances being sent her way, but she was clearly of little interest to the men in her boyish garb.

Though this encouraged her somewhat, she felt a slight anxiousness, wandering about without Marcel's leave.

Casting a glance upward at the helm, Genevieve saw that Marcel was there with Harlan. The two had their heads bent close together over something. What it was she could not make out from where she stood.

Marcel was too busy to be concerned about her every movement. Surely as long as she stayed close he could have no objection even if he was not aware of her presence. She would be able to call out to him should anything untoward occur.

The cabin took up a goodly portion of this space but there was a wide strip of deck around the outside. She should be able to follow it around until she was at the bow of the ship. From there the view of the ocean should be quite wonderful.

She started forward quickly. The rolling of the deck beneath made Genevieve slightly nervous this close to the side and she held on to the rail tightly, feeling the salt spray upon her face and hands. She realized that its coolness might have felt invigorating had she been less preoccupied, less lonely.

Once at the foremost point of the bow, she looked out over the vast expanse of the sea before them and sighed. It was all so very beautiful, the sea an endless stretch of glistening silver, the gulls dipping and diving from the enormous blue sky. The wind of their passage tugged at her cap and she made sure that it was secure atop her head.

Marcel was quite aware of the moment that Genevieve emerged from the cabin. He could not have said why, he simply glanced over from his work, expecting to see her. And he did.

That he immediately went back to what he was doing without acknowledging her did not change his awareness. When he saw her disappear at the side of the cabin, he frowned. The deck would be quite wet and slippery and the wind was brisk.

Looking up from the maps of the shoreline, he said, "We will continue this later, Harlan. I must attend another matter at the moment. Watch the helm."

If the mate was surprised at Marcel's abruptness he gave no sign as he nodded. "Aye."

Marcel then went to the ladder and slipped down to the main deck. He followed the way Genevieve had gone.

He found her at the back of the boat, her face turned up to the sun, her eyes closed. A trace of peach grazed creamy cheeks and her lashes fanned thick and luxuriant above it. For a moment as he watched her he was transfixed by her beauty, the expression of simple joy on her face.

Yet in the next instant she opened her lids, her gaze coming to rest upon his. Immediately her expression changed. In an almost protective gesture, she wrapped her arms around herself as she said, "Marcel."

He was more perturbed by this automatic response than he wished to be. It made him speak with some irritation. "You must have a care up here. You could slip into the sea without anyone knowing."

A frown marred her smooth brow. "I am not a simpleton. I know to have a care on a slippery deck. I just could not remain cooped up in that cabin for another moment and you do not wish for me to mingle with the crew." She lifted her bare hands. "My injuries are quite improved, but I could think of no way to make myself useful. I thought to come to a place where I might not cause difficulty for anyone or bring undo notice to myself. I can see that I have erred yet again." She swiveled around to leave.

Her words stabbed at his heart as he saw the sadness she attempted to hide with her anger. He spoke before he could prevent himself. "I...forgive me if I have spoken with a lack of chivalry, Genevieve. You did naught ill by coming here. I was simply worried about your safety."

She stopped and spun around to face him, her uncertain gaze searching his.

He said softly, "Will you forgive me?" And as the words were said, he realized that he was referring to far more than having spoken too roughly. In the deepest part of himself he wished that she could forgive him for what he had done that ill-fated evening in his cabin. That she had been as eager as he was of no account. She was an innocent. He was an experienced man, well aware of where such action would lead.

Genevieve replied in a voice that revealed her uncertainty and vulnerability, "Are you sorry, Marcel, are you truly?"

He deliberately hardened his resolve against the answering throb in his chest, and squared his shoulders. "Of course, you may come and go as you will. Just have a care for your safety, not only with the men, but also the ship.''

She nodded quickly. ''Oh yes, of course.'' Genevieve turned to stare out over the water.

Angry with himself for feeling as if he had somehow hurt her, he said, ''You will be glad to know that we will soon reach our destination. When we weigh anchor, you and I will go on to Glen Rowan by horse.''

She glanced at him. ''You and I?''

He nodded. ''Of course, you did not think I would leave you aboard the *Briarwind* without me.''

She shook her head quickly. ''I assumed that Constanza would be—''

He interrupted. ''She will remain aboard ship. She knows nothing of my family connections and I would keep it that way.''

She looked at him then, her eyes betraying her disapproval. ''How can you keep so much from her, Marcel? 'Tis not right. Why do you hide so much of yourself from the one you love?''

He scowled at her. ''And why should my family connections matter to the one I love, does she love me?'' He stabbed a thumb at his chest. ''I, Marcel, should be what she loves, naught else. Certainly not my name.''

As he spoke, her eyes widened and her expression grew troubled in a way that he could not explain.

He shook his head in frustration, then turned and strode away. Clearly he was unable to make her see, for she could not see him as anything other than an Ainsworth. No matter that he wished otherwise, that knowledge hurt more than he cared to admit.

* * *

Staring up at the ceiling, with only the shimmer of the moon reflected on the water outside the portal to light the darkness, Genevieve sighed with what she recognized as incredible sadness. Though he had not admitted all directly, he had given himself away. He believed she had wanted him because of his family. Now that she looked back, she knew that he had thought this from the very beginning. If only she had known she could have…could have what? She did not know how she would describe her feelings, though she did know that they were not based on her wish to be an Ainsworth. But it mattered not now.

Marcel loved Constanza. That had been made truly and painfully obvious to her. Truth to tell, she had known this before. To hear him say the words with his own lips this very day, lips that had kissed hers with such skill and tenderness was so painful, so devastating, she could barely contain the sorrow of it.

The fact that the hour was very late and Constanza had not yet returned to the cabin only added to Genevieve's distress. For it meant that Genevieve was alone with Marcel, who had come in some time gone by, his expression not inviting conversation had she been so inclined. He had extinguished the candles and gone to his own narrow bed without a word to her. That she was already abed, her eyes closed as if sleeping, was not the only thing that had kept him silent.

She knew he had no wish to converse with her on more than the most necessary of subjects.

Again, Genevieve went over their conversation earlier in the day. She was more than a little grateful for Marcel's telling her that this voyage would soon be ended. She was wearied at being cooped up here, wearied at not having a way to escape him, Constanza, or the crew in order to nurse her many wounds.

Genevieve rubbed a hand across her forehead as she tossed restlessly upon the bed he had shared with the other woman. Saints above, but she would not have such vivid notions of what had passed between him and Constanza if he had not kissed her, caressed her as she now imagined him doing to the Spanish woman.

She gasped at the pain of the images that clouded her mind. Rising up in the bed, she could only pray that Marcel had not overheard her.

Desperately she looked about the chamber. It seemed as though he was deeply asleep on the bench, if the continued silence was any indication.

The cabin was not large, and from where she sat, Genevieve could see that the blanket had slipped down to reveal his naked chest. And though the light was poor, her greedy eyes seemed to have a mind of their own as they moved over his flesh, causing her to remember how good it had felt beneath her fingers.

Genevieve knew that she had to get out into the fresh air, to escape from his nearness and the desire she continued to feel for him despite all she did to convince herself that it did not exist.

With a care born of desperation, Genevieve climbed out of the bed and made her way to the door. She was doubly careful to keep from looking at the man who slept on the narrow bench.

Once outside the cabin, Genevieve hesitated. The sounds coming from the galley told her that at least a portion of the men were still about.

Frowning, she turned toward the bow, where she earlier had met Marcel. She was reluctant to return, but it was doubtful that anyone would be there. The watch who sat atop the crow's nest would not be able to see her as the cabin would obstruct his view.

Moving around the outside of the cabin, Genevieve hastened her step. The very thought of the breeze that awaited her was heartening. For the air she breathed in seemed stale and too warm.

It was not until she had actually rounded the end of the structure that she saw them. She, in fact, nearly walked right into the two who stood there in the moonlight, locked in a passionate embrace.

Constanza...Harlan?

For the longest moment, Genevieve did not know what to do, what to think. Shock held her completely immobile.

Then realizing that she did not wish them to know she had discovered them, Genevieve cringed back against the outside wall of the cabin. As she did so, she fought to keep her breathing even.

Yet the devastation at what she had just seen continued to make her heart pound.

Constanza and Harlan!

She had no wish to know this terrible secret. She had less wish to listen to the words they whispered to each other as she stood there.

Yet she could not help hearing the yearning in Constanza's voice as she said, "Harlan, how I longed for you."

He replied, "Must we keep our feelings secret?"

She answered softly, her heartache obvious, "I have told you of his feelings, what he has asked of me. I cannot betray him now when he most needs my loyalty. You know all that he has done for me.''

The next sounds she heard were muffled, but she knew them for what they were. She and Marcel had likely made the same sorts of sound in the heat of passion. A flush stained her cheeks as she realized that she must leave. She could not bear any more.

Being careful to keep from making any noise that might attract their attention, Genevieve went back the way she had come. She did not hesitate until she came to the door of the cabin.

Pressing her lips together, she fought back tears of disillusion and hurt, realizing as she did so that they were on Marcel's behalf. She knew that he trusted both Harlan and Constanza. Each night that the Spanish woman had gone to dine with the crew, he had known she would be with his mate and had shown nothing but complete trust in them. Never would he believe they would betray him, as was evidenced by the fact that he slept so soundly while knowing they spent the evening together.

Genevieve ran a hand across her burning eyes, her heart aching for Marcel. She did not know what to do, go inside where slept the unsuspecting Marcel, or stand here where Constanza would come upon her when she left the company of her lover. Constanza, whom he believed loved him as he wished to be loved.

Genevieve knew that she could not tell Marcel what she had just seen. Never could she find it within her to hurt Marcel that way. He loved Constanza and did he ever find out the truth of her perfidy, Genevieve would not be the one who broke his heart.

No matter how hard it might be, Genevieve would take this secret to her grave.

Chapter Seven

Marcel ordered the men to drop anchor just off the coast of northern Scotland. The ship could not stand too close to land as the sea constantly battered the rugged coast. They then began to make preparations to take him and Genevieve to shore.

According to his maps, Glen Rowan lay near enough to this spot to travel the remaining distance overland in a few hours. He was certain he and Genevieve would be able to find transportation in a nearby village.

The closer he got to Glen Rowan, the more concerned Marcel grew about what he would actually do when he arrived; yet occupied as he was, he was constantly plagued by a steadily increasing sense of unease concerning Genevieve.

He could feel her watching him from where she stood beside the rail of the ship. Her gaze was dark with a mixture of emotions, the only one of which he could define being sorrow. He knew that if he was to turn and face her she would quickly look away, pretending interest in anything besides him, as she was now.

She had been behaving in this all too bothersome manner since the previous morning. It seemed as if he could not look at her without seeing an expression of sadness and regret in her face. He could only imagine that she truly regretted the embraces they had shared. No matter what her innermost longings might be, she was engaged to Beecham.

So be it, he told himself. Still he continued to be fascinated with her every motion, her every word. His gaze felt trapped as she tilted her head to listen as Charley spoke to her. He couldn't help noting the way she tugged nervously at the edges of that ridiculous cap as she always did when near a member of the crew.

He couldn't help remembering the way her eyes got dark when he kissed her, the way she...

He groaned, frustrated that he could not get the taste and feel of Genevieve's lips and body from his mind no matter how hard he tried. Though he had avoided any hint of intimacy with her since that disastrous evening when he had set out to do no more than bandage her sore hands, he had not avoided the desire for intimacy. He could not release the craving to make her his own, as his body had bade him do on that night.

Deliberately Marcel turned from her to watch the crew loading the few things he and Genevieve would be taking with them into the rowboat. As soon as he did, he felt her eyes upon him. Quickly he swung around, attempting to meet her gaze.

Instantly she turned away and he frowned in consternation.

Why her action perturbed him so very greatly as it did, Marcel could not say. He should be rejoicing in the fact that she wanted nothing to do with him. It could only make his own wishes easier to attain.

Unfortunately, he was not happy.

With a deep breath he strode away, going about the preparations for leaving the ship with far more zeal than might have been necessary. He found himself carefully instructing Harlan on what he should do if a storm was to come up. "Don't let the ship come in too close to land and…" He halted, seeing his mate's affronted expression.

Harlan looked at him closely. "I am aware of what should be done, Marcel. I am not fresh off the land."

Marcel grimaced, realizing just how much of his agitation he must be giving away. Deliberately he laughed, "Aye, you do know what to do. You will have a care for the old girl as if she were your own."

Harlan nodded. "I will from the moment you leave and throughout the voyage to Wick to repair the mast." Marcel did know that the *Briarwind* was indeed in good hands and that Harlan would return to fetch him and Genevieve in good order.

Suddenly he realized that the mate was watching him closely, his expression troubled. When Marcel looked at him in question he said, "Marcel, there is something that—"

At that moment a voice hailed them from the aft portion of the deck. "Captain, the boat is ready."

Marcel called, "Aye." He turned back to Harlan, not unaware of his mate's agitation though he was anxious to be off and see to his aunt. He was less than eager to be alone with Genevieve, and even more distracted by the fact, thus he spoke absently. "You were saying?"

Harlan shook his head, smiling tightly. "'Tis of no great concern and will await your return. You must away now while the tide is favorable."

Marcel nodded, immediately setting aside his first mate's oddness in his preoccupation over traveling to Glen Rowan with Genevieve. Because of his desire to keep the two parts of his life separate, no one else from the ship would accompany them. Unfortunately, it was just the way things had to be.

Genevieve had no intention of being any problem to Marcel. She had determined to keep Constanza and the mate's secret to herself. The fact that Marcel seemed to sense that something was amiss could not be ignored. He seemed to be watching her, studying her with far too much intensity in the past day. That he did so made her all the more agitated about keeping her silence.

While they were being rowed from the *Briarwind* to shore, she told herself hopefully that perhaps leaving Constanza behind would help to ease her difficulty. It had not been easy to keep from displaying her shock and disappointment to the other woman.

Constanza was what he wanted. Constanza and the sea.

As the boat scraped against the rocky shore, Genevieve tried to focus her attention on the sharp and wild beauty of the Scottish coastline. Her boy's garments made it less difficult than it might have been to alight quickly, with the sea thrashing the small craft against the rocks. Training her gaze on the high, rugged cliffs above them, she avoided looking at Marcel as he took their belongings from the boat and waved them away.

She was resolved to remember that Marcel loved Constanza, no matter her character. And also to remember the fact that Marcel had made it very clear he did not want her. That fact would not change if Constanza did not exist. His cold indifference since that disastrous evening in his cabin—his bed, was proof enough of that.

'Twas not Constanza who stood between her and Marcel, but Marcel himself. She would not forget this.

She told herself to be very glad indeed to be on dry land once more and free of the confines of the *Briarwind*. Nowhere on board had she been able to forget, for even a moment, that all was under the complete command of its able captain.

Marcel was somewhat surprised that they managed to get through the next part of their journey with so little said between them. He and Genevieve walked to a local village, where he succeeded in securing two horses.

It was as they halted in a quiet glen to eat the meal Charley, the cook, had sent that he found himself becoming irritated again. It was not until she took the food he handed from the bag to a stump as far from him as she could possibly go, that he could no longer contain his impatience with her. "Whatever is the matter with you, Genevieve?"

Her enormous green eyes met his. "What do you mean?"

He shook his head in utter frustration. "You have been acting strangely since yesterday morn."

"I..." she began, obviously flustered, then drew herself up, speaking with bravado, "I have been acting strangely since yesterday morn you say? 'Tis you who have been behaving strangely these many days since the night we..." She flushed and he could not be mistaken about that of which she spoke.

Her directness left him with little option but to answer in kind. "How did you expect me to behave? I had nearly done something that both of us would be sorry about for the rest of our lives."

Marcel saw the expression of hurt that passed over her face before it was quickly replaced by anger. She stood. "Aye, it is something that we would both be sorry for indeed. But you, I believe, even more than myself. For I fear you imagine that I might think your making love to me meant that you had some care for me."

He shook his head. "Can you deny that you would be pleased if I did, you who would do anything to be an Ainsworth? Even if that meant being with me?"

She stalked over to stand before him, her hands on her narrow hips. "I will not deny that my greatest wish has always been to be a true member of your family, but I would not do *anything* to become an Ainsworth." Her cheeks became flushed with more than anger and she added, "I wouldst not give myself to such as *you*, my lord, even in aid of that end."

Marcel flinched, stung by her disdain. Had he not known all along that she would eventually come to see him as beneath her? So painful were the words that he could not remark on them, choosing instead to focus his attention on her other admission. "Why, Genevieve, do you persist in believing you will only be whole when you are an Ainsworth? 'Tis not so great a thing that you should want to disregard who you are by your own birth because of it."

She ran an outraged gaze over him. "And who are you, Marcel, to say this to me, when you wish to forget what you are?"

He felt the muscles in his jaw tighten. "I do not wish to deny my family. I simply know that being an Ainsworth in and of itself is not the highest state a man can aspire to. It is what you are inside that matters."

She turned her back to him. "Can you not understand that I feel the same need to choose what I would be and not be bound to the past?"

He shrugged. "You need not be an Ainsworth to accomplish that."

"I am aware of this." She swung around to face him, her gaze direct as she tried to make him see. "But you do not know how very compelling that thought became to the young girl who came to live in your midst. I never had what you take for granted— a loving family, security of heart."

He said softly, "Our parents died when I was still quite young. Do you think I have not felt the lack of this?"

She shook her head. "But you had them until that time, had your brothers in the days afterward."

He knew what she said was true, but she did not understand the empty void that had been left when his father, who had ever seemed so large, so vital, and his mother, who had also been strong but in a soft and gentle way, had disappeared from his life. Yet he tried to listen without interrupting as she went on, for it was true that he did not know what it would have been like had he not had his brothers.

"Even before my parents' deaths my life was…less idyllic. I really had no one to depend on for aught other than physical comforts."

Marcel frowned, his own concerns forgotten, for she had never spoken of any of this in more than vague terms to him, or to his knowledge, his brothers.

"There was something…strange about my mother. She was not well in the mind. She often cried for days upon end, not eating, not sleeping, with no explanation. My father would sit with her, trying desperately to comfort her, for in spite of it all I believe he loved her greatly, for from things the servants said I understood that she had been different before my birth."

She faltered then continued. "At her best times she would notice me enough to tell me that she was sorry she was not a better mother. But she made no effort to change things, did not seem able to do so. When they died…that night was such a horror, the servants heard her screams as my father tried to rescue her…the entire keep was aroused as torches were brought to light that deep and impenetrable darkness…I stood there in my nightdress and as the light shone upon the water I saw that they were gone…both of them lost to me for always." The emptiness in her voice was shattering.

"My life did not change other than that I went to Maxim and he…he thought that any young female in his keep must be willing to succumb to his advances. When he grew tired of attempting to seduce me, he had me brought to his chamber and undressed to await him like a…bride. I escaped through the window by making a rope from the bedclothes.''

He knew a sudden and fierce rage that would have sent him immediately to kill the man had he not already been dead. His gaze moved over her face, which he found even more lovely in her distress, over her fragile yet feminine form, and he felt a tug of tender longing that near staggered him.

Desperately he fought the feelings, knowing how wrong they were as she went on. "I knew from having traveled there as a child that Brackenmoore was not a great distance away. Somehow I knew that I would find succor there. All I could think of was getting to Brackenmoore and the boys who had shown me the only real joy I had known by allowing me to trail about after them.''

Marcel shook his head, wanting to touch her, to hold her, but knowing he dared not. "Dear God, I am sorry for the misery you have known." His gaze met her anguished one. "Do not make heroes of us, Genevieve. We knew nothing of your situation and made no effort to rescue you. We were only being who we were, would have treated any other child the same way." Though he said this, he knew it was not true. As a boy he had felt that there had been something hauntingly lonely in the tiny girl with the enormous green eyes and would not be surprised to learn that his brothers had felt the same. He did not want her to know that. It was his wish to help her to see that she did not need them. Her own strengths had sustained her.

He did not want to succumb to his own undeniable

yearning, the deep core of him that wanted her to look to him for comfort, the part of him that would glory in being her strength. For both their good, he could not give in to the longing to protect and care for her that he had known from the beginning.

Clearly oblivious to his thoughts, she closed her eyes, and said, "How could I do anything but make heroes of you? Do you not see that the naturalness of your kindness to me is why I have always remembered it? Your house was one of love and peace. You simply behaved kindly because you knew no other way. Can you not see that this is why being one of you has held such an attraction for me?"

He spoke carefully. "I am honored and proud that I was a part of that for you. But what you have revealed has made me understand just how strong you are, Genevieve. You do not need the name of Ainsworth to give you honor. Your parents' acts do not define what is to be a Redgreave. Define it for yourself."

She looked at him again, her gaze dark with a forlornness that tugged at his heart. "But I do not know what that is. The lands, the monies, they are not my heritage. They are just things."

"How you care for them and your folk is."

She sighed. "Benedict cares for them far better than I ever could."

This brought on a sudden and unexpectedly painful thought. Through all of this he had forgotten her coming marriage. Forcing himself to speak with more calm than he felt, Marcel said, "That will all change with your marriage."

She gave a start, her gaze widening. "Oh yes, of

course. That is true...though he and I will most likely live upon his lands.''

He grimaced at the very thought of her ''living'' with the other man. This made him speak more sharply than he intended as he added, ''You see, you would do well to forget your obsession with the Ainsworths.''

She drew herself up to her full height. Though her head reached only the height of his shoulder, there was steel in her voice as she replied, ''Aye, you are likely correct. I must face my insecurities if I am to know happiness. You, Marcel, would do well to do the same. 'Tis as wrong for you to decry your place in the house of Ainsworth as it is for me to yearn for something that is not mine.''

He could feel the flaring of his nostrils as he said, ''As I told you, there is no similarity. I am making my own life, by my own hands. You would run from yours.''

She said not another word, but turned and stalked back to her stump. He knew she would say no more.

Truth to tell, he had nothing more to say either. What she had told him had helped him to better understand her, but he was more determined than ever to keep his distance. She had inadvertently revealed that her desire to be an Ainsworth was not dead despite her engagement. He was now even more sure that any attraction she felt toward him was brought on by her need for, not him, but his entire family.

Genevieve must become resigned to her coming marriage in spite of the fact that she had come on what she had deemed ''an adventure.'' She had to for both their sakes.

By the time they reached their destination, he was of little mind to acknowledge the fact that the countryside they had ridden through was ruggedly beautiful.

The castle of Glen Rowan itself was surrounded by a stone wall and situated at the top of a rocky outcrop. The hard appearance of the rock was softened by lush green ground cover. To one side the land fell away to a meadow that ended in a forested area.

Marcel led the way up the narrow and uneven road. The castle gate stood open and the man posted there showed no surprise when he saw them. He called down, "You would be one of the lady's English nephews."

Marcel answered with like directness. "I am."

When they drew their mounts to a halt in the sparsely inhabited courtyard, a small, richly garbed woman came to the open door of the keep and looked out. The moment she saw them, a smile lit her delicate features and she rushed down the stairs. "My dear lad, how good you are to come."

Marcel leaped from his horse and met her. "I am your nephew Marcel."

She held out her arms. "Of course you are and I am your Aunt Finella."

He had had no need of her explanation. Aunt Finella was exactly as he had recalled though he had been young when last he saw her—warm and vibrant and still quite beautiful, only smaller. He could not help wondering, as she enfolded him in a surprisingly strong embrace, if his own mother would be as youthful if she was still living. Marcel could not help feeling that she would indeed be so.

Unexpectedly he felt his heart tighten as he stepped back to look at her and took her fragile hand in his. He suddenly realized this woman was a link to his past, to his mother, whom he barely remembered. All these years he had felt robbed of her and now here, so very far from Brackenmoore and the life he had put behind him, he might very well have found a way to almost know her again.

For a moment this knowledge kept him silent beneath its awesome weight.

He saw that she too seemed to be somewhat struck by him and her eyes glistened as they traced his every feature. She said huskily, "Louisa's own lad." The next thing he knew he had again been enveloped in those surprisingly strong arms. He was assailed by feelings of yearning and vulnerability.

He was almost glad when he was released and his aunt turned to Genevieve, who now stood just behind them. "And why would you be dressed as a boy, lass?"

He felt his jaw drop even as he saw Genevieve's sea-green eyes grow round with shock. "How did you know?"

The lady laughed. "Anyone with two eyes in their head could see that you are no lad." She gave a rueful laugh as her gaze moved over Genevieve assessingly.

It was very nearly the same thing that Constanza had told him. Oddly, none of the men had seemed to realize that Genevieve was a woman, while the women had no difficulty seeing through the disguise.

He had no more time to think on that before Genevieve replied, "I am Genevieve Redgreave, Lord Benedict's ward." She cast an uncertain glance toward Marcel, who had an intense feeling of protectiveness at her unease though he wished otherwise.

"I see," the older woman said, looking back and forth between them. Marcel was forced to expend a great effort in not fidgeting under that scrutiny.

After taking a deep breath, Genevieve said, "It is very good to meet you. I have heard of you from your nephews, and hope that my presence here is not a bother to you." She looked down as she fell silent, blushing.

In spite of the awkwardness that remained between them, Marcel found himself reacting to her shyness with compassion. He knew Genevieve still longed to be accepted as a member of the family, no matter what he had said to her this very day. Quite to his surprise he found himself saying, "You need have no fear of not being wanted."

Instantly Genevieve raised uncertain eyes to his, eyes that were filled with a yearning that shocked him. His heart turned over, as he told himself that this would gain them nothing. She was to be married.

He could not allow this senseless need to make them both lose their heads. For despite his assertions to the contrary, Marcel was indeed attracted to her and with an intensity that amazed him, considering the events of this day.

Feeling Aunt Finella's gaze upon them, he looked away. His aunt continued to watch both of them as she replied, "Have no worry on that score, my dear. Marcel speaks true. You are most welcome here."

To cover his own disquiet, Marcel said, "Forgive me if I am too abrupt in changing the subject, Aunt Finella, but there are extremely important matters to attend. Namely the well-being of your grandson. Is there any news since your letter to Brackenmoore?''

Instantly sorrow darkened her fragile features. "Nay, not a word, though since writing to Benedict I have sent message upon message to his captors in the hope of resolving this nightmare.''

Marcel watched as Genevieve reached out and put a comforting hand on his aunt's slight shoulder. "Have no worry, Marcel will make all well.''

He was moved by her kindness and also somewhat surprised at the complete conviction in her voice as she spoke of his assured success, especially in light of their recent alienation. Trying to ignore his own mixed feelings concerning this, Marcel told himself that he was not as certain. He remained silent on the subject though, for his aunt turned to him with a smile of gratitude. "I am so glad you are come, lad. You lads being Louisa's sons, you are my only living family and my only avenue of hope.''

He bowed. "I will do aught in my power to see the boy returned safe home.''

"That is all I would ask of you,'' his aunt replied with a tearful smile.

"I am ready to begin as soon as possible to see it done.''

She shook her head at this and turned to Genevieve. "I will see you to your chambers and serve a hot meal before we discuss the details of how to proceed. It will serve none of us for you to neglect your own well-being. We must all be at our best to see my Cameron safe home once more.''

Marcel balked. "There is no need for…''

She hushed him with a raised hand. "I will be the

judge of that, young man. I have grown accustomed to the knowledge that all things happen in their own time. It is a lesson that first became known to me when my beloved Cameron died and then even more fully when our only son and his wife were killed a year ago. My grandson has been gone these many days. A few hours more will make little difference to him but could make a great difference to those who try to help him by way of their beginning with clear, cool heads, as opposed to tired ones.''

He settled back, unwilling to argue further in the face of her certainty. He replied with deliberate patience, ''As you wish.'' If she felt more assured of his success by seeing that he rested first, he would yield.

He realized that whatever gave the kind little soul hope was warranted. He would do as she asked in spite of the fact that he was growing more eager by the moment to face the blackguards who had sought to see their ends met by kidnapping a seven-year-old boy.

His aunt nodded. ''Come then, I will see you settled in.'' She raised a delicate hand to one of the hovering servants. ''Logan, please take my nephew up to the chamber that has been prepared.'' She turned to Genevieve. ''Please come with me, dear.''

Genevieve looked about the large airy chamber curiously. ''You did not know of my coming and yet you have the room prepared.'' She was infinitely aware of the fact that the gentle lady had asked no questions about her presence here and her gratitude was great.

After the horrible conversation with Marcel she

would find it near impossible to even try to explain. She was still distressed at the way he had spoken to her, directed *her* to heed *his* advice about accepting what she was, when he was not willing to do so.

His reminder of how happy he was at shaping his own fate had made her realize that she must continue to keep the secret of Constanza's perfidy hidden. It was very important to Marcel that he had made his own life, set his own course, and his relationship with the Spaniard was a part of all that.

His speaking of her coming ''marriage'' had helped her get hold of herself and her emotions. She must put aside the feelings that stirred in her each time he showed her the least kindness, as they had in the hall only moments ago when she had been nervous at meeting his aunt.

He meant nothing beyond what he would display to anyone in need. Their kindness was one of the things she loved most about the Ainsworths. He had made himself clear on his desire to keep distance between them and she would accept that.

She would begin doing that now, by attending to her surroundings. As Aunt Finella had said, the chamber was indeed ready for an occupant. The dark furnishings had been dusted, the hearth laid ready for the cool of evening, the heavy green damask curtains pulled back on the huge bed, the window opened wide to let in the fresh scents of the warm summer afternoon.

Aunt Finella waved a fragile hand. '''Tis Cameron's own chamber. I have kept it prepared for his return.''

Immediately Genevieve took a step toward the door. "Then I wouldst have another."

The lady halted her. "Do not speak so. He will have no objection to your occupying it, though we will make other arrangements the very moment he is released."

Genevieve nodded slowly. "If you insist, my lady. But be assured, I will be happy to give it over to him."

Aunt Finella nodded. "I thought as much. And now if you like, while you wash, I will go and see what garments I may find for you."

Genevieve knew that she did not quite hide the yearning in her gaze as she answered, "I would not put you to such trouble, my lady."

"Aunt Finella will serve me very well. And you are not a trouble to me."

Genevieve answered her smile with a tentative one of her own. She was still moved by the woman's ready acceptance of her. As ever, she felt just slightly on the outside of the family who had welcomed her into their midst. What she had revealed to Marcel this day only added to her uncertainty. She was not sure why she had disclosed so much. Yet she did know that it had only served to fuel his belief that she was attracted to him for the sake of joining his family.

Realizing that Aunt Finella was watching her, Genevieve said softly, "You have my thanks."

The older woman gave her shoulder a gentle squeeze. "Do not worry. All will be well." She then turned and exited the chamber, leaving Genevieve to wonder exactly what she might mean by that. Surely she was referring to the fact that she believed her grandson would soon be returned. She could have no way of knowing that anything else was amiss. She would certainly have no notion of the problems between Genevieve and Marcel.

As from the moment when she first met the small and seemingly fragile woman she realized the warmth as well as the core of strength inside her. Clearly this inner strength had sustained her through her grandson's abduction and continued absence. She could not help contrasting Aunt Finella with her own mother, who had been weak and utterly consumed by her own desires.

With a sigh, Genevieve shrugged and went to sit on the edge of the bed. Her life with her mother had been gone for some time. She had long since learned to put the past behind her—to live for the future.

Unfortunately, at the moment her future did not loom so bright. It was of no aid to her in the least that this was through her own fault. If only she did not desire Marcel, had not come after him. If only she had not allowed him to believe she was engaged.

She took off her cap and ran trembling hands through her hair. It felt stiff and soiled. Saints above, but she grew tired of playing the lad. As they had left the *Briarwind* she was no longer under such an obligation.

Determinedly Genevieve rose and poured water into the basin. It was cool but she was determined to wash her hair, for she had not been able to do so aboard ship. Aunt Finella would be back with the promised garments soon and she would not be caught pining away. She would go forward with aplomb, no matter what Marcel did.

Chapter Eight

Marcel paused at the entrance of the hall at Glen Rowan, viewing it with some interest. It was longer and narrower than the wide, open chamber he had run and played in as a child at Brackenmoore. The time-darkened beams hung lower over the tables. The tall stone hearth burned low and the room glowed with the light of many candles. Due to the late hour, the tapers along the walls cast more light than the tiny windows that ran along the very top edge of the outer wall. He suspected that this portion of the keep was far older than the one where the bedchambers lay, the windows there being larger and paned with glass.

He was immediately approached by one of his aunt's servants, a matronly lady of ample girth, who curtsied and said, "I am Eveline, Lord Marcel."

His brows arched in surprise. "You know me?"

"I came to this keep with my lady as her maid when she married the laird those many years ago. She has since promoted me to chatelaine. It is so grand to see one of her family after all this time. Should you have need of anything you have only to ask. I knew your mother before she wed Lord Benedict and went off to Brackenmoore. What a fine one, was the lady Louisa. Never a cross word to say to even the least of the servants, which I numbered amongst at the time. You have a bit of the look of her about your mouth, though Ainsworth has left his stamp clear enough.''

Somewhat shocked at this unexpected revelation, Marcel nodded, having to prevent himself from reaching up to touch his own mouth. So he looked like his mother about the mouth. No one had ever said this to him before. Of course, it was not so very surprising that no one would think to say such a thing to him. All at Brackenmoore had grieved the loss of his parents.

It might have helped to ease the aching grief he had known if someone had spoken to him of his parents. Someone who could have told him that his mouth was like his mother's, that she and all things like her had not been completely taken from this world. It would have helped him believe that a part of her had lived on.

He realized how odd it was to have found contact with his past in this place that was so far from anything he had known. It seemed odder still that this connection with the past had occurred on the very day that Genevieve had questioned his feelings about his family. He gave a mental shrug. He had come full circle to face his past, and it was troubling to be sure. But that did not mean his leaving Brackenmoore was an attempt to run from anything.

He had been moving toward something. An inner voice told him that a part of what he had been seeking might be found here.

He cast a thoughtful gaze over the head woman and spoke carefully to cover his feelings of disquiet. "I thank you for your kindness and welcome. What would please me greatly just now is a cool mug of wine."

She nodded quickly. "At once, my lord. First there is one more thing I wish to say. Were you not the son of Louisa I would still be happy to fetch anything you desire. You have earned the gratitude of all here for the sake of your mission in coming to Glen Rowan." She raised the hem of her apron to wipe the tears from her blue-gray eyes, and she said, "We have been so very worried for young Cameron. He was long in coming to his poor departed parents and is all my lady has."

Her words reminded him that there were more important matters afoot than his past. They weighed heavily upon him as he nodded then moved to seat himself at the high table, which was made of a dark and highly polished wood. He could only pray that he was able to live up to the faith not only his aunt but her folk had placed in him.

He was drinking from the cup of cool wine she had brought to him when Genevieve entered the hall. As she halted just inside the doorway, hesitating, he was hit by a wave of shockingly intense longing. In spite of all that had occurred and all his resolutions to control his reactions, he was not only awed but confounded by her beauty. For she was beautiful with her gold-streaked hair falling loose beneath a sheer ivory veil. Those glossy golden curls seemed relieved to be freed from the confining cap, curling about her smooth cheeks and forehead.

Allowing his gaze to dip lower, he saw that she wore what must be one of his aunt's own gowns. The fact that they were of a very similar size meant that the rich burgundy velvet was a very good fit. Yet as he took in the way her bosom spilled over the top of the square-cut bodice, he thought that Genevieve might very well be rounder in one area of her form.

As the thought came to him, he felt his body heat at the memory of the full weight of those breasts against his palms. At that moment, Genevieve's cool green gaze collided with his and he saw a flush travel from her face to the tops of those luscious curves. It was if she was reacting to his very thoughts.

That was not possible.

Immediately he looked down at his cup. Feeling the dampness in his palms, he rubbed them against his thighs, but that action did nothing to ease the erotic pictures in his mind—the heat in his body.

Groaning inwardly, Marcel realized that this reaction seemed to come each time he was least expecting it. Whenever he had managed to convince himself that he had his reactions to her under control they raised up to call him liar. Roughly he told himself that he must get hold of himself.

In spite of his resolve, he remained infinitely aware of Genevieve as she crossed the room and came to a halt beside the table. He felt her hesitation but made no sign.

Then his aunt said, "My dears," and he did at last look up.

Grateful to have anything to occupy his mind besides Genevieve, he turned and saw Aunt Finella coming across the room. She too had garbed herself more finely for the meal in a gown of soft blue-gray silk. The sheer veil and wimple she wore fluttered about her delicate and still smooth cheeks.

As before, he had an amorphous sense of familiarity as he looked at her. She moved forward and placed a slender hand on Genevieve's shoulder, where she stood beside the table. "I hope I have not kept the two of you waiting."

Genevieve answered quickly, drawing Marcel's gaze. "Not me, lady…Aunt Finella. I have just arrived here."

Marcel added, "And I had only just come before her."

The older woman waved a hand. "Good then. Genevieve, please sit. We will begin the meal." As the younger woman moved to do her bidding, she took the place beside Marcel. Genevieve was left to take the place on his other side.

The servants brought trays of food and drink, and Marcel turned to his aunt. "I would speak with you now about my cousin. I wish to see him returned safe home as soon as possible."

She put a soft hand over his. "Thank you, lad, you have no notion of how good it is to know that you are eager to see him home and that I am no longer alone in this dilemma. I have been so worried about Cameron…" She stopped, obviously gathering control of her emotions.

His aunt clearly needed someone to lean upon in spite of her inspiring strength. She put his own hand over hers and smiled reassuringly.

At that moment, a tingling along the back of his neck made him turn, and he saw that Genevieve was looking at him. The expression on her face was one of concern for his aunt, and something else that he could only describe as admiration and, unbelievably, unshakable faith.

Their eyes met and she smiled, an encouraging and strangely vulnerable sort of smile that made his heart turn over. He shifted in his seat, realizing that her belief in him moved him more than the desire he had felt earlier as she entered the hall. The knowledge was far from comforting.

He forced himself to attend the matter at hand. "What I require now is for you to tell me the details of how this came about and as much as you can about the folk who have taken my cousin."

She nodded. "There has been an ongoing dispute over a section of meadow not far from the village. My husband had been seeing to this just before his passing, but I know not what final decision he made concerning it. The McGuires insist that he verbally gave them the right to use the land after a ten-year span, which ended some months ago. The family Duggan claims this is not possible for they feel they have a continuing claim to the land as it had been let to them all along." Aunt Finella shook her head. "I do not know who is in the right. It is quite unlike my husband to settle on a limited holding without making written record of such, and there is no documentation to be found. He was very careful to keep records on all the tenants. Because of the lack of evidence on McGuire's part, the Duggans have felt justified in continuing to keep their cattle upon the lands. This has only served to make the McGuires more determined to graze their own stock there. Things became quite drastic when the Duggans confiscated several of the McGuires' cows.''

Marcel took a deep breath. ''Why do you not simply redetermine the matter in your own mind?''

She gave a rueful grimace. ''That I tried to do. Neither the McGuires nor the Duggans would hear of it and actually told me that they would not abide by such an action as they feel the laird had already chosen.'' She looked at him, her gray eyes regretful. ''Though I have been accepted by these folk in the years since I arrived, 'twas too much to think that they would so easily embrace me as their overlord when my son and his wife died over a year ago. Had my boy been alive he would have been heeded well. I am a woman, and still English in their minds, I think. And Cameron is naught but a lad. These Scots are a strong, independent people. They do not bow and scrape to their leaders as in England.'' Her voice took on a note of warning. ''Thus as we move forward in this you must have a care to treat them with the respect they take as their due.''

Marcel began to see that this situation might just prove more difficult than he had anticipated. It galled him to think of being so very careful of the folk who had kidnapped a small boy. Yet he would take his aunt's lead in his attitude toward her folk. Anything else would be foolish, and only indulging his own anger, for he had seen enough in his travels of the world to know that not all cultures were as the one he had been born into.

Thus he said, ''I will have a care for the local customs.''

She looked him straight in the eyes, her seriousness

evident. "You have my thanks. I would not have this escalate until McGuire feels there is nothing to lose in harming my grandson. At this point I feel that Cameron is in no real danger and would have it remain so."

Genevieve spoke up, drawing his attention to her deeply troubled face. "How did Cameron come into their hands?"

His aunt sighed and leaned back, her hands now rubbing the carved arms of her chair. "Cameron is so like my own beloved husband, for whom he was named. He felt that it was his responsibility to talk with them."

Genevieve shook her head. "But he is only a child."

Aunt Finella smiled, a rueful, fond smile. "Aye, only seven years. Neither my Cameron nor our son would have allowed a little thing such as that to stop them, either. Aside from that, the clan did accept him as my son's heir soon after his death. They loved and respected both my Cameron and our son after him. 'Twas not until this dispute that there has been any question of where their loyalty lay. The Scots have grown accustomed to child monarchs in recent years. King James III was only eight when he took the throne."

As she talked, Marcel took all she said under careful consideration, being fully aware of the wisdom of her words. He also could not help seeing how truly and deeply she had loved her husband. Though he had been dead these several years the thought of him still brought a light to her eyes. Ah, to love so truly. How would it feel?

Without being aware of it he found himself again turning toward Genevieve, who was watching his aunt with sympathy and concern. Surprised that this thought would lead him to her, he told himself that it was because he genuinely hoped that she would find much happiness with her intended, the gentle Roderick, in spite of the tightness in his chest.

His aunt's voice drew his wayward attention back to her. "From what I have been told, my little lad rode his highland pony right up to the door and demanded an end to the feuding, that they come together and allow him to sort it all out." The pride in her face was unmistakable. "Obviously McGuire did not accept his solution. I received a note with his demands within the hour. He has vowed to hold Cameron until I grant his family their rights. This I cannot afford them. I would only create the same degree of animosity on the part of the Duggans did I do so. Some other solution must be found and one that will suit all parties."

Marcel nodded as he attempted to put all thoughts of Genevieve from his mind. "You may rest assured that I will do all in my power to see that this is done. Without delay."

He was determined that it would be so.

He looked at his aunt for a long moment. "We must meet with these people and find out exactly what it is they expect from you. We must find some purchase for negotiation."

She nodded. "As you will, my lad. I will take your lead in this, but I offer one suggestion. They are not apt to agree to come here to Glen Rowan. The Scottish customs of hospitality would demand they leave their weapons outside the hall. Neither party is likely to put themselves in such a position, fearing treachery from the other.''

He grimaced inwardly but made no outward sign of his uncertainty. ''Then we must suggest a location that is more palatable for the blackguards.''

A frown of worry creased the older woman's smooth brow as she placed a fragile hand over his larger one. ''I know how angry you are, my boy. I myself can barely contain the outrage that fills my every waking hour. Yet, as I told you, we must go carefully.''

He could see the truth of her words in the depths of her haunted gray eyes. Was it not reasonable that he should control his own anger if she, who had faced the kidnapping of her own grandson with such courage and forbearance, could do so? He took a deep breath and turned his hand to hold her own in his. ''As I said, I will do as you have asked of me.''

He glanced away from the depth of gratitude in her gaze and straight into Genevieve's green eyes. They watched him with an expression of yearning and trust. His stomach tightened. He grimaced. God help him, why could he not armor himself against her?

He was aware of the stiffening of her body, but he was careful not to look at her again, telling himself that her anger was much preferable to any softer emotion. Deliberately he turned back to his aunt, doing his utmost to hide his agitation. There were more important matters afoot than Genevieve's reactions to him, or his to her. He was pleased with the evenness of his voice as he said, ''I will have need of writing materials.''

Aunt Finella called for a servant.

Stung at Marcel's strange change from tender regard to displeasure as his gaze met hers, Genevieve moved to get up from the table, and said, ''I shall leave you two alone to conduct this matter in privacy.''

She was halted by Aunt Finella. ''There is no need for you to leave, my dear. We have no secrets from you.''

Marcel glanced up, his expression unreadable as he met her gaze. She spoke hurriedly. ''I am quite tired.'' She could see no hint of regret in his blue eyes.

As she left the hall, Genevieve cast one last glance over her shoulder at Marcel. She could not help thinking that he would make a very capable and considerate overlord.

That Marcel did not wish to ever fill such a role, she also knew. Though Benedict had never voiced the slightest complaint as to the overseeing her own lands, Marcel's admonition that it was her own place weighed heavily in her mind. Perhaps it did behoove her to marry and relieve Benedict of these burdens.

Would that the man be as capable and levelheaded as Marcel. For despite her indignation she could not help seeing that he bore those qualities and more. By heeding his aunt's request for care in the matter of seeing Cameron returned, in spite of his own obvious anger, he had shown this day that his aptitude for careful leadership extended beyond his abilities to run his ship. There his word was law.

She knew she would want those same qualities in the man she wed.

Would that the man she married also prove to be as capable at opening her body and emotions as Marcel had. As soon as this thought entered her mind, Genevieve gasped aloud in shock.

She did not wish to think on her reactions to Marcel or the fact that she had never responded to any other man thusly. She was not sure if she was capable of doing so.

She had an instant image of Roderick Beecham. That he was handsome could not be denied. That his undeniably good looks moved her in no way was also impossible to deny.

Marcel did move her, without so much as a touch. What was she to say to that?

Once in her chamber, she flopped down on the end of the bed. She wanted Marcel and he wanted Constanza, who had proved faithless.

Perhaps when Genevieve had been returned to Brackenmoore, Constanza would realize what a terrible mistake she had made. Surely out of his love for her, Marcel would forgive her. Genevieve told herself that this was exactly what she did hope for, but the hollow feeling around her heart did not go away.

Though Genevieve slept fitfully, the morning dawned bright and clear. She went to the window to gaze out on the blue sky, saw the birds chirped loudly, dipping and diving joyfully in the depthless expanse. The scent of green things and the sounds of livestock calling out to be fed rose to invade her senses. It was almost as if nature were flaunting its unrelenting forward motion as well as its beauty in the face of her own tumultuous feelings.

A soft knock sounded upon her door and she swung about and called, "Enter."

To her utter surprise it was the very man who plagued her so. Putting a hand over her suddenly racing heart, she told herself that he had not come here for any personal intention.

This warning proved true as he said, "Messengers have already arrived in answer to our invitations." His eyes bore a hint of anticipation.

She said, "So quickly?"

He nodded. "Aye. We shall see the matter settled anon and you safely home at Brackenmoore."

She felt her stomach tighten at his words. Of course he wished to be rid of her. Determinedly she forced herself to concentrate on the matter of getting Cameron home, though she answered through tight lips, "Pray it be so."

He did not seem to heed her reaction. His next words startled her. "If it not be too difficult for you, I beg you accompany me and my aunt to this meeting. I believe she will be glad of your support of her."

Genevieve felt an unexpected tug of pleasure. She curtsied quickly, bowing her head to mask it. "If I may be of any help, I shall be happy to do so."

His glance slid away as she tried to meet it, and Genevieve flushed. She must remember that Marcel wished to keep their relationship on no more than civil terms. She asked, "When do we leave?"

He spoke without inflection. "Within the hour."

She said, "I shall not keep you then."

Marcel bowed and left with as little ceremony as he had entered.

Genevieve could not rid herself of the happiness she

felt at being asked to accompany them. Quickly she told herself there was no time for such thoughts. He wanted her there for his aunt's sake, not his. But the joy of being needed by him, for whatever reason, did not quite dissipate.

Knowing she must make haste, Genevieve looked at the gown the older woman had given her the previous night. It lay where she had carefully placed it across the chest along the wall. Being of such fine and delicate fabric it would not serve for such an outing. Thus it was with some regret that she garbed herself, once again, in William's clothing and made her way to the great hall.

She was aware of Marcel, who cast an unreadable glance over her as she entered the hall dressed as a lad. He made no remark on the subject, being very obviously occupied with the coming meeting.

Neither did his aunt say anything, though she looked at Genevieve more closely.

Genevieve followed their lead as they moved toward the courtyard and the waiting horses. Because of her preoccupation, she was not sorry that her own steed seemed less than spirited.

Once outside the castle wall, Aunt Finella indicated the direction they should take. Other than this, there was very little conversation.

The lack of conversation gave Genevieve's mind too much free reign. As she looked at Marcel's strong, wide shoulders, where he rode just ahead of her beside his aunt, her heart beat a quick tattoo. He too was mounted on one of the highland ponies, though from the look of the animal his was a bit more lively.

The small, wide-shouldered stallion danced restlessly from time to time. Marcel seemed to have no difficulty in controlling him. He handled the reins with the same sure touch that he did the helm of the *Briar-wind*.

His lack of interest in her told her quite clearly that though he had requested her presence, there was naught of an intimate nature in his doing so. Not that she had needed any proof of this.

She knew how things stood between them, yet her disappointment could not be completely denied. She fell back a distance, wanting to put some space between herself and those seemingly fascinating shoulders.

After a time, Aunt Finella turned to Genevieve and called out with gentle warning, "Please stay nearby, Genevieve. We have not far to go."

Genevieve nodded and pressed her mount forward, feeling Marcel's gaze cross her briefly. Even though she was undeniably agitated at what might happen, she could not ignore her own chaotic emotions when those blue eyes touched her.

She attempted to concentrate on the wildly rugged beauty around her. The rolling and rocky hillsides were dotted with heather, their purple blooms bright against greens of the moss and short grass. The oak and darker-hued evergreens that had found purchase in the rocky soil reached wide limbs toward the white-clouded blue of the summer sky. The air was fresh with the scent of damp and rich earth.

She watched Marcel's back, saw the stiff set of his shoulders beneath the dark blue houppeland he wore. And at the same moment she saw the uncertain glance he cast toward his aunt.

Suddenly Genevieve realized that his stiffness was worry. He was not as convinced of the outcome of this day as he appeared. Yet far from making her lose faith in his abilities, that hint of uncertainty made her faith in him all the stronger, brought on a wave of tremendous respect. It also brought an unwanted rush of a softer, even more troubling, emotion.

Marcel was not surprised to arrive at the appointed meeting place and find the others already there. He also would have acted thusly in order to be sure that he did not step headlong into a trap. It had been one of the very reasons they had chosen this spot away from the keep at Glen Rowan.

His aunt's suggestion of the ancient ruins seemed ideal for their purpose. She felt that the open lands around the crumbling walls would give cause for some sense of security on the part of her enemies.

As they approached the ruins, Marcel could not help agreeing with her. He scanned the area up ahead of them, and saw that there were indeed no vegetation or land formations that could harbor an ambush. Added to this, there was very little of the original structure left. The two stone walls that remained were nearly totally obscured by the trees and shrubs that had grown up around them, offering unconstrained exit.

Several of the sturdy highland ponies had been tied up around the outside of the area. Marcel looked to his aunt, who nodded, and they followed the lead of the others who had arrived before him.

He leaped to the ground and helped his aunt from her horse, hearing the sound of voices from inside the rubble. He was infinitely aware of Genevieve, who had dismounted by herself. He had seen that she had opted to wear her boyish garb but had made no comment on this. Perhaps it made her feel some sense of anonymity. Perhaps she simply preferred dressing as a lad in his presence. Perhaps she had guessed at how deeply her beauty had moved him the previous evening.

Forcefully he turned his thoughts to the matter at hand, preparing himself for the coming confrontation. He could not help wondering if he would feel more secure in this if he was given the same opportunity to keep his identity secret. At his aunt's directive they had been forthcoming about the fact that her English nephew had arrived at Glen Rowan to aid her in this matter in the messages they had sent. He was not sure how he would be accepted by these folk who might very well resent his Englishness. Cameron's safety might well rest upon their acceptance of Marcel's right to be here.

His aunt turned to him, as if sensing his hesitation. "You are ready to go in?"

He nodded, feeling Genevieve's steady regard as he answered. "I am—I but consider how much is at stake in this."

His aunt took a deep breath. "I would have my grandson's well-being in no other hands."

From the corner of his eye, he saw Genevieve reach out to hold the older woman's shoulder for a brief instant. He turned and their eyes met, hers filled with unshakable faith. As ever, when she looked at him that way a strange feeling of confidence settled over him.

He found himself smiling with gentle gratitude. The

smile she returned made his heart throb and it was a moment before he was able to turn and lead them forward.

Once inside he saw that there were many more people present than could be represented by the horses tied without. It seemed that each of the two parties involved had felt that they must bring reinforcements. A group of perhaps twenty men and women stood to one end of the crumbling ruins. Another group of at least equal number stood to the other side.

They had fallen silent the moment he came around the end of the wall with his aunt and Genevieve.

Aunt Finella paused for a moment, giving his arm a gentle squeeze, whether to reassure herself or him, Marcel did not know. But she did not hesitate in her step as she moved to the center of the ruins and said, "I thank you all for coming." She turned toward a tall red-bearded fellow who stepped to the front of the group to their right. "I hope, McGuire, that I need not waste time in pleasantries this day. You know why we are come. We wish to negotiate for the release of my grandson."

The man nodded. "Aye, as ye know why we have resorted to such drastic measures to see justice done."

Another equally large but dark-haired man from the other group, shouted, "See thievery done, more the like."

Marcel took this as his cue. "I am Marcel Ainsworth. As mentioned in my aunt's letters, I am her kinsman, come from England. It is to me that you will address your grievances from this point on."

McGuire looked at him with raised brows. "Ye are an Englishman?"

If it was a question, it was phrased more in the tone of an expletive. Though he cared not for this, Marcel forced himself to remember his aunt's warnings of this very attitude. He would get no respect for his position as a nobleman here.

Did these men give respect, it would be because they felt it was deserved and for no other reason. Though this did not bode well for his task here, Marcel could understand this kind of thinking.

He, in fact, preferred to be judged by his own merits. That was unless the fate of a small boy hung in the balance. In this instance he would be happy of any purchase his name might have granted him. Unfortunately, it gave him none.

He nodded with deliberate aplomb. "I am English, yes, but that is not something that should be of import here. I am, as I said, kin to your lady. If there is any disagreement with this reasoning, speak now that we might have it settled. For this is no small matter in her eyes and she would move forward with the intent of seeing Cameron returned to her as quickly as possible."

Obviously McGuire took exception to this, for he cried, "And is it not also a grave matter to me and mine? We have only gone to such ends as were needed to make our unhappiness known to those who seemed to have more important concerns on their minds."

Marcel felt his hand clench. He wanted to stalk across the clearing and give the blackguard the thrashing he deserved for taking a small boy hostage to see his own ends met. Yet this he could not do. Thus he spoke again, taking even more care to remain calm.

"We are not here to go backward but forward. At this moment why you took the child is far less important than that it come to a speedy and equitable end. Again I say, do you agree to my acting as my aunt's spokesman?" Marcel knew their agreeing was significant. He believed the men would better accept him if they felt that they had been given a choice.

At long last McGuire nodded. "Aye, I agree, but I willna take to any pompous English ways. Ye're to keep a mindful tongue in yer head and recall that yer Englishness carries no weight here."

There was a shout of agreement from the other side.

Ah, the one thing they can be in agreement about, Marcel thought with irony.

He gave no outward sign of his inner feelings as he bowed respectfully. "I will abide by that. And I have a request of my own." His gaze swept the enclosure. "I am to be taken as my own man and my nationality will not be held against me any more than I am to expect it to grant me any privilege."

There was a long silence and then the nodding of many heads.

"Well done, my lad," he heard his aunt whisper behind him. Though he did not look around at her, the words buoyed and warmed him. He risked a quick glance at Genevieve and again saw the light of confidence in her eyes.

Determinedly he turned back to McGuire, getting to the point without further delay. "What must I do to gain the boy's freedom?"

The big man shrugged. "You mun do naught but see that the land that was promised to me is given over to me."

From the opposite end of the ruins a growl of anger erupted from Duggan. "'Tis not your land, McGuire. There's no power on earth that will see me bow to your thievery. Not even to see the poor innocent lad released from your vile clutches."

McGuire moved toward him with a hand on his dirk. "Vile clutches, have I? I'll have ye know that the lad's bein' treated with more care than me own grandson."

Marcel was relieved to hear this revelation, which, because of the fact that it was spoken with such heat, was very likely the truth. Yet he quickly set aside his relief. He could not allow the two men to come to blows here. They must approach the problem of the lands with calmer heads if it was ever to be resolved.

He grasped the hilt of his sword and said with firm command, "The first man who strikes out will find himself answering to my blade. We have given a pledge of safe conduct to all here. No one will be allowed to break it."

The two men stopped and looked at him, the surprise apparent on their faces. Their surprise quickly dissolved into frowns of displeasure.

He faced them squarely. "Well, it appears that I have been remiss in making my position clear. Though this astounds me, for I felt I had already done so in my invitation to come here. There will be no bloodshed. Has anyone the right to demand blood, it is certainly my aunt. Yet she has chosen the path of negotiation."

They watched him.

Marcel was determined to make them agree to this. "Well, what say you? For there will be no further talks lest all be assured of safe conduct to and from them.'' Another silence ensued. ''Do we not want this issue resolved?''

McGuire shrugged. ''Aye.'' He shrugged even as he cast Duggan a narrow glance.

The other man faced McGuire with equal disregard for a moment before turning to Marcel with a nod. ''I will abide the terms, do ye keep that sly *clootie* to his word.''

''A sly devil am I,'' McGuire shouted. ''''Tis ye who are sly, Duggan, pretendin' ye know nothing of the laird's wishes for the meadow when ye ken full well 'twas to be mine after the ten years were past.''

Duggan growled with outrage. ''Ye lyin' bastard. The laird said na a word to me of it and he wouldna change the holding of the lands without doin' that.''

Marcel interrupted loudly. ''Have you forgotten what you both just agreed to?''

Neither of them even looked his way as they continued to shout curses at each other in not only English but their own language. The two men were, in fact, shouting so loudly that Marcel knew they would not hear a word he said. His lips thinned to a line of exasperation as he felt his own ire rise to churn inside him.

They cared nothing for anyone else, preferring to fight rather than get this settled so Cameron could be freed. Then even as these thoughts passed through his mind the two men rushed toward each other, their intent to do each other bodily harm more than apparent.

Chapter Nine

Genevieve had held her breath with dread as the two men rushed at each other. But before they reached one another, Marcel was there, between them. The fact that he did not draw his weapon but stood with no more than his own commanding presence to protect him made her heartbeat quicken with dread.

He never wavered as the two of them stopped and watched him, their anger still seething. He spoke with quiet authority. "This meeting is at an end. You will both take your folk from this place without further conflict. I will send word when I wish to meet with you again. It will not be together, but separately."

Duggan cried. "'Tis his doing. He willna speak true."

McGuire waved an angry hand. "Ye know who is at fault here, Duggan."

Again Marcel stopped them. "Go from this place. Due to your lack of self-control I see no other course of action at this time."

When the two men turned and moved off toward their respective groups, Genevieve let out the breath she had been holding in a rush. That Marcel had been able to diffuse the moment was more than slightly amazing.

She heard Aunt Finella's soft sigh of relief and realized that she too had been beset with fear. Her heart went out to the noble lady who had stood so solemnly yet bravely as they discussed the fate of her grandson. She had the sense that Aunt Finella would not wish to display any hint of weakness before these folk, no matter how disturbed she was, and Genevieve could not help admiring the strength that sustained her.

As for herself, no one seemed to pay her any heed and she was glad of the impulse to wear her boy's garments. Doing so had given her an anonymity that was a comfort in the circumstances.

As the two Scotsmen moved to their respective parties, Genevieve's gaze swept the area. The faces of those gathered registered a degree of disquiet and bewilderment that was similar to her own. This could not be easy for the families involved, for they were neighbors to one another as those who lived in the vicinity of Brackenmoore were.

She noted a most particular expression of sadness on the faces of a young man and woman who suddenly appeared around the end of the longest remaining wall some distance from the gathered groups. The two parted and moved off, one joining each party.

Even as she saw this, Genevieve dismissed the incident. There were more important concerns brewing. Surely the poor outcome of this meeting would have a negative influence on how quickly Cameron could be released.

If only they had settled down and discussed their

differences calmly. Only when they were able to do so would Cameron be released. She knew that there would be no rest for any at Glen Rowan, and likely not for the other families involved, either, until that occurred.

Again her gaze swept the tense and angry faces. How Marcel was to see this through she had no idea.

As the two groups began to exit the ruins, Marcel spoke again. "There is one more thing I must ask. Nay, demand."

McGuire looked back and ran an assessing gaze over him. "What would that be, Englishman?"

There was no wavering in Marcel's gaze as he faced him. "We have no way of knowing the condition of the boy. He has been held for weeks now with no sight of him."

The large man's head rose. "Ye have my word that he is being treated well."

Marcel smiled though Genevieve could see there was no humor in that smile. "The word of the very man who holds him captive."

McGuire seemed to see the reason of this statement for he nodded. "Very well. I have no objection to showing him to one of ye. And one only."

Marcel took a step closer. "I shall accompany you immediately."

McGuire halted him with a raised hand. "Nay, not you." His gaze scanned the three of them where they stood together, apart from the others. His eyes came to rest upon Genevieve. "I will take the lad."

Genevieve felt her heart rise up in her throat as all turned to her. Her gaze fair flew to Marcel's face.

He cast her a glance of reassurance, then addressed

McGuire. "Why should we entrust the lad to you? You have already shown that you are not above using a mere boy to gain your aims."

McGuire laughed, and shrugged. "It is ye who wishes to see how the young lad gets on, not I. Have it as ye will, Englishman. I have no need of yer English brat. I hold the one I need."

Marcel spoke calmly. "I swear to you that I will not attempt to free my cousin. I but wish to see that he is indeed well."

McGuire shook his head with stubborn resolve. "I willna allow ye near him till my rights are secure."

Heaven help us all, Genevieve thought as she realized that he would not be swayed. She did not wish to go with the wild-looking Scot, but could not see this opportunity slip away from them. Taking a deep breath for courage, Genevieve spoke up in a deliberately husky voice. "I will go, Marcel, I am not afraid."

Marcel turned and looked at her, studying her for a moment before shaking his head and turning back to the other man. "You do not understand, McGuire. Gen—"

"Is not afraid," she interrupted him forcefully, though Aunt Finella cried, "Nay. I am the one who should go."

Genevieve looked at the older woman, only reaching out to gently squeeze her slight shoulder. "We could not risk their taking you as well. I would be of little value to them." She turned to watch Marcel, pleading with him to remain silent. In his eyes, she saw indecision. She knew he was thinking that he could not allow her do this for him, not even for his aunt and cousin.

He moved to look down at her, his voice so low only Genevieve and his aunt could hear. "What will happen if they discover that you are not a lad?"

At this she grinned with true amusement. "I think they will not. I have grown quite adept at playing the lad for those who make no effort to look past the surface." Her gaze skimmed McGuire briefly. "Methinks the fellow will not see beyond the end of his nose."

Aunt Finella spoke up, though she too kept her tone low. "I cannot allow this. It will not serve us to have two of our own in McGuire's clutches."

Genevieve was moved by the older woman's referring to her as "one of our own." Deliberately she smiled and said, "Have no fear. I believe the man when he says I would be of no value to him. On the other hand my going would be of great value to our cause. I will see the boy, reassure him, tell him that we are bargaining for his release. He must be terrified and my presence will surely ease him."

She met Marcel's penetrating gaze. "Do not prevent me from doing what little I can in this. I am truly not afraid. Should the worst occur, I know you would not rest until I was free."

The words fell into a deep and searching silence in which she continued to face him directly. She whispered, "Please, Marcel, allow me to do my part. You know how much it means to me to be one of you. You say that I do not need to take the name Ainsworth to be family, I only ask to give what any family member might."

A look of understanding passed between them as she said this, and she was aware of a strange regret in those Ainsworth blue eyes. What might cause him regret she could not fathom. Finally Marcel took a deep breath and nodded, his gaze holding her. He then turned back to McGuire. "We agree to your terms."

Quickly, before McGuire could change his mind, or perhaps before she could lose her courage, Genevieve moved toward the big red-haired man. He grinned at her and swung around to speak to his party. "We're away then."

Genevieve pulled her velvet cap down tight, mindful of the fact that she must continue to play the lad.

As a group, McGuire and his followers moved out of the ruins. Those who had come on horseback mounted up. "Ye'll ride with me," McGuire told her, and Genevieve made no demure as he grabbed her from behind and tossed her on the back of his highland pony. He then pulled himself up before her.

They started off at a good clip. Genevieve had no choice but to hold on to the big man's shirt, for he made no concessions for her presence. His men followed close behind. They had ridden for only a short time when he halted and spoke to one of them. "Cover his eyes."

A tall, spare-looking young man drew his mount close, taking a strip of cloth off his plaid. The next thing she knew he had securely wrapped the heavy piece of fabric around her head.

Genevieve said nothing, nor did she make any effort to loosen the blindfold as they rode on. She did not wish to jeopardize her purpose in coming with them—which was to see the boy so she could reassure herself,

Marcel and Aunt Finella of his safety. And also to remind the child that he would be soon released.

She could only pray that this would be so.

The remainder of the journey was made without incident. There were no particular sounds to mark their passage other than a brief moment when she was aware of the thundering sound of water rushing. The sound was so quickly gone that Genevieve knew she could not gain any insight there, being unable to tell anything about that body of water in such a brief time.

When the horses clattered to a halt a relatively short time later, Genevieve was dumped to the ground without ceremony.

She stumbled and felt a rough but not unkind hand upon her arm. McGuire's voice identified him as the one who had reached out in aid. "This way."

He led her forward, telling her to step up over the stoop. The next thing she knew, the cloth was untied then taken from her face. She blinked, realizing that she was standing inside a dwelling that had been built in the style of the longhouse. Only a few people were present in the high-beamed chamber. This should not surprise her, for it was a very fine day and most of the occupants of the dwelling were likely making good use of the dry weather.

The sound of a child's laugh drew her attention to the far end of the room. She saw that two young boys were playing with several large dogs near the unlit hearth. The two boys looked up as they became aware of their entrance.

When McGuire called out, "Come hither, young Cameron," one of the boys frowned and moved toward them with obvious reluctance.

He was a slim but sturdy little fellow with a shock of red hair. He was dressed in a dark blue patterned plaid.

As he came closer, Genevieve knew this lad could be none other than Aunt Finella's grandson. His gray eyes were so like hers that he could not be mistaken. That he was not fond of his captor was obvious in his dark scowl as his eyes found McGuire, but there was no fear in his expression.

Looking at the boy as he moved toward them with a measurable degree of arrogance, Genevieve could well believe that he had taken it upon himself to confront a grown man. It suddenly occurred to her that the Ainsworth brothers had not gotten all of their self-confidence from their father's line.

His arrogance told her another, more important fact. Even if he was the bearer of a more than healthy share of self-confidence, the child would be more subdued if he were being abused. Relief washed through her, but it was tempered by a sense of disbelief as he strode up to his captor, put his hands to his hips and demanded, "Well, are you to let me go home today?"

To Genevieve's amazement McGuire laughed out loud, which only seemed to offend the boy rather than scare him, for he said, "Do not laugh at me."

McGuire shook his head though he continued to grin. "I will not release ye yet, lad, and ye know well why I willna. I have brought someone to have a look at ye for your granny and yer English cousin."

"My English cousin?" His direct gaze went to Genevieve with curiosity.

Genevieve nodded quickly. "I am a friend of your cousin Marcel who has arrived at Glen Rowan to aid

your grandmother in gaining your release. I am come
see that you are being treated well.''

"My cousin Marcel who lives at Brackenmoore?"

She nodded. "The very same."

"My grandmother has spoken of him and his brothers, of course. She has told me that I might go there
to see them one day when I am grown."

She smiled reassuringly, though the effort was
forced due to the circumstances. "Your cousins would
be quite pleased to have you. All are worried as to
your safety."

Cameron flicked an unhappy glance at McGuire but
shrugged. "I am allowed to play with Ewan."

His shrug was decidedly dejected. This prompted
Genevieve to turn to McGuire and say, "May I speak
with him privately for a moment?" She did not want
to be mistaken in what she reported to Marcel. If the
child was being mistreated but afraid to say so in front
of his captor, she must know.

The large man shrugged. "Do as you wish. You
canna escape from here, lad." He cast a glance over
Cameron. "Neither of ye."

Quickly, not wanting to give him time to reconsider, Genevieve said, "Come, Cameron."

As soon as she halted on the other side of the chamber, Cameron said, "You say you are friend to my
cousin. Who are you?"

She bit her lip, thinking quickly as she realized that
this was the first time anyone had asked her for a
name. She said the first one that popped into her head.
"Will, my name is Will."

He shook his head as his gaze moved over her in
disbelief. "Why would a lass be called Will?"

Genevieve gasped and closed her eyes. Dear heaven. Trust this child to see the truth as grown men did not. She looked at him, keeping her voice as calm and even as she possibly could under the circumstances. "Please, Cameron, have a care and do not give me away. These men believe I am a harmless boy. Their thinking so was the only reason I have been allowed to come here and speak with you. If they learned otherwise I do not doubt that they might decide to keep me here with you in retribution for being misled. I can be of no use to you or your aunt if they do not allow me to go back to Glen Rowan so that I might tell her how they are treating you. We do wish to avoid bloodshed here, and I am afraid Marcel would not greet the news of my being taken hostage with good grace."

The child nodded knowingly, and whispered in a conspiratorial tone, "I see. I will not give you away— Will!" He cast a look about them. "I am sore tired of being here though they have let Ewan stay with me and I am allowed to play with him whenever I like. McGuire is his grandfather." His voice became wistful and she saw that his bravado masked the normal fears of a young boy. "But I would like to go home. I miss my gran certain enough."

Genevieve put a comforting hand on his shoulder though she did so with deliberate awkwardness, aware of the watchful eyes upon them. "And she misses you. I came to tell you that we will get you released as soon as possible. You are to remember that and not lose heart though I know it cannot be easy. The only thing that prevents your grandmother and your cousin

Marcel from open retribution is the fear that you would be harmed.''

He shrugged again. ''I do not think—''

''Enough.'' The voice of McGuire was impossible to ignore. The steel in it bore evidence of the fact that the man was not to be underestimated in spite of his seeming unconcern about bringing her here to see Cameron.

She cast Cameron one last reassuring glance. ''Remember this, Marcel will not rest until you are safe home and—''

''Come,'' McGuire bellowed. Hearing that hardness in his voice again, Genevieve knew she could not defy him for even another moment. She moved toward the door where McGuire stood waiting, his large hands planted on sturdy hips.

Genevieve reached up to pull the cover from her eyes and saw that they had left her outside the gates at Glen Rowan. Her heart thumped with a surprising degree of relief at having come through the experience unscathed. Even as she realized this, she told herself that she was overreacting. Poor Cameron had been held in a place he did not know, far from his family, for weeks. He was but seven. If he could survive such an ordeal with as little complaint as he had exhibited, she had no justification to lament her paltry inconvenience in this.

It seemed that the guard at the gate had been watching for her, for she heard him call out the instant she removed her blindfold.

Genevieve lost no time in entering. She had a sudden understanding of how trying her experience had been when she realized that her legs were quivering with each step.

Marcel's face was the first one she saw as she entered the courtyard. His concern was evident from where he stood on the steps of the keep.

Thinking to put his mind at ease, Genevieve lifted her arm to wave and called out, "Cameron is well."

Marcel moved toward her with surprising speed, enveloping her in a tight hug that near crushed her bones. Far from being uncomfortable, the bone-crushing gesture was more welcome, more thrilling than she cared to admit. It had the effect of setting her heart to racing more quickly than ever.

She clung to him for a moment, savoring the fact that she had come through the past hours unscathed. Had come through unscathed and been met with such eagerness.

She felt a melting warmth inside her as she breathed in the scent of him, all fresh air and musky male. That pool of femininity, which reacted to no other touch besides his, liquefied and flowed through her. Genevieve closed her eyes, reveling in the rush of sensation and warmth.

She was not such a fool as to think her reaction was the result of either relief or fear. She wanted Marcel, needed the strength of his arms about her, only came completely alive in response to his touch.

She made no effort to deny the proof of her desire, which was evident in the way her breast swelled against the hardness of his chest.

He spoke in a voice that she could not describe as anything but husky with emotion. "You are all right?"

She nodded, trying her best to get hold of her own scattered emotions, which was no easy task with his blue eyes focusing on her with such open regard. Resolutely Genevieve told herself that his concern did not mean he had changed his mind about the two of them. She made an attempt to inject some humor into her voice as she said, "I am well, but McGuire proved somewhat less that helpful in the matter of gaining information. He forced me to wear a covering on my face, both going and coming."

Marcel was flooded by a wave of tenderness at her effort to make light of the ordeal she had faced. Just the waiting had been near more than he could bear.

He had been pacing the great hall since he and his aunt returned to Glen Rowan from that disastrous meeting with McGuire and Duggan. From the moment he had agreed to allow Genevieve to accompany McGuire, he had been beset by frustration that he had let her convince him to do so.

He could not even begin to explain the relief and joy that rose up inside him as he heard the cry that riders were approaching Glen Rowan. Something, some inner sense, had told him that it was McGuire with Genevieve.

He pulled her close against him once more. As he did, he felt her body meld into his. She felt so right against him, so soft and warm and alive.

Marcel could do naught but continue to hold her there for a long moment. As he did so he felt a familiar tugging inside himself, a pull of emotion that could not be denied. Urgently he tried to tell himself that gratitude was what he felt, only gratitude, nothing more. Yet he did not seem to be able to let go of her, to stop his body from reacting to the softness of hers.

Finally, with a great act of will, he stepped back to look into those dark and seemingly depthless green eyes.

Her gaze seemed to be fixed on his mouth. His breath caught and his throat constricted as his mind supplied him with a sudden and all too vivid recollection of how good, how supple and erotic her lips had felt against his, would feel on his...

Knowing that he must do something, say something to drag his wayward thoughts from such images, he tried to concentrate on his sense of guilt. He said hoarsely, "I should never have let you go with them. I have near driven myself mad with thinking what could go wrong. I wanted to come after you, but had no idea where to even begin looking. I was fool to allow you to convince me."

She blinked. "I...how could you do anything else, Marcel, when McGuire insisted that I be the one to accompany them to where they were keeping Cameron? How could you ever have foreseen that McGuire would mistake me for a lad because I had worn Will's garments again this day?"

The gentle expression in her green eyes was near too much for his slight grip on restraint. She clearly wished to absolve him of any guilty feelings. He wanted to pull her back into his arms, but some inner sense of self-preservation prevented him. He had nearly completely lost control a moment ago.

If Genevieve noted his agitation she said nothing of it, speaking instead of the matter they should be most concerned about. "I spoke with Cameron, Marcel.

McGuire spoke true. He is being treated well and has a playmate to keep him company.''

Marcel shook his head in confusion. ''I find it strange that a man could kidnap a child to gain his own ends but supply him with a companion to ease his days. Are you sure that Cameron was not forced to tell you this?''

Genevieve nodded. ''He was not forced in any way that I could detect, though I agree with your sentiment as to the strangeness of the situation. Yet odd as this may be, it seems true. I saw the lad and that he and his playmate have free run of the dwelling where he is being held. The two boys were running about when I arrived and would have had no way of knowing of my coming. Aside from that, I was allowed to speak with Cameron with some degree of privacy for a moment. He assured me that he is being treated well. No one attempted to prevent him when he talked of his grandmother and his desire to return to her.''

Marcel grimaced at the words, realizing just how out of place his reactions to Genevieve had been just a moment ago. 'Twas his small cousin he should be concerned about.

''My poor little lad.''

Marcel swung around to see that his aunt had joined them. He watched as Genevieve went to her, putting her arms around the older woman. ''Do not worry, Aunt, he is doing very well. They are treating him with far more care than I would have expected.''

The older woman pushed back, looking into her eyes. ''I have tried so hard not to worry, knowing there was nothing I could do that might not make matters worse. But when you went with them today I thought, dear heaven, now he has two of my own...I could no longer put my fears at bay.''

Marcel saw that Genevieve did not waver under that close regard. ''I can tell you with all assurance that he misses you and does desire to come home, but is in no way being mistreated other than his being held there.'' She smiled gently. ''The lad is, in fact, quite defiant of McGuire and seems to have no fear of him whatsoever.''

The older woman nodded with an expression of fondness and yearning. ''That sounds so like my little lad.''

Genevieve hugged her again and Marcel was moved at her ability to give such care to his aunt when she must have been shaken by the ordeal she had just been through. Yet the danger was now past and he must allow it to be in the past. He must not dwell too much on the subject lest he reveal more than he wished to.

Yet surely there was nothing to reveal. He was simply grateful for her safe return—nothing more.

Determined to stop worrying about Genevieve and his reaction to her, he spoke more coolly than he intended, ''Let us not dawdle here but go into the keep, where Genevieve may tell us every detail of what occurred. It is my hope that she will be able to reveal something, which might help us to gain my young cousin's release.''

Genevieve stiffened at his tone, but he made no effort to explain himself. He must gain hold of himself.

He watched as Aunt Finella pushed back from Genevieve, her gaze filled with contrition. ''Forgive me, my dear.'' She looked to Marcel. ''She must certainly come inside. But surely she should rest and take some refreshment before we ply her with questions.''

Before he could answer, Genevieve shook her head. She glanced toward Marcel and quickly away, her own voice now distant, though there was sympathy in her eyes for the other woman. ''Nay, have no concern. I am most well. I would be glad of a drink of something cool but have no great need of rest. I will be happy to relate every detail of my adventure, does Marcel wish for me to.'' She looked only at his aunt as she finished. ''I am sure that it will help your mind to be eased in this. I would save you any bit of heartache that I might.''

Marcel nodded, without meeting her gaze, and led the way into the keep.

The next hour passed with no lessening of the tension between them. As Genevieve answered his every question about her experience, he managed to keep from looking at her directly.

For her part his aunt seemed oblivious to the strain between them. He knew that the tight hold she had over her fear for Cameron had slipped and she cared about nothing so much as she did every detail of her grandson's appearance and situation.

At last he realized that, though they had learned nothing that might help him in locating Cameron's whereabouts, Genevieve had no more information to impart. Seeing the strain around her mouth and eyes brought a new feeling of tenderness. He continued to cover it with a cool demeanor as he stood and said, ''I am sorry to have kept you so long at this, Genevieve.''

His aunt added her own regrets. "Forgive us, child. We had simply hoped for too—"

Genevieve halted her. "*You* have done me no harm, my lady." Marcel was not blind to the implication in the words as she went on. "I only wish that I had more to offer. For I know nothing more than that the boy is physically sound." She reached out to the other woman with a comforting hand. "Perhaps you should go and lie down, Aunt. I will see that the preparations for the evening meal go on apace."

"But you are the one who has been through—" Aunt Finella began.

Again Genevieve interrupted her, with what he could see was a deliberately cheery smile. "I am one of the very hardiest of souls and am most well. None the worse for wear, for they did me no harm at all."

Genevieve stood and drew his aunt up. "You go up now. I will attend to what needs doing. You have had the worry of this upon you these many weeks. Pray let us attend you, for I am sure you have had very little sleep over this time. Now that you know Cameron is doing well, mayhap you will find a bit of rest."

Relief made Aunt Finella's shoulders slump. With a sigh she put a fragile hand to Genevieve's cheeks. "What a dear child you are. It is true I have not slept these many nights. You have put some of my worry to rest."

Genevieve motioned toward one of the serving woman. "Come, take your mistress to her chamber. Darken the room so that she might have a rest."

The woman moved to do as she was bid with a respectful and warm glance toward Genevieve. Marcel watched as they left the hall. The folk at Glen Rowan very clearly loved their mistress and were obviously grateful for Genevieve's consideration toward her.

Marcel found his heart swelling with pride and gratitude, as well. Despite the fact that she was obviously still perturbed with him, Genevieve was able to reach out in comfort.

Without thought, his gaze met hers. His mouth silently shaped the words *thank you.*

In spite of all her resolutions, Genevieve felt her stomach flutter. She knew that she should not give in to it. Marcel ran too hot and cold, first warm and responsive then cool and remote and seemingly without reason.

Yet when he took her arm and led her out into a small chamber that was obviously used for storage off the hall, she made no protest. He came to a halt, releasing her, but she could still feel the touch of his fingers on the arm he had held. The sensation was far from unpleasant.

It was almost as if his touch, however benign it might be, left a permanent mark upon her, made her his. Somewhere inside her lurked a demon nymph who welcomed that sense of belonging to him.

Her heart thundering, she took a step backward.

Marcel simply moved to stand close over her, and she had to close her eyes to overcome the wave of longing that raced through her at his nearness.

His words, though, made her open them again. "I...there are no words to express my gratitude for what you have done this day. You have a concern that you will never truly be a member of my family, but your actions make it so, and not only in the case of going to Cameron. Your treatment of my aunt does you no small credit. Though I haven't seen her often, I care a great deal for her. I…she makes me think of things I had not considered for a very long time…my mother.''

Her gaze found his profile as he went on, the words obviously painful. ''Mother was very like Aunt Finella. Being with her makes me feel…think of things that I had forgotten. I recall how very hard it was after Mother and Father died. I see now that was when I began to envy Benedict his position as overlord. He had things to do, important matters to distract him from the empty and agonizing truth of their absence. I knew then that I had to be my own man. I never again wanted to be in a situation where I was left with nothing but emotions to dwell on.''

She spoke gently. ''There is naught ill in being sad over your parents' deaths.''

He grimaced. ''I have been more than sad. I realize that it was when they died that I began to wish that I had something to give my time, my life to. I needed to be needed as Benedict was. It was only the passing of years that made me forget when the desire had first come upon me, when I first began to feel as if I must be of more use than my place as a third son allowed.'' He shrugged seeming to have forgotten her presence. ''I had the name of Ainsworth behind me. And Benedict said that all that I wished for would come to me. I could not tell him that the thing I most wanted, to be like my brother, could not come to me, but I learned something important. I knew then that I must follow my own beliefs, make my own life. I must earn what I desired and never use my name or position as aid. I could not use my name, or any other man—or woman—to gain what I desired.''

She said softly, ''Yet Benedict inherited the lands.''

He shook his head. ''Benedict has earned his place by his love and care for all. He was barely more than a boy when he took on the responsibilities of being baron and has fulfilled them ofttimes at great cost to himself.''

For a long moment Genevieve did not know what to say. Marcel had just given away far more than he knew. He wished to live by nothing but his own efforts in order to prove that he needed no one to succeed. He had also revealed why he had turned away from her and what they could have. If she were impoverished, with no one and no place to go, he might have cared for her. As he did Constanza. Yet she was not. She was an heiress, would bring land and fortune to her husband. And because those things were what he most desired, Marcel would deny himself the having of them.

Why must it be this way?

Why could he not see that he, Marcel, because of his many qualities of leadership and honor, would bring far more than he would gain? Without thinking, she said, ''Marcel, can you not see that it is the Fates that have brought us together on this journey? That you and I have something to offer each other. I have lands. You wish to serve as overlord, would do so with a prudence and dedication that could not be surpassed.''

His expression hardened before her very eyes. ''You mistake me, madam. What I said was no bid for sympathy, or charity. Think you that I would accept such an offer? Surely you would gain what you think you want most—my name. But 'twould serve neither of us if you tired of my bed and ended in expecting me to play the part of exalted castellan.'' With that he reached for her, his mouth closing on hers before she realized what he was about.

To her utter horror she felt desire spring up inside her, unbidden and quite unwanted, but as fierce and hot as ever. Disgusted with herself and with him, she pushed at him with all her might.

Instantly Marcel released her as her angry gaze found his. ''How could you treat me so?''

He answered with an equal heat. ''How could you treat me thusly? You have admitted some time gone that I was not your equal. Why would I ever agree to such a mad idea?''

Vaguely she recalled his having said something to that effect when they were arguing on their way to Glen Rowan, and the fact that she had not disputed him. But that had only been to keep from giving away her feelings for him. Yet she knew she would never admit this as he continued. ''I have my ship and the sea. I have…''

She finished for him, ''Constanza.''

He nodded, not looking at her. ''Aye, Constanza. And you would do well to remember that you are to marry Roderick. He is your equal in stature and lands.''

Shame froze Genevieve's blood to the very core. He had made himself quite clear. Why indeed would she ever think he would agree to such madness, to forget that he loved another? To be so carried away

by this moment of sharing and suggest something so
impossible.

With a sob of anguish she turned and ran from the
room. She cared not what anyone might make of this
if they saw her. She simply could not face Marcel and
his rejection for another moment.

Chapter Ten

Genevieve spent the next morning with Aunt Finella. The elder woman was obviously still quite agitated from the previous day's events, thus Genevieve did not try to refuse her when she insisted on bringing her all manner of garments and shoes for her use. She even went so far as to send her own maid to attend Genevieve's personal needs.

Finally Genevieve had insisted that the older woman have a rest from their labors. Only moments after Aunt Finella had gone did she realize that she could not linger about the keep with nothing to do. The thought of coming into contact with Marcel when she was feeling so very vulnerable and frustrated—and angry with him—was just too overwhelming.

Marcel did not wish to be with her, had never made any effort to imply otherwise. She had simply been so moved by what he had said, by her own recent thoughts of having neglected her responsibilities that she had been possessed by a sudden madness.

As she headed off across the courtyard, she realized there was one truth she must accept. There was very little of her relationship with Marcel that she did understand.

The previous day she had allowed herself to forget Marcel was in love with Constanza. She had allowed herself to think his confidences meant something.

He had been carried away by the feelings that had resulted from his thinking about his past. Her presence had been incidental. For her he felt only gratitude because of her kindness toward his aunt and her going to see Cameron.

His admission that Aunt Finella had brought up so many long-forgotten feelings and memories about his mother were proof of his uncommon care for her. It was that which made him seem so…vulnerable.

She would not let herself forget again.

Throwing her cloak over her shoulders, she left the chamber and made her way to the castle gate. When the guard called down to ask her business, she replied evenly, "I am only going for a walk."

Was she mistaken or was there genuine concern in his voice as he said, "Have a care. You would not wish to be lost."

She nodded and set off at a brisk pace. During the morning Aunt Finella had told her that word had gotten round the keep about her volunteering to go with McGuire to see Cameron. She had also said that the people's gratitude was great. Clearly that must be the case.

This made Genevieve feel somewhat uncomfortable for a moment and she wondered why. Perhaps, came the sudden thought, she was finally beginning to realize just how important such things were to the common folk. Perhaps she was just realizing how much they cared about the lives of their overlords. Perhaps she was coming to realize that her own folk had been without that connection since she had been forced to go to Treanly by Maxim.

After escaping him, she had been so determined to never look back on her old life that she had made Brackenmoore her home. She had not thought about the effect this might have on her tenants, trusting in Benedict's man to manage. Until now.

She was realizing more and more that she had put the onus for many things upon Benedict. Matters that were her own responsibility.

Yesterday she had understood that Marcel would be a very good and conscientious overseer. Why could she not be the same?

It was with only half her attention that she left the edge of the heather-strewn moor and entered the woods at the other side.

Here the ground was dappled with shadow and the canopy over her head was more green than blue because of the thickness of the branches, though she could see blue sky in the background along with the occasional flash of a billowy white cloud. The trail was well defined and she had no trouble following it as it led around the base of the trees, up one gentle rise to dip then in a mossy hollow. All around her she could hear the sounds of the birds as they went about the work of feeding their young.

It was the pony she saw first, one of the highland variety that were ridden by the local inhabitants. And even seeing it there tied to a tree ahead of her, it was a moment before she understood what its presence implied.

She hesitated, not wanting to intrude upon anyone.

Then as she came to a halt, she saw them. Her gaze alighted on them, and the couple, who stood locked in a fierce embrace on the other side of the same tree, realized that they were no longer alone.

Instantly she recognized the boy and girl who had caught her attention at the ruins the previous day. The tension of those moments had prevented her from paying them more than cursory attention, but she did remember seeing them enter the ruins just as the meeting was ended.

The horror on their faces now left her in no doubt as to their unhappiness at being found this way. Genevieve could not be surprised. The girl had most certainly been with the Duggans the previous day, the boy with the McGuires. His resemblance to the red-haired giant could not be mistaken. He placed a protective arm about the girl's shoulders, and demanded, "What are ye about?"

Genevieve paused at his vehemence, then replied with some indignation. "Taking a walk. Is there some ordinance against walking in Scotland?"

Clearly chagrined at having begun with what amounted to an accusation, he bowed. "Nay, there is no such law." He looked at her closely. "Do I know ye?"

Genevieve bit her lip. "I..."

The girl spoke with amazement as she ran an assessing gaze over Genevieve. "'Tis the lad from yesterday. The one who went with your da to..."

The young man's eyes widened in shock. "'Tis true. But ye are no lad. What game is this ye play, Englishwoman?"

Genevieve took in a calming breath, knowing she must try to explain the misunderstanding. "Aye, I am a woman. I had no intention of being taken for a boy yesterday. When your father did mistake me, I could not tell him the truth for fear of his refusing to take me to see Cameron."

"Why should I believe ye?" He watched her with suspicion.

She shrugged. "Only ask yourself what I might gain by deliberately disguising my identity. I am most sure your father has spoken of what happened when he took me to see Cameron. What harm did I do to anyone?"

He watched her, his expression uncertain as he considered what she had said. Finally the young man answered, "Forgive my bad humor. I..." He looked down into the girl's wide and tormented blue eyes. "We..."

Although he seemed to have a great degree of difficulty speaking, Genevieve was fairly certain she understood what he was trying to impart. He had been more upset at her having seen the two of them embracing than anything else. Clearly the problems that separated the daughter of a Duggan from the son of a McGuire were not insignificant. At the same time, Genevieve could not deny a certain frustration and anger that such ridiculous matters as birth could keep apart two people who wanted to be together.

She could not help saying so. "Clearly you two are in love." When they looked at her with wide, horrified eyes she said, "Do not allow your families, or anything else for that matter, to keep you apart. Your love is something special and wonderful. It will sustain you if you but allow it."

The girl shook her head in dismay. "You do not understand."

Genevieve met her gaze with a long and assessing look. "Aye, I do. More than you will ever know. I cannot convince you of what really matters if your love for each other cannot."

This she knew was true. If a man and a woman were not prepared to overcome the obstacles that kept them apart, there was no hope for them.

She knew all too well that if Marcel was not willing to see that the things he imagined to be problems were nothing more than his imaginings, then there was no use trying to convince him otherwise. Even if he had not in love with Constanza, they would have little hope. Unless wholly given, love—or even the strange inexplicable bond that she and Marcel shared—could not have a chance to flourish.

So thinking, she spoke with more affront than she ever would have if her thoughts had been less distressing, "Do as you will, then. If your love is not strong enough to defy the unfairness of your families, it simply is not." She then turned her back on them in preparation to leaving them to their own worries.

The young man's voice halted her. "Ye think I am afraid to deny my father. I tell ye Englishwoman, the McGuire is not so fierce that I would not face him."

Genevieve swung back around with a gasp, for it was even worse than she had thought. McGuire was the lad's own father. He went on watching her with a scowl. "It is Fiona's father that I fear. I would not have him denounce her."

Genevieve took a deep breath, realizing that she had no right to plague these two with her opinions when she could not resolve her own life. She replied softly, "Pray, forgive me for my utterly capricious condemnation of you when I really know nothing of your situation. I would have no leave to judge you if I did. I…my own troubles cloud my thinking."

The girl spoke up. "My father might very well kill Robert if he knew that we had been together. It is for him that I fear, not myself."

Genevieve sighed. "Again I beg your forgiveness and reiterate that I have no right to pass judgment upon you." Her gaze met the girl's tormented eyes earnestly. "Upon either of you."

How sad was a world where love was not allowed to flourish where it may. How tragic that it could not dwell unchecked in hearts that longed only for the embrace of the beloved.

This time as she turned to go, Genevieve could not completely deny a sudden sting of tears. Though why they would come she could not quite explain.

What she did know was that she would speak of this to no one. The young lovers had the right to their secret.

Marcel tossed restlessly upon his bed.

He should be able to come up with a solution for bringing Cameron safe home. He tired of this waiting game, wanted to hunt the countryside high and low until he found his cousin, destroying those who had taken him in the process.

Yet here he sat attempting to think of how to get Duggan and McGuire into the same room without the constant gibes that only made the situation worse. His private audiences with the two men this day had ended in much the same way as the initial meeting in the ruins.

"God rot them." He rubbed an agitated hand over his hair.

He was hampered, not only by his aunt's pleadings for a peaceful solution, but also by his own realization that he would gain nothing with self-indulgent rage. By Genevieve's own words, the boy was being kept safe and reasonably well. He could not jeopardize that because of his own frustration.

For if he were honest with himself, he knew his agitation was not entirely due to his feelings of having his hands tied in the matter of dealing with McGuire. He had other equally burdensome thoughts pressing upon his mind.

In spite of all reason and good sense, he wanted Genevieve more than he ever had. Why he could not find the strength within himself to crush these feelings he could not understand.

Her offer of herself and her lands was far greater than he would ever have her know. He had kissed her simply because he was so filled with longing at the thoughts her words evoked that he could not contain it. It had been the depth of his own response that made him reject her with such vehemence.

He'd been overwhelmed when she'd spoken of Constanza, and he had been hard-pressed for a moment to recall who she was.

He could not succumb, and for the very reasons he had admitted to her. Yet he seemed to have no ability to control his mind, his very dreams.

His nights were haunted by images of the two of them together, doing, saying things that left his body bathed in sweat and his heart racing. He only wished he could convince himself that the passion Genevieve displayed in those erotic dreams was nothing more than imagination. The ardor she had shown each time he touched her left him with the unwavering certainty that to lie with her would be to bring reality to each and every heated image.

His dilemma was all the more difficult because of the fact that it became harder to hide his feelings with each day that passed. In spite of the fact that Genevieve had managed to avoid addressing him directly even once in the two days since their confrontation, he was more aware of her than ever.

He knew that it was wrong of him to allow her to go on thinking he was in love with Constanza. Dear God, what kind of man did she believe him to be that he could react so strongly to one woman while loving another? But he could not see what there was to gain in telling her the truth now.

He had come to realize that his feelings for Genevieve must be dealt with moment by moment.

The note fell open on the floor, where it had slipped from Genevieve's trembling hands. Heaven help her, what had she done?

When the message had been delivered to her chamber only minutes ago she'd had no indication of what might be contained therein. Yet the parchment, obviously penned by some cleric, and signed by young Robert McGuire explained all. The lovers had run away together and all because of what she had said.

'Twas sheer folly. They should never have heeded anything she might say. No one's life was in more turmoil than her own. She could not control her desire for a man who wanted nothing to do with her. She'd run after him witlessly only to discover that he loved another.

They should never have listened to her. She should never have spoken to them as she had, all that crazed talk of love and following one's heart.

Yet they had heeded her words. What was she to do?

Suddenly she knew that she could not keep this to herself. She must tell Marcel and immediately. When the lovers' families learned of their running away together, the repercussions might very well impact one poor captive boy who had no blame in any of it.

So thinking, she reached down and picked up the note, shrugged into the robe Aunt Finella had supplied. In the same haste she picked up a candle and hurried from the room, afraid she would lose her courage if she did not act now. Marcel would surely be angry with her, and justifiably. She would not shrink from that anger. 'Twas no more than she deserved.

Yet at the door of his chamber she hesitated, her heart thumping, her throat dry.

Then taking a deep breath, Genevieve drew herself up and knocked upon the door.

It was jerked open after only a moment by a barechested Marcel. When he saw who was standing there, he took a step backward. "Genevieve."

Her gaze took in that too oft remembered golden expanse, which seemed to almost glow in the light of the one candle he held in his hand. He pulled his robe more closely about him, seeming uncomfortable with her close regard.

Genevieve felt herself flush to the tips of her toes. She took another deep breath, forcing herself to concentrate on what she must say. What was wrong with her that she could not control her reaction to this man in even the most dreadful of circumstances?

Especially when his displeasure with her interest was so very obvious.

Quickly she began, attempting to pretend that the last moment had not taken place, though she was not unaware of the huskiness in her voice. "Marcel, I have come here because I have something of import to show you." Abruptly she held the missive out toward him.

He reached to take the parchment with a perplexed frown, and she cried, "I have committed the most dreadful of follies."

One quick glance at the signature at the bottom of the page prompted Marcel to pull her inside without another word. As he read the dratted note, she set her candle on the table and busied herself with looking about the room. She took in the one tall window, the same as the one in Cameron's chamber, the high, heavily curtained bed, the table, which bore a cup and pitcher, the softly glowing candle. Anything was better than seeing the condemnation that would come into his eyes the moment he realized what had happened.

The fact that it would only be made worse when she admitted that it was indeed her own fault did not help.

He lowered the note and turned to her with puzzled

eyes, asking, "Why are they thanking you for helping them to see that they must do this mad thing?"

She sighed. "I am to blame for all, Marcel. I spouted some ridiculous gibberish about love being all and that they should have the courage to face their families if they really loved one another. I have ruined everything. For now, when their families learn of this, they will be even more at odds. How are we ever to get Cameron released?"

Holding up both hands, he took a deep breath. "What are you talking about? How do you even know them?"

Briefly she explained how she had come upon the couple in the forest and her subsequent foolishness in telling them that they should not allow the wishes of others to stand in their way. She ended by turning her back to him, saying, "Thus you see I have brought about this horrid state of affairs."

Before she knew what he was going to do, Marcel had put his hands to her shoulders and turned her to face him. His tone was surprisingly reasonable. "Did you advise them to run away together?"

She looked at him with misery. "Nay, I did not go so far. Yet 'tis my fault that they have done so. Have you not heard me? I told them that true love should overcome any obstacles. I had no right to speak thusly. I was only thinking of my o—" She halted, realizing that she had been about to divulge the truth of her own confused and unresolved feelings for him.

He shook his head. "This is no fault of yours. You spoke from your heart. Obviously they do love one another enough to risk the wrath of their families. They only needed the courage to act on what they wished to do. People will always take another's advice if it aligns with their true desires. Only the most weak-minded will do so under other circumstances.''

He paused and, when he went on she felt his words sink into her in spite of her guilt and confusion. ''You have met many of the folk here about. Would you term them weak-minded?''

Genevieve found herself shaking her head. ''Nay, but…''

''There is no but. You did not make this happen. If there is one thing I know of a certainty in this world, it is that you would not deliberately harm or manipulate anyone.''

She watched his eyes, so deep and intensely blue, so sincere, and felt a now familiar ache of longing rise up inside her. She put her hands over her face, trying to hide the desire he would surely see. Why did he say such things to her, make her want him in spite of all the hurt that lay between them?

He reached out and pulled her hands away, and when he did, their eyes met. In those blue depths she thought she saw…heaven help her, she could not help seeing, could not ignore the fact that his gaze had changed. There was a heaviness to his lids, a barely leashed heat in those blue orbs.

Her breath caught and she felt a tremor of desire race through her as he passed a trembling hand over her hair and spoke her name with quiet desperation. ''Genevieve.''

The raw need of that one word emboldened her to reach out and put her hand against his chest, slipping inside the folds of his robe. Her eyes told him what her voice could not, that she wanted him, too, had always wanted him. From the beginning of time it seemed this wanting had been smoldering inside her.

When he gasped as her fingers inadvertently found his nipple, Genevieve felt another wave of longing so intense it weakened her knees. She closed her eyes, becoming aware of her madly thrumming pulse.

Marcel could no longer fight his need to touch and hold this woman. He had been so shocked to see her at his door, looking tousled and oh so lovely with her gold-streaked curls falling about her. He had grown too accustomed to seeing her garbed as a boy of late. Each time he saw her looking so softly feminine, her beauty nearly rendered him speechless. It was especially difficult given the path of his thoughts this very night.

Then as she had spoken to him, shown him the letter, he had made himself concentrate on her words, forget how his blood heated when her gaze brushed the skin of his chest as he'd opened the door. When he'd realized that she felt herself to blame for the actions of the young couple who had run away, this had brought such a feeling of compassion and protectiveness that he was shocked by it.

But it was not until he saw the path of her thoughts that the tight control he had on himself began to dissolve. He'd seen the yearning and, yes, need in her gaze. Feeling the spark of awareness that passed between them, Marcel could no longer ignore the need inside him. When her cool fingers touched his nipple it hardened, sending a flash of heat through his body that would not be denied.

The only thing he could do was take her in his arms. Genevieve found herself crushed against the wall of his chest. She pressed against his hard length, her body seeming to meld itself to his. He held her there for a long moment, and she felt the pounding of his heart beneath her ear, the shallowness of his breathing with senses that were both heightened and numbed by the sheer enormity and wonder of what was taking place.

When he drew back slightly, she opened dazed eyes just in time to see his face above hers. Then as his lips closed on her own, there was nothing but sensation, a spinning, whirling abyss of pleasure that spread through her limbs and left her clinging to him as if her very life depended upon it.

And, in truth, did it not? For she knew somewhere deep inside her that if he did not touch her, hold her, ease the ache in her belly, that she would surely go mad.

His hands traced the curves of her hips and she groaned, pressing her mouth and body more fully to him. She wanted to be a part of him, Marcel, the man who turned her blood to flame.

He slipped one hand inside her robe and her belly fluttered against his fingers. Her breasts swelled, aching with anticipation. She caught her breath, her whole being becoming focused on the path of that warm hand as it passed over her belly, her ribs, the undersides of her breasts, tracing, exploring, seeming to memorize the curves of her flesh as it went. When he finally touched one breast, his hand closing with gentle assurance over that aching mound, she sighed, sagging against him as he began to massage it through her shift. Her nipple hardened, becoming so sensitive that even the soft fabric of the shift seemed abrasive.

She could not keep her own hands still, the desire she felt growing inside making her restless and eager to experience the feel of his skin beneath her fingers. She groaned with impatience as his robe hampered her efforts to touch him as she wished. She wanted nothing between them but their own flesh, and pushed back from him in frustration.

She met his passion-darkened eyes. Her breath came quickly through parted lips as did his.

That blue, blue gaze seemed to be asking a question. She answered him directly, unable to play the coy maiden in the face of her own overwhelming longing. She dropped her robe to the floor. "I want to feel your hands on me. To put mine on you."

He groaned, needing no further encouragement. Without a word he pushed his robe back from his shoulders, stepping away from it and toward her as it dropped to the floor.

She gasped with wonder as his magnificent body was revealed to her in the glow of the candles. His wide shoulders, flat belly, narrow hips and long muscular legs were enough to inspire any warm-blooded maid to a covetous response. It was the rise of his manhood that brought a strange liquid warmth to that secret place betwixt her thighs. Though why this should be she was not sure, for Genevieve knew no more details about the act of joining than the ribald confidences that women sometimes shared as they worked about the keep at Brackenmoore.

Yet it seemed as if in some deep part of herself her body knew, understood that this proud part of him was to somehow become a part of her. It told her the pleasure to be gained in that act of joining would surpass even what she had experienced with him thus far.

Genevieve was ready for this joining, would let nothing—not modesty, not conscience, not the devil himself—stand in the way.

She reached down and pulled her shift over her head. When his breath caught and his eyes seemed to scorch each part of her, she knew only elation. He spoke in a voice that was harsh with wanting. "You are lovely. More lovely than I could have imagined."

Her own breathing stopped as she reached out to him. Marcel took her up against him once more, their flesh and hands no longer restrained by the constrictions of clothing.

When he slid his hands down her back, she pressed herself close against him even as his hands found her hips. His strong fingers closed around her firmly and drew her into full contact with the hard rise of his manhood.

The warmth inside her lower belly thickened, the ache making her shift restlessly against him.

Wanting more of him, she lifted her face for his kiss and he bent to her, his mouth parted. She answered his invitation by sliding her velvety tongue along his lips, and he shuddered.

When he lifted her in his arms, Genevieve's heart hammered against her ribs. His gaze held hers as he moved. She did not have to watch where he took her to know that he carried her to the bed.

She did not look away as he lowered her to the pillows, wanting to see his reactions, wanting this with every fiber of her being.

When he bent to kiss her once more, Genevieve

pulled him down to her, her hands urgent on his shoulders as she attempted to bring his body into closer contact with hers once more. But Marcel was not yet ready to comply with that urging.

His lips left hers to trail over her face, her neck, then down to the curves of her breasts. As he dipped his head further to take one turgid nipple in his mouth, she gasped, her hands tangling in the hair at his nape. He laughed huskily, reveling in her reaction to his caress and deepened the pressure, suckling her.

She cried out, squirming beneath him, "Oh please, I am afire."

He reached out to run his other hand across her belly, then down, his fingers stilling in that nest of golden curls. When he slid his fingers lower into the wet, silken folds of her, she reared up beneath his hand.

Gently he plied her, knowing that this was her first time, determined to prepare her for his passage.

Genevieve could not breathe, could not think, nor reason. She was falling, drowning in a sea of sweet, sweet pleasure that only seemed to rise higher and higher above her as Marcel caressed her burning flesh. And then for an infinite moment, she felt as though she were hovering on the crest of ecstasy, her body arched high. Then the crest broke and she was sliding down inside it, crying out with wonder and joy as she, Genevieve, became ecstasy itself, a mindless being of delight with no thought but that of her own bliss.

Marcel was both awed and emboldened by her response. Only when she stiffened, crying out in mindless wonder did he reach to take her in his arms, holding her against him as her shudders eased, feeling an overwhelming tenderness along with the unmistakable drive of his own hunger.

When she looked up at him, her voice was hoarse with wonder as she said, "There is more?" He knew he could no longer hold himself in check.

He rose over her and, as he did so, she opened to him, offering the dark secrets of her body without demure. His touch had indeed prepared the way, for there was only the slightest of barriers to his manhood. She pushed up to him, breaching that boundary without hesitation, encouraging him with the movements of her body. As he slipped inside her, felt himself engulfed in that velvet sheath, he lost all sense of aught but the sheer rapture of it. He groaned as they fell into a rhythm as old as pleasure. He was not unaware though of the quickening of her form beneath his, nor the pace of her breathing as she built toward another completion that only served to enhance his own. When the sweetness burst inside him, filling him with an earth-shattering delight, he heard her soft cry of joy and cried out his own in wonder that he had moved her again so easily.

Only when the ripples had passed did he roll to lie beside her, his heartbeat still a throb in his ears as he pulled her into his arms. Neither of them said a word. Marcel did not know if there were any words that could ever describe the sheer depth of his feelings and wondered if she felt the same. When he gently raised her face to look at her, he saw that she had fallen asleep.

He should not be surprised. If Genevieve had experienced even a portion of the tension he had known over the past day, this physical release had left her limp, as it had him. Marcel sighed, closing his eyes.

He knew he had to think, to understand what must be done now, but just for a moment he...

Chapter Eleven

Genevieve opened her eyes, instantly recalling the events of the night. And why would she not, for they had changed her life forever. She reached out to feel the space beside her and found it empty. An unpleasant apprehension passed through her as she sat up and looked at him, holding the bedclothes close against her breast. Immediately her gaze found Marcel where he sat in the chair beside the cold hearth.

The harsh light of morning poured through more than the window, casting its full illumination on Marcel's face. The guilt and sadness on that all too handsome countenance could not be mistaken. Sorrow washed through her, and she said, "There is no need to say anything. We have made a dreadful mistake by giving in to this terrible, unexplainable passion. There is no need for you to tell me again that you are not interested in my inheritance or that you are in love with Constanza."

He looked at her blankly, obviously so filled with guilt that the mere mention of his lover's name left him dumb. "I…forgive me."

Genevieve closed her eyes, for the urge to tell him the truth about Constanza, the secret hope that doing so might make him turn to her, was so strong it weakened her. But she knew she could not do that. She would not wish to have him that way.

Not out of guilt that he had made love to her. If Marcel did not want her, Genevieve, more than any other, then to have him would be nothing.

Without another sound she rose and picked up her robe. She was past shame, past caring if he looked at her or nay. All she was aware of was the great and agonizing pain inside her.

Only as she went to the door did Marcel seem to realize that she was leaving. He made a halfhearted attempt to stop her. "Please, Genevieve, we should talk."

She looked at him, seeing the emptiness in his eyes. It felt as if she were looking into a mirror of her own misery. She spoke harshly. "Nay. There is nothing more to say. We both know what lack-wits we have been. Neither of us has ever been foolhardy enough to profess that what exists between us had aught to do with love or any such emotion. Let us not belabor the situation, but attempt to salvage some semblance of pride."

He said no more to stop her, his lips clamping tightly as if to keep himself from speaking.

Marcel said not another word until the door had closed behind her. When it did, he let out an expletive so foul that it would have shocked half the members of his crew aboard the *Briarwind*.

When he'd woken to find Genevieve in his bed,

Marcel had been overcome with equal amounts of joy and agony. He had risen from the bed, his mind filled with an image of her face, so lovely and innocent in sleep.

Dear God, what had he done? He knew it was wrong to take her as he had. He'd simply lost himself in her, in his need for her, in her passionate and unashamed responses to him.

She had spoken of his love for Constanza and he had nearly told her the truth—that he did not love the other woman, that there was in fact nothing between them.

Her stopping him as he began to speak had brought him to his senses. Marcel had nothing to offer Genevieve. A woman like her with her great wealth and position should only wed a man who was her equal in status.

He knew that right now Genevieve thought she wanted him, that she did indeed desire him with a passion that had brought him to his knees. But it would not last. Passion was not love and neither of them had ever professed to feel anything more than passion.

If he were to do the right thing here and ask for her, as he should after having taken her virginity, they could never be truly be happy. Genevieve had been honest enough to tell him that she did not love him.

Beyond that, Marcel told himself forcefully, he would only come to resent the infringement upon his freedom. He would always feel that he had been given something he had not earned. Nay, he shook his head. 'Twas best left as it stood, even though it hurt him more than he would ever have imagined to see the betrayal in her gaze as she left him.

The frustration and unhappiness Marcel felt over the disastrous situation between himself and Genevieve was only compounded by the fact that he continued to make no gain in his efforts to make peace between the two feuding Scots. The two men had learned of the marriage of the offspring and it had only heated their hatred to a fevered pitch. His every attempt to reason with either man over the past days had ended in shouted accusations of the other's treachery.

His disposition was not improved by the fact that Genevieve had not spoken to him since the morning she had woken in his bed. He knew that he could not fault her for her anger. Neither could he easily bear the brunt of it, especially when his every contact with her made him long with a fierce and aching need to take her back to his bed and love her until both of them were sated and exhausted.

Yet that could not be. Nothing had changed, nor would it.

These thoughts rode hard on his mind as he returned from his third failed effort to persuade McGuire to hear Duggan out. Truth be told, he had spent more time thinking of Genevieve than in concentrating on the matter at hand. He knew that things could not continue as they were. He would most certainly go mad.

He must settle matters here in Scotland and return Genevieve to Brackenmoore, where she belonged. It was his only hope of putting his life in order.

Marcel spurred his mount toward Glen Rowan. When he arrived, he went immediately to his aunt after being told that she was in her own chambers.

He opened the door at her command and saw that she was not alone. Genevieve sat in a chair next to hers and the two women appeared to be sewing on different portions of the same garment.

Genevieve's gaze met his for the briefest moment before she quickly looked down at her needle. Yet that moment was not so brief that he failed to see the hurt in her sea-green eyes.

He forced himself to turn to his aunt, who took on an expression of dread as she saw his face. "Has something happened?"

He shook his head, "Nay, neither good nor ill." He laughed without humor. "Have no worry on that score. I learned nothing new at my meeting with McGuire." He went on speaking with as much compassion as he could in deference to her fears for Cameron. "Yet I have come to a decision. This situation has gone quite far enough, Aunt Finella. I know that you do not wish for me to act openly against McGuire for fear of his harming Cameron, but I cannot continue to sit idly by knowing that he is keeping the boy and seems to have no intention of letting him go at any near date."

She raised trembling hands to her cheeks. "What do you mean to do?"

"I mean to find my cousin and bring him home. Any further negotiations with McGuire and Duggan will take place when that has been accomplished. Neither of them has any intent to be swayed from their tediously fixed positions. They must be forced to do so. I would not have my cousin at the mercy of such men for another moment."

He could feel Genevieve's steady regard and turned to her. "Pray, Genevieve, help me in this. I need know if there is anything more you can recall that might help me to locate the place where Cameron is being held."

She took a deep breath and nodded, obviously willing to put her anger with him aside in the name of this cause. "As I told you, I was blindfolded for most of the ride there and all of the return to Glen Rowan. If only I could recall something new, but I fear I have told you all." Her open regret told him just how much she did wish to remember something new.

Earnestly he held her gaze. "Aye, I know you have tried your best, but think one more time, Genevieve. You are our only hope. The only one who has been there. Any small hint, no matter how seemingly irrelevant might end in being greatly significant."

She pushed her hair back from her forehead as she clearly fought to drag something from her memory. "There was really nothing. Nothing that would be specific enough to find the location again. All I could hear was the sounds of the horses' hooves…then men exchanging very few words…mostly one-word orders from McGuire…" She shook her head again. "Water rushing loudly for a moment…"

Aunt Finella interrupted softly, her voice intent. "Water rushing?"

Genevieve looked at her in surprise, nodding. "Yes. I do not know where, and it was only for a moment, not even long enough to tell how large a body, though the sound was quite loud for that one moment."

She watched Genevieve closely. "How long was it after hearing the sound of water that you arrived where my grandson is being held?"

Genevieve frowned in concentration. "I...saints above, I am not sure. I did not know that..."

Marcel spoke more harshly than he intended, understanding by his aunt's expression that the reply could be very important. "Think, Genevieve." As she turned her wounded gaze upon him, he apologized quickly. "Forgive me, I know you are doing your utmost. It is simply that it seems this information might give Aunt some clue as to where you were taken."

His aunt nodded. "It might, indeed. For if your destination was close onto hearing this sound I believe I may know the location. For there is a very old structure, built in the fashion of the Vikings not far from Clananaught Falls."

Genevieve frowned pensively. "Aye, I do believe it was not long before we arrived."

Aunt Finella clasped her hands together, her face registering hope, joy and fear all at one and the same time. She looked to Marcel. "Then I can surely direct you to the place I am thinking of." She took a deep breath, before adding, "Though Genevieve has given us this clue, there is no surety that it is the correct location. I could be misinterpreting what she heard."

Marcel shook his own head. "However uncertain, 'tis a better hope than what we had." He looked to Genevieve, his gaze warm in spite of knowing that he should keep his emotions close to him. "You have my thanks."

The regret and sadness in her gaze made him turn away.

Knowing that he could not allow himself to react to this, Marcel concentrated on what he must do now in connection to his cousin. As he did so he realized just what this information meant. Should fortune smile upon him, he might, by stealth and surprise, go to this place and take the lad before anyone could prevent him. On the other hand should their supposition prove wrong and McGuire learn of his attempt, he would get no second opportunity. They would certainly make sure that Cameron was taken to an even more secure position than the one he was in now.

There could be no mistakes.

Yet he must act. With the two feuding families now even more immersed in their anger toward one another at the marriage of their wayward offspring, there was no telling how long it might take them to come to their senses.

He would not make the little boy wait in the hope that they would overcome their anger toward one another. Both men had displayed a stubborn disregard of Cameron.

The summer night was very still, too still. No birds twittered in the trees, no small animals scuttled about in the underbrush. The moon in the sky overhead shone all about the silent earth with a brightness that caused Marcel no small amount of discomfort. Though it lightened the way ahead well enough, any sentries that might be waiting in the forest would be able to see the small mounted party with little effort.

Firmly he told himself not to let his imagination wander to mishaps that might occur. No matter what, if Cameron was at the location, he would succeed in rescuing him.

To even contemplate other possibilities was to only invite trouble.

Connor, one of his aunt's most trusted men, rode his mount up beside Marcel's as a sudden thunderous rushing of water came from his left. The Scot pointed off toward the sound, his voice so low as to barely be audible as he said, "Clananaught Falls."

Marcel nodded and they pressed on again. The noise ceased almost immediately. No wonder Genevieve had thought it such a strange and unidentifiable sound. The falls must lie at the back of a narrow chasm or the like.

Genevieve. The mere thought of her brought a rush of melancholy. And longing.

Quickly Marcel concentrated on where he was going. No good could come of thinking about Genevieve.

He had pressing matters to occupy him. He hoped against all reason that they would be able to gain Cameron's freedom without bloodshed. Though he was angry and frustrated with the whole situation, Marcel was also infinitely conscious of the fact that his aunt continued to plead for restraint. He would not betray her by destroying all possibility of seeing this feud to a peaceful conclusion.

It seemed a very short time later when Connor raised a hand for them to halt, again drawing near to Marcel. "'Tis just ahead through those trees."

Marcel nodded, whispering back, "Conner, we must waste no time once the dwelling is breached. You know our intent. If Cameron is not within we must try to learn of his location. If you think it can be gained, go there immediately. Once we have taken this step, we can no longer be completely assured of the boy's safety.''

Connor nodded his dark blond head, his strong face grim. Glancing at the other four men, Marcel could see that their expressions were equally grave. They cared for the child and for their mistress.

Marcel spoke again, with the same care for quiet. ''We will leave the horses here.''

The men obeyed him by dismounting and tying their animals to the lower branches of the yew trees. He did the same.

All the while he was ever watchful for any sign of unwanted company. The forest continued to lie still and silent around them.

In single file they moved from the shelter of the trees, Marcel in the lead. With the stealth born of sheer necessity he approached the building, which was highlighted by the moonlight. It was a long, single-story, windowless structure—as Genevieve had described it.

The wide oak door appeared to be unmanned. Marcel became more incredulous at this seeming lack of security by the moment. He did not drop his own guard, for to do so would be to court disaster.

He signaled for the men to approach the door. Maintaining an almost preternatural silence, they took up positions on either side of the portal. Marcel joined them, cautious, listening, trying to anticipate any threat before it arrived.

There was no sound, not one clue as to what they would find within. Anxiety stretched his nerves as taut as the string of a drawn bow.

Taking a deep breath, Marcel moved to the door and with as much care as possible, he lifted the latch. Obviously bolted from within, it would not budge. Again he motioned with his hand and four of the men went into the woods, coming back a moment later with a short but heavy looking log. Marcel stood back and dropped his hand.

They surged forward, the sound of the log pounding against the portal ripping a hole in the silent darkness. With a resounding crash the door fell inward, torn from its hinges.

Instantaneous chaos erupted inside as dogs began barking, women screamed and men cried out in surprise.

Not wanting to give them time to gather their forces, Marcel took his sword from its sheath and yelled, "Follow me."

He then ran forward across the fallen door, hearing the men right behind him. He could only pray that he was not leading them to their deaths.

The sight that met his eyes was one that made Marcel stop still and assess the situation. As he watched, someone was lighting the torches that hung in the wall near the empty hearth. In their wavering light he saw several women and men standing down at the far end of the room. Dogs that had been chained beside the hearth leaped and thrashed about, barking with great furor. All of them were clearly suffering from complete surprise.

His gaze narrowed as one of the men suddenly raced across the floor and took up a sword from the bedroll where he must have been sleeping prior to their arrival. Another man hurried to do the same.

Marcel strode toward them quickly. "I would think twice were I you, my friends. You are outnumbered." And it was true. The two men and three women would be no match for the six of them, especially as Marcel and his party had surprise as their ally.

With a disconsolate glance toward each other, the two men dropped their swords to the floor with a clatter. Marcel motioned to Connor, who moved to collect the weapons as the men went to stand beside the huddled women.

As he watched this, Marcel was hard-pressed to credit what was taking place as true. Who would have imagined that no more than two armed men had been left here to guard Cameron? Obviously McGuire had not expected a rescue attempt. He had been far too sure of his own supremacy in this situation.

And all to Marcel's benefit.

Or perhaps not, Marcel suddenly thought. He had not seen Cameron. He was not, in fact, even certain that his cousin had ever been here, though passing the waterfall had given him fair hope that it was so.

Yet Marcel knew he would best be served in this by acting as though he knew what he was about. Thus thinking, he growled, "Where is Cameron?"

There was an uncomfortable ripple amongst the group.

Marcel was not sure whether to take this as a sign of good or ill. He spoke again, still acting as though he knew what he was doing. "I want the boy and I want him now. Lest you hold your lives in little value you will release him into my care."

The man who had first taken up his sword said, "Why do ye think he is here?"

Marcel moved closer, again aware that his aunt's men were right behind him. It was a good feeling, knowing they were with him in this, their allegiance unwavering.

Marcel smiled, hiding his uncertainty as to whether his cousin was indeed being held here. "Suffice it to say that I know he is here and you will produce him." His heart was hammering with the hope that he had not made a dreadful mistake that could very well put the lad in serious jeopardy.

The man who had spoken before said, "Ye are mist—"

He was interrupted by a scuffling noise from behind him. With a nervous glance toward Marcel he went on quickly saying "mistaken" in a louder voice. But it was too late. Marcel had heard that noise, which was followed by another that could only be taken for a gasp of pain.

Striding down the length of the chamber, Marcel pushed the small group near the hearth aside. Now he could see why they had all been standing there huddled together as they were. They were attempting to hide the heavy wool curtain that hung behind them. It was from behind this curtain that the noises had come.

Marcel grasped the drapery, ripping it from the wall. Behind it lay a small alcove that held a bed. A man stood against the wall beside the bed. In his arms he held a hand over the bottom half of the face of a squirming auburn-haired lad that indicated to Marcel that this could only be Cameron. Behind them in the bed was a boy with a thatch of red hair and wide green eyes.

Rage filled Marcel, spreading through him in a hot

tide as he saw the way the little lad fought against the burly man's strength. His eyes narrowed and he raised his sword. "Release him and I may spare your life." He was surprised at the depth of cold fury that was revealed by his tone.

So angry was he that Marcel was almost disappointed when the man let go of Cameron without hesitation. Marcel felt a need to release the fury in his belly. He resisted the impulse, sending a reassuring glance to his cousin, who stood staring up at him, his gaze uncertain.

Still keeping most of his attention on the other man, who now backed toward the others, Marcel spoke in a voice that was deliberately gentle. "Are you well, Cameron?"

The boy nodded. "I am. Have you come to take me home to Glen Rowan?"

Marcel would answer, but wanted to make sure they were secure first. He called out to his aunt's men, "Bind them all."

Seeing the men hurry to do his bidding, Marcel smiled down at Cameron. "I have come to take you home."

The blue eyes rounded with pleasure and relief. "Who are you then?"

"I am your cousin Marcel."

"Ah, I thought you might be." A gamin smile curved his mouth. "The lady who came before spoke of you. She did not say that you would be coming for me."

In spite of the fact that they must still get out of here and away before he would begin to feel at ease, Marcel could not withhold an answering smile. "She did not know that I was going to do so at the time. For I did not know myself.''

Cameron nodded with charming wisdom. ''I see. 'Tis always best to think on your feet.'' He grinned at Marcel again. ''Or so my father told me.'' He looked around the place where he had been held prisoner over the past weeks. ''I was trying to do just that when I came here to settle the troubles between Duggan and McGuire. It did not work. I suppose it is a good enough creed if one has the swords to back up one's good ideas.''

Marcel nodded. He could not deny that the lad had a winning nature, as Genevieve had said.

Connor called out. ''All's done, my lord.''

Cameron looked over to the boy who still sat silent and frightened in the bed. ''What of Ewan?''

Marcel looked at him then, having forgotten the lad's existence. The obviously frightened boy's eyes widened even more. Marcel said, ''You are McGuire's grandson.''

The child nodded.

Would it not lesson McGuire if he were to repay the man in kind with the taking of someone he loved? Aye, he would have a great point of bargaining in taking the lad.

Marcel sighed, knowing he could not do such a thing. The troubles that he must solve were between men and would remain between men, if he had any say in it.

Marcel bent over and spoke very softly to the boy in the bed so the others would not hear. ''You are Cameron's friend, are you not?''

The boy nodded.

Marcel reached out to ruffle his cousin's auburn hair, pulling him close. "Cameron and I, we would ask boon of you."

The boy nodded.

Marcel raised his brows as he continued, "Think you that if we do not bind you, you might delay long enough for us to be well gone from this place before untying the others?"

The red-haired lad looked at him with uncertainty. "You are not going to take me?"

Marcel shook his head. "Nay, I have no wish to make you a part of things you do not understand and have no say in."

The boy turned to Cameron and said very softly, "I am not strong and it might take a great time to undo the knots."

Cameron smiled. "Soon we will go fishing at Glen Rowan."

His friend smiled in return. "Aye."

"My lord." Connor called.

Marcel knew he was waiting for the order to leave. It would serve none of them to forget that they were in the camp of their enemy in spite of the fact that they had faced no real opposition as yet.

Marcel gave the order to leave and saw the men move toward the door. He turned to Cameron and said, "Come then, cousin. Let us away."

"Fare you well, Cameron," the boy in the bed called out softly.

Cameron nodded.

Then as if with one mind he and Marcel swung around, and raced through the hall behind the others and out the door.

* * *

Genevieve was startled by the sounds of excitedly raised voices in the courtyard beneath her open window. She had not slept since watching Marcel and five of his aunt's men depart from this very window what seemed an eternity ago. Rising hurriedly, she went and leaned out to see what was amiss.

In the light of many torches, she saw Marcel and, mounted before him on his horse, a much smaller figure. Her heart soared, for who could it be but Cameron?

Hurriedly she shrugged into the robe Aunt Finella had provided for her use. She then raced through the darkened keep, seeing the many people who were beginning to stir as she went. Obviously word of their return was already spreading, for there was no mistaking the excited tone of the people's voices as she passed through the hall.

Somehow, unbelievably, for Genevieve had fair flown from her chamber, Aunt Finella had arrived in the courtyard before her. Genevieve watched Cameron jump down from his place before Marcel and run into his grandmother's waiting arms.

Feeling her heart swell with emotion as the two grasped each other tightly, Genevieve looked up into Marcel's blue eyes. Their gazes locked and held, his damp with the same intensity of feeling that had swept through her. It was the first time he had actually looked at her without looking through her since...

When Marcel smiled at her, her heart thumped in response. She told herself that this change in his attitude was brought on by his joy in having succeeded in the rescue of his cousin. Yet in spite of knowing this, she was overcome by her own response to the simple gesture. Genevieve glanced away, unable to hold that gaze for another moment for fear of giving away the fact that her own reaction was not solely due to her happiness at seeing Cameron home where he belonged.

When she raised her gaze once more she expected him to have turned away. But he had not. He had dismounted from his highland pony but was still watching her with an expression that she did not even dare try to name.

Her breath caught and her heart throbbed in her chest.

At that moment, Aunt Finella moved to block her view of Marcel, her eyes bright with unashamed tears. As he turned to his aunt, the moment was broken. The older woman said, "Thank you, thank you, Marcel. You will never know how grateful I am that I had my nephews to call upon."

She hugged the boy again tightly and then reached to put an arm around Marcel.

It was a touching family scene, one that did not really include her. Genevieve took a step backward, feeling suddenly shy.

Marcel seemed to sense her unease for he motioned to her and said, "Genevieve, come and make your greeting to Cameron. You have certainly aided in bringing him home. It was because of your recall of the waterfall that we were able to fetch him."

Still she hesitated, feeling shy as she glanced about and realized how many of the castle folk had now gathered. The faces around her were sheathed in happy smiles and those smiles did seem to include her.

When Aunt Finella turned and held out her arms, Genevieve went into them. She hugged the older woman, then stepped back and turned to Cameron. "It is so good to see you here."

He nodded. "Aye. I am most happy to be back. And I have you to thank as well as my cousin."

Genevieve bowed her head, acknowledging his thanks. When she looked at him again, she suddenly became aware of the weariness on his young face. It seemed that his grandmother had also taken note of this for she said, "Come in then, my lad. It's a bit of rest that you'll be needing before anything else."

In spite of his obvious fatigue, he looked to Marcel and said, "But..."

His grandmother interrupted in a tone that while kind brooked no further discussion. "You will to bed, and now."

Genevieve hurried before them as they went into the keep. "I will remove my things from your chamber."

Cameron looked up at her. "What?"

She said, "I have been sleeping in your chamber. I am most happy to return it to you."

His grandmother spoke hurriedly. "Nay, you will not. I know I said as much when you first arrived. I would never allow my grandson to behave with such a lack of chivalry. We shall find him a place to sleep."

"But..." Genevieve began.

She was interrupted by Aunt Finella, in much the same way the boy had been when he attempted to argue with his grandmother. "There shall be no talk on the subject. We will trouble you only long enough to remove some of Cameron's garments. Then the room shall be yours, and most happily so until such time as you are ready to leave Glen Rowan.''

Until such time as they were ready to leave Glen Rowan. The unexpected words struck her like darts.

The older woman moved away, her back held stiffly with determination to have her way done. Genevieve took a deep breath. With Cameron home, it was unlikely that she and Marcel would remain much longer.

That meant it would not be long before she was back at Brackenmoore. Her devastated gaze went to Marcel's face. Thankfully he did not appear to be aware of her disquiet, for he was occupied in telling the men to post extra guards on the chance that McGuire might retaliate.

She did not think the man would do such a thing. With his hostage gone, Genevieve suspected he would be much more malleable. Marcel would be glad. He would wish to have the matter of the dispute between McGuire and Duggan settled quickly so that he might be on his way.

In spite of her wishes to the contrary, her gaze was full of yearning as it moved over his masculinely beautiful features. Though she knew that he did not want her, that he did indeed love another, he would always hold a special place inside her.

He was the man who had shown her what it was to be a woman. And he had done so with such a shattering thoroughness that no other man would ever be able to take his place.

Chapter Twelve

Genevieve slept very little that night, rising early with an urge to quit the confines of the keep for the open air of the moor. She met Aunt Finella in the hall.

That fair lady ran an assessing gaze over the warm cloak she had donned, then her face. Genevieve was hard-pressed to meet that searching look for she feared the signs of her sleepless night would be visible in her face.

It seemed they were, for Aunt Finella said, "Why do the two of you play this unhappy game?"

"Pray what do you mean, my lady?" As she said the words she knew far too well what they implied.

Aunt Finella shook her head. "Do not pretend you know naught of what I speak. Clearly there is love between you and Marcel and yet you wish to deny it."

The older woman's directness forced Genevieve to speak more frankly than she wished. "You do not understand. Marcel does not love me, has no regard for what I would bring to the man who loved me. He loves another."

Folding her arms across her bosom, Aunt Finella shook her head. "I do not believe it."

"He has told me so with his own lips."

Aunt Finella sighed with exasperation. "You are fools, the both of you. Love is all that matters. The love we give and the love we receive. The rest of it doesn't amount to a handful of sand. I'd give it all away, each and every stone of this keep, my name, all in my possession for one more hour with my Cameron. None of those things have ever given me a glimpse of what it felt like to be held in his arms, to know that I was loved and that I loved in return." With that she turned and stalked off across the chamber, her head held high.

Genevieve was left staring after her, her insides a whirl of confusion. The well-meaning woman had completely misunderstood the whole matter.

Marcel did not love her. And she certainly did not love him.

What they felt was powerful, compelling, even ungovernable at times, undeniably so. Yet it was not love.

Nay, never that!

Marcel tried to concentrate on the food on his plate, but he found he had no appetite for the roast, fowl and game. Casting a surreptitious glance about the high table he saw that neither his aunt nor Genevieve seemed to have any more interest in the meal. Only Cameron was eating with any enthusiasm, professing that he was quite hungry after spending the whole day explaining to all what had occurred while he was gone.

Marcel only wished he could be as relieved as his young cousin seemed to be. Even though Cameron was home at Glen Rowan, Marcel's duty here was not done. McGuire would be angry—enraged.

For his own part he cared naught for the man's good grace or lack of such, would gladly call him out in man-to-man combat. Yet he was aware of his aunt's precarious position in this. She would be the one to bear the brunt of the family's rage. For much as he had to admit that he had gained great satisfaction from helping his aunt, he could not remain indefinitely.

He had to get Genevieve back to Brackenmoore. For the good of both of them.

The night they had shared together seemed only to have whetted his appetite for her. It was a craving he could not indulge. Not if he was to retain any self-respect.

She believed him the worst kind of knave. He had taken her innocence and all the while allowed her to believe that he loved another. That Genevieve had given up her innocence with such eager and wild abandon did not make him easy on the matter. It only served to make Marcel the more ashamed of his deceit.

Marcel was distracted from these troubling thoughts by the sound of a voice at his elbow. "My lord, McGuire is come to speak with ye."

As Marcel swung around to face the soldier who had obviously run from his post, if his labored breathing was any indication, he felt Genevieve's steady gaze upon him.

He was glad to be able to face his young cousin, who said, "Has he then?" The boy sat up in his seat, his face set, his head high. Marcel was not oblivious to the signs of fearfulness in the lines around his mouth and the tightness with which he clenched his small hands into fists.

Marcel looked at his aunt. Her expression was clearly troubled. He did not look at Genevieve but felt her anxiety as well. He nodded to the servant. "You may bring him in." As the man left, Marcel turned to Cameron. "You will go to your room, please."

Cameron frowned. "I am not afraid of him."

Marcel smiled gently. "I thought no such thing. I simply prefer to let the blackguard know that he will deal only with me now."

Aunt Finella said, "Do as your cousin asks, Cameron."

Marcel was grateful for her support, for the lad's frown did not disappear, but he did get up and stalk from the hall. And none too hurriedly, for he clearly wished them to know that he was not afraid to face his kidnapper.

Marcel felt somewhat guilty for sending him away. He well recalled what it was like to feel that your fate had been placed in the hands of others. Yet he wanted McGuire to be clear in the fact that it was he, Marcel, who would decide this matter. He was not a young boy who could be held at the mercy of a grown man.

"He will be fine," Genevieve said quietly.

With surprise Marcel faced her and saw the understanding in those green eyes. Somehow, at times such as this, she managed to find it inside her to be decent, to set aside the anger she felt toward him, in spite of his ill treatment of her.

He was glad to be distracted from his own unexplainable sadness at this by the arrival of McGuire himself.

As he watched the older man enter the hall, Marcel felt a pensive frown crease his brow. Contrary to the expression of fury he had expected McGuire to be wearing, he seemed almost…chagrinned.

Aunt Finella addressed him politely, adhering to the Scot custom of hospitality. "Will you sup with us, McGuire?"

"Nay, Lady Finella, I willna. That is no' why I have come." The big Scot turned to Marcel, losing no time in getting to the point. "Ye took the lad."

Marcel shrugged. "I did, indeed. Did you imagine that I would simply loll about here waiting for you and Duggan to come to terms while my cousin was kept from his home and family? Methinks not."

Again there was a hint of chagrin in the older man's gaze as it flitted away from Marcel's. Suddenly those eyes widened and Marcel looked around to see what had caused this strange reaction. It was Genevieve who seemed to hold McGuire's rapt attention.

He pointed to her. "Ye are the lad."

She raised her chin high, flushing. "I am no lad as you can see. And 'twas not I who said I was a boy. You simply assumed as much and we did not disabuse you of the notion."

"Ye were dressed as a lad. Ye tricked me well enough."

Genevieve flushed again. "My garb had naught to do with you whatsoever. If you will recall 'twas you yourself who insisted that I accompany you. Marcel did his utmost to dissuade you." Marcel was proud of not only her candor but the accuracy of her assessment. "You but seek a distraction from your own crimes by speaking of it."

McGuire scowled blackly but Marcel could see that he had no answer for this. It seemed that even the ill-humored Scotsman could not argue with the truth.

He swung around to glare at Marcel and then, to his utter amazement, said, "Ye did not take my grandson."

Marcel blinked at this abrupt change of topic. "Nay, I did not. I do not harry children with the troubles of men."

McGuire blanched but spoke with arrogance. "I suppose ye expect my gratitude for that."

Marcel shook his head. "I expect nothing. I simply could not bring myself to put your lad through the ordeal that Cameron had been subjected to. For in spite of the fact that he is full of bravado and refuses to admit his anxiety over being held against his will, he is still just a small boy. Thus he is susceptible to the fears of a small boy." Marcel's gaze was unrelenting. "What you did was inexcusable."

McGuire blanched again and his demeanor changed before their very eyes as his shoulders slumped. "God forgive me for the taking of that boy. May he also forgive me for not coming right out and thanking ye for not putting our Ewan through the same ordeal. For beggin' yer pardon was what I came here to do. God, when I found out ye had been there...that ye could have...I felt sick with the dread of it."

Marcel sighed. "Now you know how my aunt has worried these past weeks."

McGuire looked at Aunt Finella. "I dinna ken how grave a thing I had done. The lad seemed so defiant and played about with our Ewan as if he had not a care.''

''That is what children do,'' Marcel told him. He could well recall how he had played and laughed and behaved as normally as he knew how to after his parents died, though he had felt empty and afraid inside.

But he did not want to think about that now. It was far in the past.

What he needed to concentrate on was the startling transformation in McGuire's attitude. He would never have believed that this great a change could come about.

Whether this contrite mood could be parlayed into some kind of truce between McGuire and Duggan remained to be seen.

Marcel watched the older man, trying to gauge just what might come now. He was not entirely happy when the next words from his adversary's lips were not encouraging ones. ''What has happened has not changed my thinking about Duggan. Not only has he laid claim to land that is mine, as ye well know his temptress of a daughter has lured my own son off to wed wi' her.''

Marcel spoke to McGuire in a tone that brooked no argument. ''It is my aunt's intent to take all opinions under consideration and make her own decision concerning the lands under dispute. After doing so, she will render her judgment and will expect that judgment to be adhered to.''

''But…'' sputtered the other man.

Marcel halted him. ''Enough. You have done grave ill to mine. I would have you know that it is only by my aunt's good grace that you have done so without serious consequence to yourself. For I am most certain that kidnapping is considered a crime in Scotland. You will not be allowed to transgress further. Nor, as she is the guardian of the new laird, will you be allowed to make any further demands upon my aunt's dignity and authority. Your concerns over your son's marriage to Duggan's daughter will also be settled in a peaceful manner. Make no more trouble with your neighbor and leave the disbursement of the lands to your lady.''

McGuire turned to Aunt Finella with narrowed eyes. ''Why should I do that when ye have shown your anger with me? However justified it might be, 'twill color your decision.''

Aunt Finella spoke with quiet certainty. ''You have my word that I will not allow my personal feelings about my grandson's kidnapping to sway me in this. It is my intention to be a fair overseer to my grandson's lands until such time as he is able to hold them. I will, despite what you have done, decide on only the merits of the facts. As I may or may not be able to uncover them.''

McGuire looked anything but pleased at this. Yet Marcel thought he also recognized a hint of respect in those eyes. The older man stood, nodding, then left the hall.

Genevieve had felt as if she could barely breathe through most of this unbelievable interview. It was only after McGuire had been gone for several seconds that she was able to take what felt like a normal breath into her lungs.

What an unexpected turn of events. The dour man

had been almost contrite as far as Cameron was concerned.

Marcel had seemed cognizant of that fact, even understanding. Yet he had also been very commanding, more so than ever before. It had been quite clear that he would accept no more such acts as the one that had been perpetrated against Cameron. Though he had said that the decisions would be Aunt Finella's, it was made very obvious that Marcel would be happy to see those decisions enforced.

Not for the first time she found herself thinking that Marcel was a natural leader. The responsibilities seemed to sit quite easily on his wide shoulders.

If only she knew that such a man would be at her own side. How good it would be to know that she would be listened to, respected for her own mind, as Marcel did his aunt, but also aware that his strength was beside her.

Unbidden came Aunt Finella's assertion that there was love between them.

Unconsciously Genevieve turned to face Marcel, realizing as she did so that he was watching her. She flushed, looking away, glad that he could not read the madness of that thought in her eyes. That their attraction was strong, she could not deny. Yet again she reminded herself that it was not love.

She was surprised when Marcel spoke to her. "You have no need to continue to feel guilty about the wayward newlyweds. McGuire and Duggan need make peace on that subject. Their anger serves no one. And judging from his relief at my not taking his grandson, I would say he has a great love for his family. I suspect that Duggan is very likely the same."

She nodded. She had been slightly shocked to hear him mention the couple, but she no longer felt culpable on that matter. Marcel had helped her to see the truth of that on the night that...

She felt the color rise in her face. That night was something she did not wish to think on at all. Nodding curtly, Genevieve said, "I no longer feel responsible, Marcel, though I thank you for your concern." She was surprised at the coldness of her tone, though she knew that it was caused by the tight control she had on herself and her emotions.

His silence made her look up at him and she saw the consternation on his handsome face with some degree of regret. He said shortly, "Forgive my presumption."

Sadness swept though her, but it could not be helped. She would not explain herself. Were she to do that, Marcel would know how very badly she wished that things were not as they were.

With a quick nod she said, "You will excuse me now. I find that I am weary."

Aunt Finella said, "Oh, please do retire, my dear. There has been far too much excitement of late." Looking at her, Genevieve could see that she was clearly distracted by what had just gone on with McGuire.

Genevieve touched her shoulder briefly before she turned to leave the hall.

She had just stepped onto the bottom step of the stair leading to the upper chambers when Marcel's voice halted her. "Genevieve." As she turned and their gazes collided, she saw, dear saints above, a completely unexpected and naked longing in those blue eyes. The sheer shock of it halted her in mid-motion, made her own blood run like heated wine in her veins. Her voice seemed too husky as she queried, "Yes?"

He hesitated, his expression troubled. "I...I am sorry for what happened between us in my...I would not have you hate me. Perhaps if things were different...perhaps if Constanza did not need me so desperately." His face closed up and her heart plummeted. "But you understand that she does need me. I am all that she has."

Breathing quickly, she tore her gaze away. "Of course, Marcel. You need not concern yourself. I am fine. You have made yourself clear on more than one occasion."

His brow creased with consternation, but he said nothing more as she turned and left him. Though she felt Marcel's attention upon her back, she did not look to him again.

Surely, she told herself, still feeling the heat and weight of that gaze long after she was gone, 'twas only for the best.

Yet hours later Genevieve was still pacing the confines of the chamber. Had she ever actually thought this room large? It seemed a cage this night, the walls coming closer and closer with each long hour that passed.

She wanted to scream in frustration, angry with herself and the Fates. Even as she cried aloud, asking herself what was wrong with her, she knew.

Marcel.

She could think of little else either night or day. And he, God help her, though she could not explain it, he seemed to want her, too. He wanted her in spite of his love for Constanza and all the unpleasantness that had passed between them.

That made her own desire all the more difficult to deny. Suddenly Genevieve was not sure why she should deny herself what they both wanted. Surely she could understand Marcel's feelings, because of the lack of reason in her own. He was in love with another woman yet found himself attracted to her, had admitted just hours ago that if he were not responsible for the other woman that...well, Genevieve knew something that he did not. Constanza was not completely dependent upon him. Marcel's denial of his desire was unnecessary.

Against all reason she wanted Marcel with every fiber of her being. Knew with a shattering certainty that she would never again want any man as she did him. Not if she dwelt five hundred years upon this earth.

She recalled what Aunt Finella had said about love being all. Well, that might prove true for them if they were in love. Yet perhaps love was not the only emotion that created its own truth. Did not this overwhelming passion deserve some concession?

In this moment Genevieve was not inclined to put their desire second to his love for Constanza. Genevieve was still resolved that she would never tell him the truth, but she felt no great compunction to bestow great honor upon such a love, either.

Was not she, Genevieve, deserving of some pleasure, some measure of happiness? For she knew that there would be little enough of either once Marcel sailed out of her life.

Before she could stop herself, she rose and took up her candle.

In some ways, what she was about to do reminded her of the first night she had gone to Marcel's chamber. This night her purpose was very different. Tonight she intended to make love with Marcel. It would not be out of an overwhelming need of the moment. Tonight she would make love with Marcel because, she, Genevieve chose to do so. This night would be hers to remember for all the days of her life.

As she reached his chamber door, she hesitated for a brief moment. Something, some inner sense of confidence rose inside her, stopped her from knocking. Taking a deep breath, she turned the latch.

The portal swung inward on silent hinges.

Her gaze went immediately to Marcel where he sat in the chair beside the low-burning hearth. He looked up, seeing her even as he rose. "Genevieve."

She faced him directly, her gaze unwavering on his. "Marcel." Their eyes held and that now familiar awareness passed between them, making her stomach tighten.

He ran obviously unsteady hands over his thighs, drawing her gaze to their muscular length. "Why have you come?" he asked, making her look into his face again.

She did not hesitate. "Methinks you already know the answer to that question."

He sucked in a quick breath of surprise at her directness. At the same time she noted that his blue eyes darkened, his lids becoming hooded as his gaze slid over her.

Marcel did indeed know the answer to that question.

Had he not, the stirring in his own blood as he looked at her, clad only in that diaphanous white gown, her golden hair falling about her in a wild tangle would have told him.

Genevieve moved forward and carefully placed her candle on the table near him. He saw that her hand was steady, as was her gaze. He was very aware that her calm was at direct odds with his own demeanor. He could not deny the trembling in his body as she then came to stand in front of him.

Marcel swallowed hard as his gaze moved over her lovely face, saw the heightened color along her high cheekbones, the flutter of her pulse at her throat as she raised her head to look up at him. Those two subtle signs told him that she was not as unmoved as it might appear.

She interrupted his thought, whispering, "Would you have me stay?"

There was no mistaking the meaning of that breathless query.

She was so beautiful. The perfect contours of her form were not truly concealed by the gown, only tantalizingly veiled in hints of light and shadow. His body tightened and his breathing quickened as he recalled how lovely she was, how soft the flesh that covered the curves and planes of her body.

Again Marcel swallowed, knowing that he wanted what she offered more than he had ever wanted anything in his life. He held out his arms, for there was naught else he could do.

Genevieve went into his arms, only realizing as he held them out to her how very afraid she had been that he might turn her away. Her relief that he did not do so left her limp and weak in his embrace.

But only for the space of a heartbeat.

Genevieve had no intention of wasting even a moment of this time. For she knew that it was stolen from another woman no matter how undeserving. Closing her eyes, she lifted her face to his.

Marcel's mouth found hers, his lips supple and warm, igniting a flame that raced through her and made her breath quicken. She raised her arms to hold his head down to her, standing up on tiptoe as she fitted her body to the hard length of his.

When his hands moved down her back to settle on her hips, she moaned, her body arching into his. She felt the hardness of him against her belly with a thrill.

Unlike the first time, Genevieve knew exactly where they were headed in this dance of desire. She stepped backward, urging him with her body to move toward the bed.

Marcel stopped her, his breath hot on her ear as he turned and whispered, ''Nay, my eager beauty, not so fast. First we will play.''

She closed her eyes on the wave of heat that was engendered by those words. Then she opened them again as she felt herself being turned in his arms.

''What...?'' she cried, subsiding as she felt the press of his firm body against her back.

He made no verbal reply, only easing away slightly, then slowly drawing her gown up the length of her body. Sighing, she raised her arms, her breathing labored when he passed the garment over her head, then tossed it to the floor. Her breath caught and she ran her tongue over her suddenly parched lips as he drew her back against him, his palms on the flat plane of her belly.

"I want to touch you," he told her, his mouth close beside her ear, the heat of his breath warming her as it had before. When he slowly began to trace his hands up her sides, she sucked in a breath of pleasure and anticipation. His hands at last closed over her breasts and she moaned aloud, sagging back against the wall of his chest as his thumbs found her already erect nipples.

Gently he plied her breasts with his two large, warm hands, circling, squeezing gently, knowing just the right pressure to apply to those yearning tips. Thick, sweet honey spread from the two sensitive points, seeping through her body to form a delicious pool of delight in her lower belly. When his hand moved lower, tracing over her ribs, the flat plane of her stomach, then paused in the nest of golden curls, she held her breath. As his fingers slipped into the moist warmth of her she gasped aloud, her knees buckling, only managing to stay upright because she could not bear for the pleasure to stop. Her head fell backward on his chest, allowing him better access to her throat as his warm lips sought that tender flesh. Without conscious thought, she rubbed her bottom against his manhood, heard him gasp, and her lips curved with a smile of sheer sensuality.

Marcel was aching, dying for her, and before he had even begun to awaken her as he wished to. The unadulterated joy with which she took her pleasure near drove him mad with need and an undeniable wonder.

Never in his years had he met such a woman, a

woman who was neither ashamed nor demure about taking such joy in the sensations of her body. He reveled in her reactions, felt his own pleasure was heightened by them tenfold.

Genevieve's body ached, throbbed, with the pleasure of his touch. But she was not ready to give in to the pounding of her blood. She turned in his arms, feeling a need to touch him, to bring him to the same level of desire that raced through her own veins.

As she raised her hands to slide them over his belly, it was his turn to suck in a gasping breath. She looked up at him, saw the fire that lit the depths of his blue eyes and leaned forward to place her lips where her hands had touched him.

His fingers tangled in the heavy fall of her hair as she kissed his chest, her lips soft, sensuous and shockingly confident on his flesh. When they closed over one of his hard nipples, he groaned and gently but firmly pulled her away, then bent to kiss those beautiful lips.

He kissed her until his own head was spinning, his body aching with need.

Marcel knew he could wait no more. He picked her up and moved toward the bed, his eyes on hers, seeing the gladness—the eagerness in those lovely green eyes.

Genevieve continued to hold his gaze as he lay her back against the pillows. She wanted, needed, to know that Marcel was thinking of her and her alone as they made love to each other for the very last time.

When he ran a hand down her bare side, she shivered, her lids drooping. His voice was husky with passion as he said, "You are so lovely. You take my breath from me, Genevieve, and leave me with nothing but insignificant words to describe what is indescribable.''

"Oh Marcel, there is no need to talk. I understand, for I feel the same way." She took his hand and raised it to her left breast. "Can you not feel the way my heart beats from the very sight of you?"

He groaned and dipped his head to suckle at the very same breast. Now it was she who cried out with wanting, "Please Marcel, no more. You must make me yours."

He went into her arms, his body sliding along the length of her slender one. Her flesh was like silk against his, their two contours seeming to meld into one perfect form as he slipped between her silken thighs.

When she shifted her hips to accept him into her body, he felt himself slide into her. Her body was so wet, yet seemed to grasp the length of him, holding him with gentle pressure. The sensation was indescribably pleasurable, making him sob with the sheer intensity of it as it rippled through his body.

Genevieve was afire, her body awhirl with the sensations aroused by Marcel's touch. Yet she wanted to watch him, to see him reacting to her, to hear the hoarse sound of his voice and know that he was driven so far beyond himself because he was with her.

No matter what might come in the years ahead, she wished to have this time with him to relive, to ease the loneliness of her days. Thus it was Marcel she concentrated on, his expressions, the shallowness of his breathing as she moved beneath him, deliberately drawing him as deeply into herself as she could before withdrawing again.

And then he stiffened above her, his face beautiful as the power of his passion took him, and she was no longer able to control her own response. She closed her eyes, driven by the shudders that took her as she too dissolved in the glorious culmination of their love-making.

Yet even before the delight had completely eased, she reached out to hold him to her. He pushed back, rolling to the side, putting out his own hand to brush the hair away from her face in a gesture so tender it made her heart ache. She looked into those blue eyes. They were lit with a gentleness as warm as his touch and even more moving. Such dearly beloved eyes. How was she ever to survive without him, to accept the reality of never looking into that gentle gaze again?

Her heart stopped then for one infinite moment as the truth of her own thought was revealed inside her. Marcel was beloved, indeed, more beloved than she had ever imagined any being could be.

Yet he did not love her. What she saw in those eyes was no more than the remnants of the passion they had shared. Only moments ago that passion had been enough…yet now…now that she realized how much she loved him it was a source of unfathomable pain.

Knowing she could not allow him to see the truth, she called upon reserves of strength that she had not even known she possessed. Taking a deep breath, Genevieve pushed back and sat up.

Marcel protested softly, his confusion evident, "Genevieve?"

She did not look at him. "You need have no worry, Marcel. I do not expect anything from you beyond what just took place. I realize there is nothing more than this between us, that it is of no great account."

"I see." Had she not known better she would have thought there was disappointment in his tone. But she did know better, knew full well that Marcel loved Constanza.

He said harshly, "You believe that what we have done together would not matter to the man you will wed?"

She took a deep breath. "There is to be no marriage."

"You must not let what happened here prevent you from marrying Beecham. He is a good man...will make a fine husband."

Still without looking at him, she said, "I lied to you. I never was going to marry him."

She could hear the confusion in his voice. "But Benedict said..."

Genevieve shrugged. "I may have told you a falsehood. I am certain Benedict did not do so. You have only to think on what he did tell you, to know that."

"But why would *you* lie to me about such a thing?"

She cast him a brief glance, saw the confusion on his handsome face. "That is another question you could answer did you but wish to." Feeling she had said far too much, but too miserable to care what he might make of it, Genevieve left him.

Chapter Thirteen

Marcel was awoken by the sound of pounding at his chamber door. He raised up in bed and looked to the pillow beside him, instantly remembering all that had passed between himself and Genevieve during the night.

Ignoring the wave of misery that washed though him, he jumped up and shrugged into his robe. He yanked open the door with a scowl. "What is it?"

One of the servants stood there, his brown eyes wide with amazement, which Marcel understood when he began to speak. "The Lady Finella has sent me to fetch you, my lord. They have come. The both of them, Duggan and McGuire are below in the hall, my lord."

Marcel did not wait for further explanation, but said, "Tell her I will attend her anon."

He then closed the door and sought his clothing.

When he reached the hall only a short time later, he saw that it was indeed true. His aunt was seated at the head table, her less than worthy subjects on the opposite side and directly across from her. She looked to Marcel with a calm smile as he came toward them. "Ah, my nephew."

"You sent for me, Aunt?"

She nodded. "McGuire and Duggan have come here to speak with me. I ask that you attend my audience with them."

Marcel said, "Of a certainty." He watched the two men, saw their chagrin as they avoided eye contact. Intrigued with this turn of events, Marcel seated himself next to his aunt.

Aunt Finella turned to him, and though her expression was even, he could see a hint of excitement in her gray eyes. "These men tell me they have come to discuss a peaceful solution as to the disposition of the meadow that has brought such trouble of late."

Marcel nodded, though he too was hard-pressed to hide the glimmer of amazement that rippled through him. What, he wondered, had brought about this change of heart?

His unspoken question was answered by McGuire. "Lady Finella, it is right that your kin be here this morn. For it is due to his actions that we are come to speak with ye about the meadow."

Marcel felt his brows raising. His aunt spoke evenly. "What might he have done to bring about this change of heart?"

McGuire turned to Marcel, his scowl belying his words. "Firstly as I told ye afore, I am thankful that he dinna take my wee Ewan when he had the chance. Second he hasna taken revenge against me or mine for doing such a grave ill."

Marcel held his tongue, not bothering to say that he would gladly have done the latter in the form of calling McGuire out. He allowed his aunt to answer. It was she who would be here to deal with these men in the future as Cameron was growing to manhood.

She replied softly but firmly, "What you say is true. You did me a grave ill to keep the boy and I longed for his return every moment that he was gone. Yet I remembered you were one of our own folk and told my nephew that you should be dealt with in as peaceful a manner as possible." She looked into his eyes. "I remembered that your former laird, my own dear Cameron, had called you friend."

Marcel watched as McGuire had the grace to blush, dropping his eyes. "He did indeed, my lady. And I have no defense save that I was near driven mad by my anger at this one." He cast an unhappy glance toward Duggan, who scowled back at him.

Now Marcel felt that he must step in. "You will not begin all afresh, either of you within reach. For make no mistake, now that I have the two of you I would not be averse to locking you in a chamber together till such time as you either killed each other or made peace." When they turned to frown at him, he simply smiled. "Do not think that I am too soft to do so because I did not take young McGuire. Neither of you is innocent in this, as Ewan was. I would feel no regret whatever."

The men looked at each other and Duggan replied, "There will be no need of that. We have come to an agreement."

"Have you then?" Marcel could hear the disdain in his own voice and regretted it. He was angry with the two of them, it was true. Yet he had to admit, if only to himself, that a great portion of his agitation could be credited to his unhappiness over his relationship with Genevieve. He became more guilt ridden with each hour that he allowed her to believe he was in love with Constanza. Now he found himself with an overwhelming urge to tell her that he did not, had never loved, the Spanish woman.

Yet he could not do so. In some deep part of himself he was afraid, afraid that his desire to tell her the truth came from that newly reawakened desire to have all that a joining with her would offer him. This time with his aunt had reminded him anew of just how much he wished to fulfill the duties of an overlord. It was true that he gained great satisfaction from his command of the *Briarwind,* but the men were not bonded to him in the same way that those at Brackenmoore were bonded to Benedict, or that the people here at Glen Rowan were bonded to his aunt. Being here, being a part of setting things right here had brought him full circle, made him recall the deep longings of his boyhood.

Feeling a prickling along his nape, he looked up, seeing none other than Genevieve standing at the entrance to the hall. She was looking at McGuire and Duggan with no small amount of surprise on her lovely face.

Then, as if sensing his attention on her, she turned. Her gaze collided with his. Seeing the blush that stole up her neck and pale cheeks, he was reminded with startling clarity of seeing a similar flush spread over her as she reached the culmination of her passion. Only then he had been privy to the fact that the becoming color had covered far more of her than was now exposed to his view.

He knew a wave of longing so intense that it took every bit of his will to keep from groaning aloud. But that longing was mixed with horror, for there was nothing to be gained in giving in to such mad desire. The odd way she had left him last night, the absence of emotion in her eyes, had told him she was done with him.

He did not know why, not after the way she had just made love to him with a thoroughness that left him weak with passion.

"Marcel." He blinked. Hearing his name spoken made him realize that he must wrest control of himself. The matter at hand was of dire importance to his aunt and her folk.

Taking a deep breath, he turned to Aunt Finella. He attempted to be unmoved by the fact that he was aware with each and every fiber of his being that Genevieve was coming across the room, that she would soon reach the table where they were seated.

His aunt was looking at him with a puzzled frown. "What say you, Marcel?"

Having no notion of what had been said, he nodded. "I yield to you in this matter, my lady aunt."

She nodded in return and swung around to face McGuire and Duggan.

He was more grateful than he could say that the others did not appear to be aware of his inner struggle.

As his aunt spoke, he forced himself to concentrate on what she was saying, in spite of the fact that Genevieve now stood beside the table, her hip so near his elbow that he could brush her did he wish to. Silently he groaned.

With a great act of will he listened as Aunt Finella

told the two men, "I will hear what you and Duggan have concocted. We really must see this matter settled for all our good, and the fact that you are here together gives me cause to hope you have actually devised some workable solution. But I must add that, considering your recent behavior, in the future you will first come to me over any dispute."

The men fidgeted beneath her level gaze, then nodded each in turn.

Just as Marcel felt Genevieve step back a pace, his aunt's gaze swung to her. "Please, dear, stay, we have no secrets from you."

Stiffly Genevieve bowed as Marcel turned to watch her reaction to this statement. "I...I wouldst not, Aunt. I simply wished to know if you would like me to arrange for refreshments. I can see that you are too—"

Marcel spoke up quickly. "Aye, that is an excellent suggestion, Genevieve." He did not believe he could make sense of any of it with her seated next to him, and that was precisely where she would be forced to sit lest she crawl across him to reach his aunt's other side.

Genevieve nodded. "I will see to it."

He was relieved and bereft at her absence at one and the same time. Marcel gave himself a mental shake, unsure as to just what had come over him this morning.

He looked to McGuire. "You say you have come to an agreement. What might that agreement be?"

It was Duggan who replied. "We have decided to allow Robert and Fiona to make use of the meadow as a sort of a wedding settlement, if ye will." He glanced at Aunt Finella, bowing. "That is, we propose this, if it dost meet with your approval, my lady?"

Aunt Finella smiled. "Prithee it does. What a grand notion."

Marcel told himself he was glad, overjoyed to have this matter settled and the two adversaries so tamed. Yet he felt no elation. He could think of nothing save the fact that he now must return Genevieve to Brackenmoore.

The mere thought was agonizing.

As she traversed the passage that led to the kitchens, Genevieve paid little attention to where she was going. Her mind was awhirl as she had been quite aware of the tension in Marcel's body as she stood next to him and, heaven help her, she could not help feeling the tautness within herself at just being near him. Could feel the longing to...

She drew herself up. She would not think about that. Marcel had made his opinion of her quite clear last eve when he mentioned her coming marriage.

Why, she thought, would he believe anything else of her? If she was truly promised to Roderick Beecham, her behavior would be worse than reprehensible.

He did not know that it was he, Marcel, whom she was completely and hopelessly in love with.

It had been because of Marcel that she had been so shocked and devastated to see Duggan and McGuire sitting in the great hall. There could only be one reason that would bring them to the keep. They were ready to reconcile their differences.

She and Marcel would be leaving Glen Rowan.

A shattering numbness had gripped her and she had not even thought about whether or not she should approach those gathered at the table. It had only been when Aunt Finella had spoken to her that she realized she must display more care. She had no right to listen to their discussion, in spite of the kind woman's invitation.

Marcel did not wish her to be present. It was obvious in his too hurried agreement to her quickly considered offer to seek refreshment.

Again she felt a stab of grief so overwhelming it made her stomach clench in a painful knot. They had shared so much, joined together in a way that she knew would never happen with another man.

She looked up as she realized that she had come to a halt in the middle of the passage. Luckily no one was about. She went on, entering the kitchen and seeing the women as they bustled about, unheeding of her sorrow.

What, she wondered silently as she hesitated at the entrance to the long narrow chamber, would happen now?

Why, Marcel would take her home to Brackenmoore. When he took her back to Brackenmoore, he would walk out of her life for good.

The thought was so painful that she was forced to hold on to the end of the counter for support. The feel of that oft-scrubbed surface beneath her fingers reminded her of just why she had come. She moved to the far end of the room, where the women were working near the large stone fire. Eveline swung around at her approach.

Looking up into the curious gaze of the head

woman, Genevieve felt as though she were hearing her own voice from a great distance as she said, "Please see that refreshments are taken to them at the high table."

The woman nodded. "Aye, my lady."

Genevieve was not blind to the concern and respect on the woman's face and smiled with studied care as she said thank-you and turned away. The castle folk had been quite kind to her since that morning when she had ridden to see that Cameron was faring well. Yet this day she was unable to summon her usual pleasure in this fact.

A creeping numbness was beginning to descend upon her. And she was not sorry. Anything was preferable to the pain of loving Marcel.

She would not allow herself to think about her love for him.

She must try to focus on the future. For when she returned to Brackenmoore she intended to tell Benedict that she had made the decision to go home, to Harwick. It was past time to take up the duties of her position. One thing she was grateful to Marcel for was his having helped her to see that she had a duty to those who depended upon her. His sense of the rightness of such obligations was one of the things she loved most about him.

She could no longer convince herself that they needed her at Brackenmoore. The keep had a very capable mistress in the form of Benedict's own wife, Raine. It was wrong for her to avoid doing what she must simply because of her childhood. The past was the gone and she could not allow it to determine her future.

She knew that someday she would even be forced to marry. Her responsibility to her heritage demanded that she do so. That was another thought that she could not bear to face at this moment.

There would be more than enough time for that in the lonely years ahead. Years in which she would nevermore be near the only man she would ever love.

When Aunt Finella came to her chamber the next afternoon to tell her that a man and a woman had arrived from the *Briarwind,* Genevieve knew who they would be. When she went on to say that Marcel had requested her presence in the hall, Genevieve stiffened from the top of her head to the tips of her toes. It was difficult enough to think of facing Marcel without having to do so in front of the two people she knew had betrayed him.

The elderly lady seemed to sense the apprehension Genevieve felt. She gave her an unexpectedly fierce hug, though she said nothing more before leaving.

Genevieve garbed herself as finely as the garments Aunt Finella had given her would allow. She was not prepared to play the boy before Marcel's crew any longer. She was very conscious of the snug fit of the bodice of the sea-green gown, but there was no help for that. She must concentrate on holding her head high. She refused to bear any shame for having taken what she could of the only man she would ever love. The fact that his heart was given to another meant they would never truly be together as she wished they could be, but the moments they'd shared were hers and hers alone.

Genevieve entered the hall and saw Constanza and

Harlan sitting there. Yet it was not the mere fact of seeing them that made a great wave of dizziness take her. It was that they were sitting close together, their arms entwined. Like lovers.

And they were doing so right under the very nose of Marcel.

For a moment she forgot she was so angry with Marcel, that she loved him and he cared not in the least about that. He loved another. Loved this woman who would so brazenly stand before him with his own friend.

Yet the very thought of this made her anger and hurt return with a crushing force that made it difficult to breathe. No matter what occurred, no matter who loved him, or betrayed him, or otherwise, Marcel did not love her. He would never allow himself to love her or anyone like her.

He would never see that he could not run from what he was. He, like his brothers, was an Ainsworth. The very blood that made them responsible and caring men, offering aid to those who needed them, also ran through his veins. It made him wish to care for others, not some sense of greed that he must resist in order to retain his self-respect.

As she stood there, Marcel looked up and their eyes met. His bore an uncomfortable expression that she could not even begin to fathom. It was almost as if he were feeling…guilty about something. But that made no sense whatsoever. He did not have enough care for what she thought to feel guilty about anything. Furthermore, why should he feel guilty about the fact that the woman he loved hung upon the arm of another man?

Telling herself that she was mistaken and confused because of her own feelings, Genevieve moved forward.

When Constanza followed the path of Marcel's gaze, her eyes widened and she blanched. With perceptible chagrin she eased away from Harlan's side.

This only served to make Genevieve even more confused. She was not ashamed to show her perfidy before Marcel. Yet she was clearly shamed to have Genevieve see them together.

Her brow creasing with confusion, Genevieve paused. As she hesitated, Marcel rose and came toward her. He took her arm and she again noted that he seemed to be looking at her strangely. His voice, as he spoke, only seemed to further expose his uncertainty. "Please, come and talk with us, Genevieve. There is something that you must be told."

Feeling more unsettled by the moment, she tried to push down her discomfort. She raised her head high as he led her forward to where the others waited.

Harlan bowed as she came close. "Lady Genevieve."

She nodded in return, registering slight surprise that he knew her name. Harlan answered her unvoiced question. "Constanza has told me of your true identity."

Genevieve looked at Constanza. "Has she?"

Marcel spoke up at her side. "All is well, Genevieve. Constanza has done *nothing* that I would not have her do."

Genevieve could not help hearing his stress upon the word nothing. What was he attempting to tell her?

Marcel went on, clearly oblivious to her thoughts.

"Constanza and Harlan have come to share their most happy news with us. They are wed."

Genevieve could feel her eyes widening in utter shock but could not seem to control the depth of her reaction as she looked from one face to another in abject confusion. "They are wed?"

Constanza spoke softly, her cheeks flushing as she admitted, "I have just recently realized that I am with child. When I told Harlan, he insisted that we must marry while we were in port getting the mast repaired. He did not wish for the babe to be a..."

Genevieve shook her head with a disapproval and horror she made no effort to disguise. "That you would come here so openly and admit your betrayal of Marcel without one bit of regret does you no credit, madam."

Constanza paled and Harlan frowned, moving to place a protective arm around her. It was clear that he was working very hard to keep silent.

Marcel put his hands on Genevieve's shoulders and turned her to face him. "Please, Genevieve, there is no need to speak so. You defend me wrongly. Constanza owed me nothing. It is I who should bear the brunt of your anger."

She faced him with confusion. "I do not understand."

He frowned, his gaze dark with regret. "Constanza and I have never been aught but friends."

Her tone was bitter. "As we have been, Marcel?"

His blue gaze held hers as he spoke so low that only she could hear him. "Nay, not as we have been." His meaning was clear, but the words did nothing to ease her outrage.

Her gaze swept the three of them with disdain, coming to rest on Marcel's unhappy face. "So the whole time it was nothing but a falsehood. You and Constanza were never...together?"

He nodded with obvious discomfort. "That is correct."

She found her voice had grown louder when she went on. "You deliberately misled me."

Again he nodded, with even more clearly displayed chagrin. "Aye."

Genevieve had heard quite enough. She turned and left them without another word. But Marcel was not finished. He caught her on the stair, his hand clasping her arm, and he said, "You must hear me out this once."

She stared at him, her anger rolling up inside her like a tide. He had lied to her, tricked her into believing he and Constanza were together. There could be only one reason for that.

She found her voice was far calmer than she had expected as she said, "I will not ask why you lied. The reason is obvious. Are you so full of your own conceit, Marcel, that you felt you must lie to me about being involved with another woman in order to protect yourself from my unwanted attention?" The very memory of how she had given herself to Marcel the previous night made her heart ache at knowing this. The deep flush that stained his neck was answer enough. "Did you think yourself so irresistible that I would not take no for answer? What a pitiful fool you have taken me for."

Quickly he interjected, "That is not true. I did not think you pitiful or anything of the sort. I..." He raised his hands in appeal. "I know that it was wrong to lie to you. Yet I saw what you assumed of Constanza and myself and felt that it would be best for all of us if you continued to believe it."

She could not even begin to control the rise of emotion inside her as she looked at him. Anger, hurt and pity warred in her belly, each feeling as overwhelming as the others. She looked at him with incredulity. "And you thought that this would be best for me?"

Marcel shook his head. "I knew what you wanted, Genevieve, and it was not truly me. You have wanted to be a part of my family from the very beginning."

She faced him with amazement. "Do you truly think this of me after all we have been through?"

He raked a hand through his hair. "What else was I to think when you had proposed marriage to Tristan for the purpose of becoming a member of my family? Then you turned to me after finding out that Tristan was in love with Lily. You spoke of your renewed hope to be an Ainsworth."

She took a deep breath, attempting to quell the urge to thrash him. "I turned to you because of your kindness to me. It is true what you say of my relationship with Tristan. But was I not honest with him on that? Did I ever make a pretense of wanting to marry him for any other reason? Are you so blind that you think I do not know my own feelings?"

He frowned, saying nothing.

She shook her fist at him, only further maddened by his expression. "Had I wanted you to marry me for such a reason, I would have told you the truth of it, Marcel. I would not have pretended an attraction toward you. I can hardly credit that you believe I would be so sly.''

He said hesitantly, ''Not deliberately sly, never that, but sometimes when we want something badly enough we are able to convince ourselves of things that are not completely true.''

She was beyond caring what she revealed by her next words. ''You believe I could simply summon the degree of attraction I have felt for you in order to meet some unconscious need?''

He frowned again. ''You lied to me as well. You allowed me to think that you were to wed Beecham. What of that?''

Now it was her turn to blanch, but she made no effort to prevaricate. ''I told you that lie, yes, but I did so in order to hide my feelings for you from you. You lied to me, but it was not for the reasons you give. You lied in order to hide your feelings from yourself. You are afraid, Marcel, afraid that you will not be able to resist the secret desires of your heart if they are offered to you, which is to be in position of responsibility and leadership of your own lands.'' Genevieve paused to look at him closely. ''Aye, I have loved being a part of your family. Perhaps I have even wanted it too much. But I have not wanted you because of it. I wanted you for the reasons that any woman would want a man. I find you more than pleasing to look upon. You have merely to touch me and my body reacts. You are kind and gentle and intelligent. You would be a considerate and wise overlord to my lands, not just to my folk, but also in the matter of listening to my own opinions and desires. Dear heaven, are you so unsure of yourself that the only justification you can imagine for my attraction to you is my wish to be an Ainsworth? Aye, I have wanted to be an Ainsworth, but even I would not go so far as to fall in love with a man who did not want me.''

He stopped still. ''You love me?''

She paled but faced him openly. ''I did love you. Praise God that 'tis gone, for the affliction has brought me no joy.''

With that, she swung about and stalked away. She could see no point in continuing their discussion. She had revealed all there was to reveal.

It was now up to Marcel to be honest with himself. As she had told him, he had lied to her about Constanza for reasons he was not willing to accept. He was not so enamored of himself that he felt he was irresistible. He, in fact, seemed to hold himself with too little regard.

Aye, he had wanted something other than to hold her at bay. Yet his discovering just what that might be was not her worry.

She was well and truly shed of him.

Unfortunately, in spite of what she had told him about her love being gone, her battered heart did not appear to understand this. For it ached in her chest as if it might never cease.

As he watched her go, Marcel ran a shaky hand over his face. Genevieve loved him.

Had loved him. Dear God, what had he done?

For her words had made him realize what he had not been able to admit before. God help him, he knew it was true. He loved her. Had always loved her.

That he had destroyed her love because of his own fear brought a pain to his chest that was crushing.

He knew he did not deserve her love. What she had said was true. He had not been able to be honest with her because he could not be honest with anyone, least of all himself.

Marcel realized that he must stop denying what he was and how he felt. The first thing he could do to change that was to tell the truth about who he was.

He would begin by telling the two people who had become his friends. After what they had just heard between himself and Genevieve he did not believe his disclosures would come as a complete surprise. If they treated him differently because of being an Ainsworth, so be it. He was who he was.

He knew that this must be resolved before he could even think of approaching Genevieve, begging her forgiveness. He did not even consider begging for her love. Forgiveness was almost more than he could hope for. If she refused to forgive him for the way he had treated her, that too he must accept. For it was of his own making.

He squared his shoulders and went back to the hall where they were still seated. "There is something I must tell the two of you. For there are many things that I have kept from not only Genevieve, but everyone."

Their expectant eyes met his.

Genevieve went immediately to Aunt Finella's chamber. The elderly lady looked up from her sewing, her face registering concern the moment she saw Genevieve's expression. "Whatever has happened, my dear? Has that nice couple from the *Briarwind* brought ill news?"

Genevieve wasted no time in niceties. Neither did she try to hide the hurt she felt as she said, "In truth they have not, but their coming has forced me to see what I must do. Please, I beg your aid. I must leave this place and with all possible haste. You were right in what you said to me before, though I did not know it at the time. I was in love with Marcel. Yet I can no longer be near him for he has no such feelings for me."

Aunt Finella came toward her with her arms outstretched. "Oh, my poor lamb. How could he fail to love you?"

Genevieve closed her eyes, refusing to shed the tears that burned behind her lids. "I beg you, kind lady. Do not force me to speak of this in more detail. I can bear no more hurt than he has just dealt me. If you cannot help me then I must find another way."

"Of course I will help you. You are so dear to me already, child." She smoothed a gentle hand over Genevieve's heated cheek. That gesture of kindness was nearly her undoing. But she kept the pain inside, forced herself to keep control. For she could not risk losing control now. If she did so, she might never regain it.

She must keep her head long enough to quit this place and the man who had hurt her beyond all bearing. Genevieve spoke as evenly as her aching throat would allow. "I must depart this very night."

Aunt Finella frowned pensively. "Whither will you go, child?"

Genevieve took a deep breath. "To Brackenmoore. It has been home to me these many years. Marcel will not follow me. He has no desire to return there."

The older woman nodded, obviously seeing that Genevieve's mind was set. She said matter-of-factly, "I will see that you are able to depart this very night."

Now it was Genevieve's turn to reach out and hug her. "You have my most heartfelt thanks. I will never forget your kindness to me."

The other woman held her for a moment before she pushed back and looked into her eyes. "Follow the road your heart tells you to take, Genevieve, and you will never err. It is what I have done in my own life."

Genevieve nodded. She meant to do just that. She would go home, first to Brackenmoore and the folk who had given her a family. Then on to Harwick. She had a duty to her folk. They were not responsible for the pains of her childhood, nor those of her adulthood. They worked the lands, loved and died. It was through their work that she prospered. Their efforts were not to be treated with disregard.

She would make a new life for herself that had nothing to do with Marcel. She would remove him, and the memory of his touch, from her mind, heart and soul.

Even if it took the rest of her days.

Chapter Fourteen

Neither Constanza nor Harlan had seemed the least bit surprised to learn that Marcel was a nobleman. Constanza's only reaction had been to call him every kind of a fool for letting Genevieve slip through his fingers.

He could not find it in him to deny her words, for he knew they were all too true.

It was not until the next morning that he went in search of Genevieve. He balked at the delay, lying awake through the whole of the night, but he felt he had put her through enough for one day without pressing his apologies upon her.

When he did not find her after seeking her out in every conceivable location, he sought out his aunt.

She answered his question before the words were even spoken. "I am sorry, Marcel, but Genevieve has gone. She left last night."

Marcel swayed.

"Gone?" The sorrow on his aunt's face told him that what she was saying was all too true.

Genevieve was gone. "I must stop her."

Aunt Finella shook her head. "You'd not find her. She's with several of my most experienced men. They have been instructed to have the utmost care in disguising their route."

"But why?"

Her gaze did not waver. "Because she asked it of me and I could not deny her, seeing the pain she was in."

Marcel raked a frustrated hand through his hair. She'd walked right out of his life as unexpectedly as she had entered it only weeks ago. Though the time had been short, the impact she had had on him and his life could not be measured did he spend the rest of his life trying.

He loved her, as the moon loved to see the silver sheen of its light upon the sea at night and knew that his life would never be complete without her. That he might have hurt her too badly for her to ever forgive him he knew.

Surely he must try. Although she no longer loved him he realized that it was his only hope of happiness. Perhaps if he had not been so blind and foolish, bent on taking the course he had set no matter what the cost, he would have seen sooner, before he had destroyed her love.

Marcel's tormented eyes met his aunt's sympathetic gaze.

She returned that look in full measure. "I no longer require your presence here at Glen Rowan, though I have taken great joy in having both you and Genevieve, my lad. You have done what I asked you to do and more. I have no real fear that there will be any more trouble from McGuire. Methinks in fact that judging from his recent demeanor he might very well act as the champion I may require in future.''

Marcel took a deep breath of both relief and regret. This dear lady had helped him to come to terms with his past, however unwittingly, and he would always be grateful, no matter the outcome of his relationship with Genevieve. ''You have my love, Aunt, and always will. Should you ever need me again, I will gladly come.''

She hugged him close and he returned her embrace for a long time before stepping back. He sighed. ''Though I know not what Genevieve will say, I must go after her.''

She smiled, gently laying a hand on his arm. ''I was praying that would be your decision, lad. You never know what might come of things lest you try.'' She went on encouragingly. ''I think the lady will not be averse to seeing you.''

He took another deep breath, his voice filled with doubt and undeniable longing. He could not give credit to her words, but in the deepest recesses of his heart he felt a flicker of hope. Quickly he snuffed it. He had no right to hope for anything.

Marcel had made the journey back to Bracken-moore with all haste. Yet even then he had far too much time to think. And because of that he realized that he must be willing to offer Genevieve all of himself, his heart, his hands, his life—and without reservation—no matter that the possibility of her accepting him was nil. She must see that he was willing to risk all.

And he would gladly do so. He had nothing to lose.

If Genevieve would not have him he had no future. Thus he did not care how he might appear to his crew, his family or anyone else.

Benedict had been more than a little surprised when he had informed him that he no longer wished to be captain of the *Briarwind*. He'd ended by saying, "If it is agreeable, I have given the position of captain to Harlan."

Benedict shrugged. "You have no need to ask my permission about anything concerning the *Briarwind*."

Marcel frowned. "And why would I not?"

Benedict smiled. "I have long since signed ownership over to you." Marcel sat very still in his chair. He faced his brother across the table in the library and shook his head. "You need not have done that. You inherited the *Briarwind,* not I."

"Marcel, you have paid for the cost of the *Briarwind* many times over in the years you have captained her. Never in the years previous to your stewardship did she bring in such profits. I have collected enough for my own share to commission the building of another ship. How many ships should one man own on the work of another, especially if that man is his brother? I give you nothing that you have not earned. You went from Brackenmoore determined to prove yourself your own man, and though there was no need for you to do that, you have surely done so even by your own standard."

Looking into Benedict's earnest face, Marcel realized he would be wrong to refuse this gesture. Benedict spoke true of his efforts and he also spoke true of the fact that Marcel would not wish to gain one of his brother's efforts while giving nothing in return. And Benedict spoke true on another matter. Marcel had proven himself. But in the end he had only done so by realizing that there was nothing to prove. His worth had never come from outside himself, for he could have accomplished nothing if it had.

He nodded. "I thank you, Benedict." He paused for a long moment, then looked at his brother with an ironic grimace. "I find that I have been a fool, Benedict. That which I set the most store in, I had all along. That which would bring me the most joy in gaining, I ran from." He was not surprised by the depth of sadness in his own voice.

Benedict's black brows drew together in concern. "What has brought you such pain, my brother? Is there aught I can do to ease it?"

Marcel shook his head and said, "There is only one thing I would ask of you. I would ask your permission to wed your ward, Lady Genevieve."

Though there was still some degree of confusion on his face as Marcel said this, Benedict's happiness could not be mistaken. "You have it and gladly. I have long hoped that you would come to your senses on that matter."

Yet when Benedict began to congratulate him, Marcel was quick to halt him. He shook his head. "Do not spend your good wishes yet, my brother. I do not know if the lady will have me."

Benedict smiled. "Of a certainty she will. Genevieve has loved you these past two years."

Marcel sighed. Had he been the only one who was blind to the truth? "She may have loved me at one time, but I am not certain that love still exists." He met his brother's blue gaze without wavering. "You know that she preferred to return to Brackenmoore overland rather than be with me." When he had arrived the previous evening, Marcel had said as little as possible concerning this, and thankfully his family had accepted his brief explanation.

"Aye, you said that she was angry with you." Benedict shrugged. "Women do these things."

He did not hide his guilt as he admitted, "Genevieve is completely justified in her anger. I have hurt her terribly. If she never forgives me I will not fault her."

Benedict shrugged. "But you have asked me for her hand?"

"Because I must try to win her. I love her and am ready to set aside my pride. I care not how mad I might appear should she refuse me. I must show her that nothing else matters to me. All will be in readiness for her arrival. The priest, a gown, a feast, everything."

Benedict's brow creased with concern. "Must you go to such lengths before she can even answer you?"

He knew that the depth of pain in his eyes was bared but could no longer summon any ability to hide it. "I must. If she refuses me, my life is worth nothing."

Genevieve was tired—so tired that she was numbed in mind and body. The journey from Scotland had not been an easy one, for she was determined to reach Brackenmoore as quickly as possible. Yet the difficulty of the journey could not entirely account for her condition.

She knew that the reason for her dazed lethargy was the fact that she had experienced more pain in her last hours at Glen Rowan than she was able to absorb. Even after the way he had hurt her, leaving Marcel had been the hardest thing she had ever done in her life, though she knew it was the only thing she could do.

She had told herself that these feelings would pass, that in time she would come to feel alive again.

Yet they had not. Aunt Finella's retainers had attempted to make the many long hours easier by way of conversation, but she had found she had little to say. She felt as though she was locked in some dense fog from which she could not escape. Eventually they desisted, watching her closely as they did all they could to make the arduous trip as comfortable for her as possible.

Even here on the last leg of her journey, with Brackenmoore castle within sight, she experienced no lessening of the dense fog of nothingness that encircled her. Genevieve attempted to enliven herself, to concentrate on the future, on the fact that she intended to tell Benedict that she was ready to go home to Harwick now.

But the thought of taking up her proper position as heir to her lands had no effect upon her. Though she would do so, and with her best effort, it meant nothing.

That her nights and days would be spent in the absence of the man she had loved was all that mattered.

And love him she did, despite what she had said to him about her love being gone, with all her being. For she did not seem to be able to do anything else. It was as if somehow, somewhere, a force bigger and far more powerful than herself had decreed that she would love Marcel and Marcel alone until the day she died.

Thus it was with no sign of relief that she, along with Aunt Finella's long-suffering retainers, approached the castle gates. Her mare, seeming to sense that they had reached the end of their travels, did quicken her pace and Genevieve neither encouraged nor discouraged her.

Marcel was ready for the call when it came. A party had been seen approaching Brackenmoore and they were riding the Scots' ponies. His heart thudded to a halt in his chest as he realized that it could only be Genevieve and her escort.

He rose from where he was sitting and started across the great hall, then hesitated for a long moment, his legs feeling as if they were made from lead. In the days that he had been anticipating Genevieve's arrival, Marcel had thought he would go mad with the waiting. Now that she was here he was beset by a nearly debilitating anxiety.

What if she refused him? How would he live without her?

He took a deep breath and raised his head. He simply would do so, because he must. He was not so mad that he actually believed she would do anything but refuse him.

Again he reminded himself that he was willing to accept her feelings whatever they might be.

Yet as he reached the courtyard and saw her riding through the open gate, sunlight glinting off her gold-streaked blond curls, his heart soared. The last days had seemed an eternity apart from her. Come what may, he would see her this one last time.

With a sigh, Genevieve glanced up. Immediately her gaze lit upon a head full of black hair that shone like the wings of a raven in the bright afternoon sunlight.

Her breath caught, for there was no mistaking that man. It was none other than Marcel.

Even though his brothers and he were so alike in coloring, the shock of awareness that raced through her would not be denied.

Marcel, here? Why?

Then as he came toward her, she told herself that the why of it mattered not in the least. Marcel had lied to her, hurt her, would always do so in order to protect himself from caring too much for any woman.

Yet as these thoughts passed through her mind, she could not help seeing the uncertainty in his face as he moved to stand at her mount's head. His gaze seemed to near drink her in as he looked up at her.

"Genevieve." His voice was husky and filled with a note she was afraid to even attempt to identify. For it sounded almost like—longing.

She faced him squarely, telling herself not to fall into the trap of imagining more than he was capable of giving. That was what she had always done where he was concerned.

To her own detriment.

Yet when he went on she felt herself stirring inside, awakening as she had not been awake since the day she left him in Scotland. "Genevieve, I am so…glad to see you. So very glad." Again she felt as if that dark blue gaze might indeed devour her.

Then in spite of herself and all her good intentions, in spite of all she knew to be true, Genevieve felt a stirring of hope. She was not prepared to reveal that hope to him—to do so would only be to open herself up to the agony she had known at his every rejection of her.

She said evenly, "I am sorry if you worried for my safety, Marcel. There was no need for you to come all this way. Your aunt's men have been quite diligent in their care of me."

He frowned. "I was not...well, I am most glad to see you safely here."

He paused then, as if not knowing how to go on and she looked at him closely, moved in spite of herself by his seeming self-consciousness. She glanced away from the troubling uncertainty in those eyes and realized that the courtyard was filling quickly. The men who had accompanied her from Scotland had been joined by many of the castle folk already, and more seemed to be arriving by the moment. There was a decided expectancy in their faces that left her feeling even more confused.

Marcel met her gaze, his own still appearing somewhat unsure. Then he took a deep breath and said with unmistakable emotion, "Genevieve, I am not here because I was worried about your safety, though I was indeed concerned for you."

She answered slowly, softly, aware of all those watching eyes, afraid to imagine what his changed demeanor might mean. "Then why are you here, Marcel? Have we not said all that could possibly be said to each other?"

Consternation creased his brow before he drew himself up. He too seemed somewhat overwhelmed by their audience for he also spoke quietly. "No, Genevieve, we have not said all that we could. At least, I have not. I have not said the one thing that is most important for you to know."

He stopped then, his gaze growing soft with undisguised longing. Suddenly she could not hide the breathlessness in her voice as she replied, "What then is it that you would have me know?"

He reached out a hand in supplication. "That I love you. That I have loved you for longer than I know, for I cannot for the life of me recall a time when I did not love you."

"You love me." The barely audible words escaped from stiff lips. The sea of faces faded to a blur and she felt as if she were trying to see him though a sea of sludge.

She forced herself to concentrate on his words. "Aye, I love you, Genevieve, with my whole heart and soul."

She was aware of his warm fingers closing around hers, but could not seem to drag herself from the depths of her own shock. The words came again, as if of their own accord. "You love me."

Marcel realized that something was dreadfully awry. Genevieve seemed dazed and completely confused, almost as if she were far removed from what was happening. The fact that she repeated what he had said did not encourage him, as it was as if she did not fully understand what the words meant, but simply chanted them back at him.

He clenched her hand tightly in his. "Genevieve,

dear heart, pray tell me what is wrong? If I have hurt you so badly that you cannot forgive me only say so and I will leave you in peace. But please, answer me.''

When she said nothing, only sat there staring down at him as if not seeing him, he could bear it no more. He reached up to pull her into his arms. ''Genevieve, Genevieve, God help me, what have I done to you?'' He cared not what anyone might make of this, he cared for nothing but this dear, beloved woman in his arms.

He raised her face to look at her and she whispered, ''You love me?'' The words were the same, but this time there was difference in her. This time there was a trace of life in her voice.

With some relief, he replied, ''Yes, I love you for now and for always. I only hope that you will forgive me for all I have done to hurt you.''

She shook her head, her gaze holding his. ''I forgive you. How can I not forgive you? Yet what am I to make of this? What I am, what I hold, has not changed. Surely you will eventually come to fear your care for me as you have in the past.''

The accusation, however gently spoken, stabbed at his heart. He looked at her, knowing he was baring his soul for all the folk who had gathered in the court-yard and not caring one jot. ''I will never again treat you with anything but the love and care you so deeply deserve.''

She whispered, ''What are you saying?''

He took her hand in his. ''Marry me, Genevieve?''

''Marry you?''

''Aye, this day. This very hour.''

She looked at him closely. "There is something I must tell you before I answer. My saying yes to your proposal would greatly change your life even further than you have imagined." She took a deep breath. "I do not mean to go on living at Brackenmoore, nor could I make my life aboard the *Briarwind.* Through your help I have come to realize that I must go home to Harwick. It is my duty. The man who weds me must accept a place beside me there."

His eyes did not waver as he replied, "I no longer feel the need to deny myself what I want most, not you, my love, nor the satisfaction I would gain at looking after your folk."

"What of the *Briarwind?*"

"'Tis in Harlan's very capable hand and will remain so."

She took a deep breath, unable to look away from those blue eyes so filled with a love she had never thought to see. "I...know not what to say."

He faced her without wavering. "Only say what you will. If you do not want me, cannot forget how I have wronged you I will leave you in peace."

She was silent for a very long time. Marcel felt his own nerves stretch to the breaking point.

Finally she replied, "I would not have you go away, Marcel. I will wed you."

His heart soared and he cried out in exaltation.

As he did so, Marcel heard a shout of happiness. He looked up to see Tristan, Lily, Benedict, Raine and Kendran all standing on the steps of the keep. Their faces were wreathed in joyful smiles.

Benedict called out, "I shall alert the priest."

And now the others gathered in the courtyard joined in, adding their calls of happiness.

He turned back to Genevieve, seeing the way she blushed at his reaction. She carefully avoided his gaze and he realized that despite her agreeing to marry him, she had made no declaration of love. But that, he knew, he must earn. Perhaps, eventually, if he loved her enough, showed her in each and every moment how precious she was to him, she would in time come to have some care for him in return.

For now it would be enough that she had not turned him away.

The bathing and preparation, not to mention the ceremony itself passed in a daze for Genevieve. She could not believe that only several short hours ago she had thought never to see Marcel again and now he sat at her side at the high table, both of them garbed in their wedding finery. With awe she touched the sleeve of the white gown with its heavy silver threads. The fit had been perfect, the silver veil that had accompanied it more flattering than she could have imagined.

Marcel's own houppeland of deep blue velvet was also adorned with the same fine silver threading about the sleeves and neck. He was so handsome with his dark hair and strongly molded features, so utterly masculine and yet retaining that trace of boyish uncertainty she had noted in the courtyard. He had made no move to touch her in any way, and his blue eyes were almost shy as he addressed her with a reticent care that startled her. His manner only added to her sense of unreality.

She looked about the hall, seeing their family and folk, who gathered about them smiling, laughing, telling ribald jests. The tables fair groaned beneath the weight of the feast that had been laid, but she could eat very little.

It all seemed so inconceivable. And yet, lest she be dreaming, it was indeed true. She and Marcel were wed before God and man.

When the cry for the bride to be carried to the bridal chamber went up only a moment later, she made no demure or reply of any kind. Only when she was at last sitting back against the pillows, with only her hair and the bedcover to hide her nakedness, did anyone remark on her silence.

Lily bent close to her. "Are you well? Is this marriage what you truly desire?"

Feeling Raine's steady attention, as well, Genevieve nodded. "Aye, it is."

Both women smiled, and Raine said, "We will leave you alone then to await your husband."

She had not long to wait once they had gone. She heard Marcel enter and the soft sounds of his disrobing. Yet she did not look at him until he said, "Genevieve."

She turned to him, her gaze widening as it fell upon him. Marcel's body was all gold and strong in the light of the candles and she felt a blush staining her cheeks. Dear heaven, she reminded herself anew, this beautiful man, the one who had awakened her body to desire, was hers to do with as she wished.

No one would come through that door and interrupt them. She had no need to rise and leave before the sun could light their windows.

Marcel moved toward the bed and their eyes met. It was with some surprise that she saw the anxiety that colored his handsome face as he sat down on the coverlet. He spoke hesitantly. "Genevieve, if you prefer that I wait...that we do not..."

She felt a puzzled frown mar her brow. "What do you mean? Are you saying that you do not wish to..." Another flush heated her face and shoulders.

His gaze grazed her shoulders, the edge of the coverlet where it dipped low over her breasts. With seeming haste, his eyes found hers once more. "Nay, not I. I but thought that if you would prefer to wait and see if your love for me might return..."

She stared at him in amazement. "Wait for my love to return? Marcel, if I loved you more I wouldst surely expire of it."

His expression lit with a joy so powerful that it made her own heart sing, and his strong hand trembled as he reached out to smooth the curls back from her brow. Marcel's voice was filled with a wonder that sent a thrill of unutterable longing through her as he said, "You love me."

She brought his hand to her cheek, turning her face to kiss it. "I do not seem to be capable of not loving you."

"But when you found out about Constanza, you said..."

She felt sorrow stab her anew at the memory, and she whispered, "I was so very angry and hurt. I did not mean the words when I said them. I had only to set eyes upon you again and I was lost."

His breath caught, and he bent to place a soft kiss beside her lips. When he leaned back, she felt the heat of his gaze course through her, lighting that familiar fire in her belly.

He had not even touched her yet.

And still he did not as he went on, seeming to need to cleanse his soul. "You had every reason to be angry with me. You were right about everything. I did not lie to you to protect you but to protect myself from my own feelings. I was afraid my love for you would rule me if I ever gave in to it. And rule me it does, body and soul."

Even as she heard this wild declaration of his love with exultation, she felt a twinge of anxiety. "Pray how will you bear that, being ruled by your love for me?"

He spoke without compunction. "With rapture, for I have become a willing subject. If self-governance is only to be had without you, I want it not. Do with me what you will, my love, my Eve."

Wonder filled her as she put a hand to his well-sculpted cheek. "I want only to love you. For I feel the same. I want no peace if peace is not to be had with you."

He leaned closer to her, his eyes becoming hot with longing. "I have found myself in your heart, my love. And you are at long last a part of the Ainsworth family."

She rose up before him, allowing the bedclothes to fall about her knees. As his hot gaze raked her, she put her arms around his neck, her body fitting itself to his hard one. "You, my lord husband, are the only thing I truly care to be a part of."

He kissed her then, long and hard before pulling away, his eyes taking on a roguish gleam as his husky voice whispered, "That, my lady wife, can be arranged."

* * * * *

If you enjoyed Catherine Archer's

SUMMER'S BRIDE,

you'll love the next story in her exciting
SEASONS' BRIDES *series:*

AUTUMN'S BRIDE

Available Autumn 2001

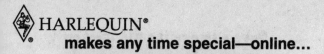

HARLEQUIN®

makes any time special—online...

eHARLEQUIN.com

shop eHarlequin

- ♥ Find all the new Harlequin releases at everyday great discounts.
- ♥ Try before you buy! Read an excerpt from the latest Harlequin novels.
- ♥ Write an online review and share your thoughts with others.

reading room

- ♥ Read our Internet exclusive daily and weekly online serials, or vote in our interactive novel.
- ♥ Talk to other readers about your favorite novels in our Reading Groups.
- ♥ Take our Choose-a-Book quiz to find the series that matches you!

authors' alcove

- ♥ Find out interesting tidbits and details about your favorite authors' lives, interests and writing habits.
- ♥ Ever dreamed of being an author? Enter our Writing Round Robin. The Winning Chapter will be published online! Or review our guidelines for submitting your novel.

Take a trip to the Old West with four handsome heroes from Harlequin Historicals.

ON SALE JANUARY 2001

MAGGIE'S BEAU
by Carolyn Davidson

Beau Jackson, former soldier/rancher

and

BRIDE ON THE RUN
by Elizabeth Lane

Malachi Stone, ferry owner

ON SALE FEBRUARY 2001

SWEET ANNIE
by Cheryl St.John

Luke Carpenter, horseman

and

THE RANGER'S BRIDE
by Laurie Grant

Rede Smith, Texas Ranger

Harlequin® Historical

Visit us at www.eHarlequin.com

HHWEST11

Tyler Brides

It happened one weekend...

Quinn and Molly Spencer are delighted to accept three
bookings for their newly opened B&B, Breakfast Inn Bed,
located in America's favorite hometown, Tyler, Wisconsin.

But Gina Santori is anything but thrilled to discover her
best friend has tricked her into sharing a room with
the man who broke her heart eight years ago....

And Delia Mayhew can hardly believe that she's
gotten herself locked in the Breakfast Inn Bed
basement with the sexiest man in America.

Then there's Rebecca Salter. She's turned up at the
Inn in her wedding gown. Minus her groom.

*Come home to Tyler for three delightful novellas
by three of your favorite authors: Kristine Rolofson,
Heather MacAllister and Jacqueline Diamond.*

HARLEQUIN®
Makes any time special ™

Visit us at www.eHarlequin.com   PHTB

PRESENTS

SIRENS OF THE SEA

The brand-new historical series
from bestselling author

Ruth Langan

Join the spirited Lambert sisters in their
search for adventure—and love!

THE SEA WITCH
When dashing Captain Riordan Spencer arrives in
Land's End, Ambrosia Lambert may have
met her perfect match!

On sale January 2001
THE SEA NYMPH
Middle sister Bethany must choose between a
scandalous highwayman and the very proper
Earl of Alsmeeth.

In June 2001
THE SEA SPRITE
Youngest sister Darcy loses the love of her life
in a shipwreck, only to fall for a man who
strongly resembles her lost lover.

AWARD-WINNING AUTHOR

GAYLE WILSON

presents her latest
Harlequin Historical novel

ANNE'S
PERFECT HUSBAND

Book II in her brand-new series

The Sinclair Brides

When a dashing naval officer searches for the
perfect husband for his beautiful young ward,
he soon discovers he needn't search any
further than his own heart!

Look for it in bookstores in March 2001!

Available at your favorite retail outlet.